VICIOUS PROMISE

M. JAMES

PROLOGUE

SOFIA

"Your father is dead, Sophia."

My mother says this to me in her thick accent, still more Russian than American, despite how often I hear my father telling her that she needs to work on blending in. Even at twelve years old, though, I know it would be impossible for my mother to blend in anywhere. She's the most beautiful woman I've ever seen, lithe and long-necked as the swans that we see swimming around the lake in Central Park on our daily walks, blue-eyed and blonde-haired, everything I'm not. I'm short and round even for my age, with dark hair and thick eyebrows like my father.

My father. The man who always smells like vanilla tobacco, who picks me up every day when he comes home from work and spins me in a circle, who brings me books, who encouraged me every day since I was eight and decided I wanted to play the violin. Every day he asks me what new thing I learned, asks me to show him, even though I know he's very busy. He must be, because there's always men at the house, important-looking men in expensive-looking suits, men who look at my mother disapprovingly and whisper to my father.

But now my mother is telling me that he's dead. *Dead.* It's such a final word, and it feels impossible. My father can't be dead, he was too full of life. It's impossible to think that I'll never hear his boisterous laugh again, never play the violin for him again, never breathe in the rich scent of tobacco from his shirt collar when he picks me up and swings me around.

I don't cry. I can't. I know I should—my mother is crying, her mascara running down her face in thick black streaks, but the grief feels like a knot in my throat, a wall in my chest, hot and heavy and choking. I can't believe it. I won't.

I don't realize that I've screamed those words aloud until my mother recoils, letting go of my hands just long enough for me to run to my room and slam the door behind me. *In here,* I think, *none of this can find me. None of it will be real.* I pick up the latest book my father brought home for me, an illustrated copy of *Grimm's Fairy Tales,* which my mother said was too dark for a twelve-year-old. My father took it away from me, and then when she was gone, winked and handed it back. "Find a good hiding place for it," he said to me. "There's a lesson in that book, an important one."

"What is it, papa?" I'd asked, taking the book back. The cover was smooth and new, the pages still full of that new-book smell. I couldn't wait to breathe it in.

He'd leaned down, pushing a loose piece of hair out of my face, and smiled sadly. "All fairytales have a dark side."

I hadn't read it yet. But now I clung to it, pressing the book against my chest as if it could keep me safe, as if it could change everything that my mother had said to me. In here, surrounded by my books, my violin, everything that my father and I shared, I can pretend that it's not true.

But somewhere deep down, I know it is.

* * *

I STILL CAN'T BELIEVE it at the funeral, either. Not when I see his body in the casket, his face waxy with makeup, and not when they lower him into the ground. Not when more of the important men in suits come to talk to my pale-faced mother, and I hear the name that I've so often overheard when they come to our house—*Rossi*. I sneak close enough to hear snippets of the conversation: *you'll be safe...provided for...Giovanni took precautions...his daughter...*

But safe from what? My life has always been safe and comfortable, full of joy and love from both of my parents. My mother shows it in a different way, she's always been more stoic than my father, more reserved. But they love each other, too, I know it. I see it in their faces when they look at each other, in the way my father sneaks kisses from her around corners when they think I can't see.

Used to sneak. How will I ever get used to thinking of him in the past tense?

I can't bear it. I think that I'll be able to get away from it all when we go home, but our house is full of people all draped in dreary black, the women carrying casserole dishes and comforting my mother. I can see the women looking sideways at her after they console her, though, whispering about her behind her back. Two-faced, she would call them.

I hate them all.

At the first opportunity, I run upstairs to my room, intent on hiding from the crowd downstairs. But only a few minutes have passed when there's a knock at my door.

I ignore it, but it comes again. "Go away!" I yell, hating how choked my voice sounds. "Leave me alone."

The door opens anyway. A tall man walks in, one that I don't recognize, but that I saw at the funeral with the other important-looking men. He's very handsome, with a thick mustache, wearing a wool greatcoat that looks expensive. He steps inside and shuts the door behind him, crouching down so that he's at my level.

"This must be very hard for you," he says in a low voice. "You must have loved your father very much."

I look away. I don't know who this man is, but something inside of me pings nervously at the sight of him, some instinct that tells me he's dangerous. That something about him, and the other men who come to the house, is connected to why my father is dead.

Why he'll never come home again.

The man lets out a long sigh. "I don't blame you for not wanting to talk to me. But I came to bring you something. Your father gave this to me the night that he died, for you. Read it when you're ready." He sets something down on the floor, a few inches away from me, as if I'm a small dog that might bite if he comes too close.

And then he stands up, and leaves without another word.

I reach for the envelope. It's thin and light. At first I don't want to open it. These are my father's last words to me, the last thing he'll ever say. It's beginning to dawn on me that he's really gone, that no amount of pretending can change it, and once I read this letter, everything that's left of him will truly be in the dirt of the cemetery a few miles down the road, rotting into nothingness.

So I stand up, and slip the letter into my violin case. I'll read it one day.

But not yet.

SOFIA

EIGHT YEARS LATER

"You have practice *again*? Sofia, it's Friday night. For fuck's sake, live a little."

My best friend and roommate, Anastasia Ivanova, is propped up against the stack of pillows on my bed, painting her nails a brilliant shade of crimson.

"You're just going to have to take that off before class on Monday," I tell her dryly, nodding at the bottle of polish.

Anastasia, or Ana to me, is one of the top ballet students at Juilliard, where I study violin. We're both the top in our class, actually, but that's where the similarities end. Ana is naturally blonde, tall, and impossibly thin, with a list of numbers in her phone a mile long and a date every night of the week. I dye my hair platinum blonde, I'm just shy of 5'6, and although I definitely lost my baby fat when I turned sixteen, I have more curves than Ana does. But beyond that, I can't remember the last time I was out on a date. I've never had a boyfriend. Ana spends every weekend out at the elite Manhattan clubs, flashing her fake ID to anyone who dares question her right to be there, and I spend my weekends getting in extra practice sessions with the rest of the string section.

How she remains the shoo-in for the next prima of the New York

City Ballet, I'll never understand, other than the fact that she's ridiculously talented. I've seen her dance a handful of times, and it takes my breath away every single time without fail. Watching her dance is like watching a fairytale come to life.

All fairytales have a dark side.

For a brief flash of a moment, I hear my father's words echo in my head, in his deep and kindly voice, and a shiver runs down my spine. I bite my lip hard to keep my eyes from welling up. It's been eight years, but I still can't hear my father's voice in my head without wanting to cry.

"Did someone walk over your grave?" Ana asks, glancing up at me with the brush hovering over her finger. "You look like you saw a ghost."

"I'm fine." I pull my hair back into a ponytail, still watching her. "Your teacher is going to have a fit, Ana."

"I'll take it off before class." Ana insists. "But I'm not going out with bare nails, or worse, painted some frumpy pale pink." She swipes the brush over her pinky nail, caps it, and then sits up, waving her hand in the air. "Come on, Sofia," she says again, her voice pleading. "We never go out. And it's my birthday month."

I can't help but roll my eyes. "You don't get a whole month, Ana. No one does." I gingerly lay my violin in its case, carefully setting the bow beside it and zipping it up. "I'll go out with you for your birthday though. I promise."

"I'd rather you go out with me tonight." She pouts, pursing her lips, which are painted with the same shade of lipstick as the nail polish. "Come on. You can borrow something out of my closet."

"Nothing in your closet would fit me," I point out. "There's not a chance."

"You're still thin. Just because you have boobs doesn't mean you can't fit into anything I have. There's one dress that I always wear a pushup bra to fill it out—"

"Ana, no. I promised my group—" My phone goes off then, and I dive for it before Ana can pick it up off of the nightstand. The preview of the text on the screen makes my heart sink.

Ana catches the look on my face before I can smooth it over. "They canceled, didn't they?" she asks triumphantly. "Now you *have* to go with me."

Desperately, I try to think of another out. It's not even just that I don't want to go out, even though that's part of it. It's that I know the kinds of places Ana likes to go—the fanciest, most expensive clubs and bars that Manhattan has to offer. It's not that I can't afford it, either. It's just that I don't want to spend the money.

Every month, like clockwork, an embarrassing amount of money shows up in my bank account. I don't know where it comes from or how, and I've tried every way that I can think of to dodge it. I've changed banks multiple times, but it always shows up again. I've tried to get a job, so that I won't need to use it, but most of the time I never even get a call back, even for the simplest of retail positions. When I do get a call, the position somehow is always filled before I can go in for an interview.

And then there's my tuition to Juilliard. Every semester, it's paid in full, before I can even try to call and set up a payment plan of my own. When I tried to get the receptionist in the registrar's office to tell me who had paid, they'd said it was an anonymous benefactor. Even when I'd tried to move into the dorms, I'd gotten a call the day before telling me that a two-bedroom apartment in an expensive pre-war building near campus had been leased in my name, with the first year's rent paid in full.

It was all very mysterious, very frustrating, and made me feel both anxious and curious as to who, exactly, was providing all of this. I'd spent one night alone in the too-big apartment before putting out an ad for a roommate, which Ana answered almost immediately. Since the place was already paid for, I just asked her to chip in for groceries and utilities, which she was more than happy to accept. All I wanted was a quiet roommate who didn't party, didn't disturb me, and didn't have boys over very often if at all.

That didn't turn out to be Ana in the slightest. But somehow, despite the fact that she's as extroverted as I am introverted, as much of a partier as I am a homebody, and could rival an opera singer with

7

her moans every time she brings a guy home, we rapidly became friends. Part of it, I think, is due to the fact that I don't *have* any other friends, and part of it is that Ana, with her slight Russian accent and willowy frame, reminds me of my mother, just brunette instead of blonde.

Ana taps her fingers on the nightstand. "Earth to Sofia. Come on, I know they canceled. Are you really just going to stay in tonight instead of going out with me and seeing the most eligible bachelors that Manhattan has to offer?"

"I'm not interested in dating," I say almost automatically. "You know that."

"Yeah, but *I* am." Ana hops off of the bed, linking her arm through mine. "Come on. You can be my wingwoman. Drinks are on me."

I can see that I'm not getting out of it. And a *tiny* part of me, ever so tiny, is curious. I've never been in this world that Ana inhabits on the weekends, full of expensive cocktails and glamorous men and women and neon-lit clubs. It doesn't really appeal to me, but shouldn't I experience it just once? The spring recital is only two months away, and just after it, graduation. Then I'll be leaving Manhattan for good, and that means Ana, too.

So maybe it wouldn't hurt to indulge her, just a little.

"Okay," I relent, and her entire face lights up.

"Yes!" She claps her hands excitedly. "I've been wanting to make you over since I moved in. Come on, we'll dig through my closet."

"O—okay." I can tell there's no use in arguing, as Ana eagerly drags me out of my room and down the hall towards hers.

Half an hour later, I don't quite recognize myself. The black dress that Ana stuffed me into is Gucci, with a bustier-style top that I more than fill out and lacing up each side, giving a peek of a sliver of bare skin through the lacing from my breasts all the way down to the hem. It means I can't wear a bra with it, and although the cups in the front are supportive enough, it makes me feel more bare and vulnerable than I've ever been. "If there's a stiff wind outside, you're going to be able to see my nipples through this," I complain, but Ana just shrugs. "And it's so tight." Thankfully my stomach is flat enough that the dress lays perfectly over it, but it hugs me so tightly that you can see every curve. "You can see my underwear lines."

"So wear a thong."

"I don't *own* a thong," I retort plaintively. "And *don't* tell me I can borrow one of yours, that's going way too far."

"So go without." Ana shrugs.

"What?" I turn a shade of red that could rival a stop sign. "I can't do that."

"Sure you can." She grins at me, fishing two pairs of heels out of her closet and bending over enough that I can see the flash of a lace thong up *her* skirt. The dress she's wearing is the same cherry red as her lips and her nails. She called it a "Hermes bandage dress," which means nothing to me, but is evidently a big deal, based on her tone.

A moment later, Ana emerges with the shoes, a pair of silver sandals for her and black pumps for me, both with the red bottoms that even I recognize. "I can't wear these," I protest. "What if I fall? What if I break a heel? These probably cost as much as a month's rent."

Actually, if anything happened to them, I *could* technically more than afford to replace them. But I don't like admitting that. I've felt weird about the money in my account since the day I turned eighteen and it started appearing, and I don't feel any less uncomfortable about it now. If I told Ana about it, she'd rightfully have a million questions, and there's no way for me to explain it when I don't even have the answers.

Of course, I'm talked into the shoes and out of my underwear exactly the way I've been talked into everything else, and as I totter to the bathroom in my new six-inch stilettos and an uncomfortable awareness that I'm wearing absolutely *nothing* under this dress, Ana prepares to do things to my hair and face that I've only ever seen in movies. There's products spread across her entire bathroom counter, from one end to the other, and I stand mutely in front of it as she goes to work.

When she's done, I have to admit, I look incredible. My hair is curled into thick spirals that fall loosely around my face and make my hair look twice as thick as it ever has, and she's done something to my eyes that makes them look huge and full and round, with a thick, sharp cat eye at each corner. Topped off with the same cherry red lipstick, I look like a Hollywood actress.

"You look gorgeous." Ana looks thoroughly pleased with herself. "You're going to be the envy of every woman in Manhattan tonight."

"I'm pretty sure those women have panties on," I mutter, gingerly touching one of the fake eyelashes that she applied. They feel heavy and strange on my face, but I have to admit they make my eyes stand out.

"I wouldn't bet on it." Ana gives me a cheeky grin. "I already called our Uber, so we've got to head down." She caps the lipstick and tosses it into her small silver purse, then hands me a sleek lacquered black clutch. I open it to see another tube of lipstick, a thin sleeve of tissues, and nothing else.

"Don't I need an ID? I'm not old enough to drink for another two months—"

"You've got nothing to worry about," Ana says confidently. "No one will question you. You're with me tonight."

Something about the way she says it makes me nervous. I shrug it off as anxiety about going out, and it's not until we're already in the Uber and headed into downtown Manhattan that I recognize the feeling. It's the same one that I had eight years ago, when a man I didn't recognize brought me a letter from my dead father.

That feeling is a warning.

I just don't know why, after all these years, I'm feeling it now.

LUCA

$\mathcal{M}$y head is pounding, loudly enough that I don't think I heard a single word of what my secretary just said to me. It's been pounding since I woke up this morning with the hangover of the century, sandwiched between two gorgeous naked blondes, breathing in the heavy scent of perfume and sex.

That, in and of itself, was strange. I don't usually allow women to sleep over—I prefer having my California king all to myself, and no questions to answer in the morning. No *what are we* or *when can we do this again* or even *will you call me?* No awkward breakfasts in which I pretend that I'm going to call and she—or they—pretend to believe me.

Most of them don't come home with me expecting more than one night of passion, though. I've been Manhattan's most notorious playboy since the minute I was old enough to legally fuck, and even more so once I had a penthouse to call my own. At thirty-one, I've had more nights with one or more women in my bed than without. They just rarely stay over. In fact, I can only think of a few occasions—and those were usually somewhere else, on weekend benders when I did little other than stay in bed, fuck to my heart's content, and order room service and champagne in between.

Eight years ago, I was given a get-out-of-jail free card, a pass on holy matrimony for the rest of my life, and I've enjoyed it to the fullest. I intend to continue doing so—but these days, there's more meetings and business trips and fewer hazy weekends in Ibiza.

Which brings me back to my pounding headache, and the secretary that I should probably be paying attention to.

"Franco called—he wants to know if you've got his bachelor party booked. He was very insistent that it be out of the country, somewhere with fewer restrictions on—"

"I'm sure I know what Franco wants." I rub a hand over my face. "Look, just make the arrangements, and run them by me before they're finalized, okay?"

"Yes sir." The secretary—I think her name is Carmen---shifts from one foot to the other. "And the engagement party—"

I look directly at her, bypassing her generous cleavage to gaze straight into her eyes. "Let me be clear, Karen."

"It's Carmen, sir."

"I don't care." I sit back, wincing as another bolt of pain shoots through my temples. "I don't give a fuck about the engagement party. Call Mrs. Rossi. It's her daughter's party, for fuck's sake."

"Yes sir." She almost bobs a curtsy before fleeing out of the door, and I make a mental note to check when she was hired. I vaguely remember my last secretary being more capable.

I peer at my computer screen, flipping to my calendar, and that's when I see exactly why Karen—*Carmen*—brought up the party. It's tomorrow night, and I have to be there, even though I'd rather put my balls in a vise than go to Caterina Rossi's engagement party. But I don't have a choice, because not only is she marrying my best friend, but her father is my boss. The Don of the Rossi family, head of the Northeast chapter of the Italian Mafia, and the boss of New York City.

And I, like it or not, am his heir.

It's a fate that I would have avoided if either my father had lived, or Rossi's wife had given him a son. But my father, Rossi's underboss, died seven years ago hunting down his best friend's killer, and Rossi

VICIOUS PROMISE

has only one daughter, a point of contention between him and his wife.

Without some sort of tie to the Rossi family, my life would be in danger the minute that Don Rossi went six feet under. I have no blood ties to the family, only Rossi's fondness for my father and insistence that I should be his heir. In a perfect world, I would marry his daughter, giving me the unquestioned right to his seat. But I've been promised since I was twenty-two to a woman I've never seen and will almost certainly never marry, bound by a vow that our fathers made without ever bothering to ask either of us.

So instead, my best friend and future underboss, Franco Bianchi, is marrying Caterina. With her husband as my underboss, there will be no chance of a civil war breaking out among the underbosses who would want a shot at the highest-ranking seat. They would have to get through Franco to get to me, and once he's married to Caterina, no one will question his right to his position.

If anything, marrying her should get him *my* future spot as the Don. But I would trust Franco with my life—and I will be, once Don Rossi dies.

But for now, Rossi is alive and well. My responsibilities, however, are still extensive, which is why I'm still in my office at nine p.m.. As I toggle away from my calendar, an automated email alert pops up, letting me know that a deposit has been transferred to another account, under the name of Sofia Ferretti.

Sofia. I hover the cursor over the alert for a moment, and then move it away. There's no point in looking at it—I know the exact amount, the same that's been transferred to that account for the last three years, ever since Sofia turned eighteen. It pays for her housing, her food, and her utilities, with plenty left over as an allowance. Her tuition is paid separately every semester. And once she leaves Manhattan, as I've been told she plans to do, the money will follow her to whatever bank account she opens next.

I've also been told that she's tried to evade the money a number of times, which seems irrationally stupid to me. The idea that anyone wouldn't want such a large sum is baffling, and if it were up to me, I'd

13

be happy to put a stop to it. But I can't, because of a promise. The same promise that tied me to Sofia eight years ago, a girl then and a woman now who is a complete stranger to me.

I don't even know what she looks like. I remember a chubby, round-faced pre-teen, with acne and a proclivity to keep her nose buried in a book. Not exactly the erotic picture that one would hope for when thinking of one's future wife. I would hope that she's blossomed into something more palatable since, but in the end, it doesn't matter. The circumstances that would lead me into wedlock with her will almost certainly never occur. And until that day hopefully never comes, I'm free to do whatever I like, without the burden of marriage. When I die, my seat will pass to Franco's eldest son, and the position of Don will once again belong to a son with Rossi blood in his veins.

It's all very neat and tidy. But there is a certain faint curiosity that I feel every time I see the alert. *What does my fiancée look like now? What sort of woman has she grown into?* Her mother was astoundingly beautiful, and if she took after her even a little—

But now, as always, I shake the thought away. I have the attention of nearly every woman in Manhattan; I don't need one more. Especially not one that would tie me down for life, turning me into the husband and father that I was never meant to be.

No, it's better if Sofia Ferretti remains a mystery to me, and I to her.

Still, as I pack up and prepare to leave my office for the night, I can't quite shake the memory of a pale twelve-year-old girl, staring at her father's coffin as it was lowered into the earth, and the look on her face as she clutched her mother's hand.

There was a promise made on that girl's behalf, a promise that I inherited.

And if the day does come, I'm going to have to make good on it.

SOFIA

To my relief, we start out simple. The first place Ana takes me is an upscale martini bar on a rooftop, where we bypass the line waiting to get in and all Ana does is tell the bouncer her name. The moment her last name slips out of her mouth, his face changes, and he doesn't even glance at me as he ushers us both inside.

I'm shocked at how it makes me feel. I've never cared about any of this, but a strange sort of elation washes over me as the bouncer waves me past, as if I've just been admitted into a world that I was only vaguely aware even existed. The bar is full of women dressed in everything from expensive business suits to tight-fitted dresses like the ones Ana and I are wearing, with sky-high heels and perfectly done hair and makeup. The men are elegant and sleek too, clean-cut in suits that I can only imagine are tailored just for them, fitting so well that I can't help but feel a slight buzz of desire as I look around the room. It's impossible not to—the bar is thrumming with sexual energy, every man in here an alpha predator looking for his prey for the night. I can feel their gazes traveling over me like electric sparks on my skin, and I'm not sure that I like it. I feel too exposed, and I desperately wish that I didn't only have one layer of too-tight fabric between my skin and their hungry eyes.

"I need a drink," I hiss in Ana's ear, and she grins.

"I'm on it." She grabs my hand, pulling me towards the gleaming bar. There's a handsome man in a white-button down and no tie standing behind it, his dark hair slicked back. He's making something elaborate for a pencil-thin, beautiful woman leaning on the bar, swiftly moving the cocktail shaker from one hand to the next and then pouring it from several inches above the glass, finishing with a flourish before adding a wisp of lemon rind and setting the glass on the bar.

"What do you want?" Ana perches on one of the mahogany stools, pushing a long curl out of her face. "I'm having a gin martini, extra dirty."

"I don't even know what that means."

"Just try it." She smiles flirtatiously at the bartender, pushing a lock of silky dark hair out of her face. I can see his eyes flick immediately to her full lips. *There's a certain kind of power in what she does,* I think, but I don't understand how Ana and women like her wield it, how they can be so confident in their beauty and their sexuality. I know that I'm beautiful by the definition of the word, but all I feel right now is out of place and awkward, uncomfortable in my thin dress and exposed by everything I don't have under it. I don't know how to feel powerful like this.

The bartender slides the two martinis across to us, and Ana picks hers up. "To an exciting night out in Manhattan," she says with a grin, tapping the thin edge of her glass against mine. She takes a sip, leaving a crimson stain on the glass.

Gingerly, I lift my own martini to my lips. It smells like a pine tree, and when I take a sip, I cough immediately. There's a faint saltiness from the olives, but aside from that it just burns all the way down to my stomach.

Ana frowns. The bartender looks at me with a small smirk, and I can feel myself turning red. *I should never have agreed to this.*

"Here." The bartender pushes a drink across to me, his face slightly more sympathetic. "Give this a try."

I smell that same piney scent, this time mixed with lime, and when

I take a sip this time it's much more palatable—a bit sweeter, and tinged with enough lime that I think I actually like it. "That's good," I manage. "What's that?"

"Gin and tonic," the bartender says. His eyes are glued to me now, flicking over my breasts in the bustier-style top of my dress. "Ask for that at any bar with extra lime and top-shelf liquor, and I guarantee you'll like it. It's a hard drink to fuck up." He winks at me. "Just a little tip."

"I'm sure that's not the only *little tip* he's got," Ana whispers in my ear, giggling as he walks away.

"I think he's sexy." For once I let myself actually look at a guy in a sexual way, wondering what would happen if I asked him for his number, or gave him mine. "He's got a nice ass."

Ana frowns. "Don't get distracted by the first pair of tight pants you see, Sofia. You can do a hell of a lot better than a bartender."

"What if I don't want to, though?" Truthfully, I'm not really interested in dating anyone. But the predatory men all around this bar don't turn me on, they frighten me. All I can think is that any woman with one of them isn't a girlfriend, she's a possession.

"Come on," Ana says, finishing her drink and setting it down. "There's a lot of night ahead of us."

We hit two more spots, a futuristic bar with a lot of dry ice and neon lights, and a smoky whiskey bar with leather seating and mahogany throughout. I feel out of place in all of them, and I'm just about to beg Ana to head back to the apartment—or at least go back on my own—when she comes back from the bathroom with a huge smile on her face.

"My friend Devin just texted me back," she says, leaning in towards me conspiratorially. "She gave me the secret password for this new club. It's supposed to be *wild*."

Wild is exactly the opposite of what I want. But Ana is already paying the bill, an excited look on her face. "I've been hearing about this club for months," she says. "It's super exclusive. And crazy shit happens there."

"I don't know if I'm down for *crazy shit*," I start to say, but by then

Ana is signing the receipt and grabbing my hand, pulling me out into the busy street again as she flags down a cab. "This is going to be the best night of our lives," she promises. "I'm *so* having some really freaky sex tonight."

Also not something I'm interested in, I think dryly as a cab pulls up to the curb and Ana tumbles inside, pulling me along. I can only imagine what this place that she's taking us to must be like. Ana is fearless, down for anything, and I have to admit that sometimes it's a trait I'm envious of.

But how can I be fearless, when I know all too well what's out there to be afraid of—that there are monsters in the dark streets of the city, the kind of men who would snatch away a girl's father, and leave her half an orphan at twelve, her mother so brokenhearted that she didn't have the spirit to fight off the cancer that struck her a year later? The doctors said that we just didn't catch it in time, but I knew the truth. Even I wasn't enough to keep my mother tied to this Earth, with my father gone. Not when she believed that his spirit was somewhere out there waiting for her.

I touch the small gold cross laying against my skin, crusted with the tiniest of pave diamonds along the sides. It's the most valuable thing that my mother owned, other than the pearl earrings that my father gave her for their wedding, and she gave it to me just before she died. It was a gift from her own mother, back in Russia. Ana wanted me to take it off tonight, but I haven't removed it since her funeral. I wasn't about to tonight, just to avoid putting someone off. I'm not even a little bit religious—her funeral was also the last time that I was in a church, but nothing in the world could convince me to take off the last thing my mother gave me.

The cab pulls up to the edge of the street again, jolting me out of my thoughts, and I climb out as Ana pays the driver. The street we're on is dark, and less busy than others, and I feel that pinging sensation again, the warning that something is off. But Ana is already heading towards the wall in front of us, where I can't even tell that there's a door until we're right in front of it, and I can see the thin seam.

Ana knocks three times quickly, and the door cracks open.

"Preispodnyaya," she says, her accent thickening as she says the password aloud. It's the first time I can recall hearing her speak Russian, and it sends a shiver down my spine. I rarely ever heard my mother speak it, and I recall overhearing my father tell her than she couldn't teach me, that she shouldn't even speak it at home. He'd said it kindly, but still, it was one of the few times I ever saw my mother cry.

The door swings open, and Ana steps confidently inside. I follow, nerves churning in my stomach, and I catch a glimpse of the man standing in the shadows by the door—tall and dressed all in black, his craggy features undefinable in the darkness.

I can hear the heavy beat of the music as we descend down the steps, and I see a red glow ahead of us. By the time we reach the foot of the stairs and stop in front of the archway that leads into the main room of the club, locked behind iron gates, I can feel the music vibrating through my body and shaking the floor beneath me.

Two impossibly thin girls dressed in red latex push the gates open, and Ana grins at me as we walk into the red glow.

"Welcome to Hell."

SOFIA

*E*very part of me wants to run back up the stairs and flag down a cab, taking it straight back to the apartment.

Hell, which is apparently the name of the club—a bit too on the nose, in my opinion—is comprised of a huge dance floor, in which latex and leather-clad men and women are writhing against each other all across it, in boots that could crush someone's head or put their eye out, and more spikes than an entire Hot Topic. It's a change from the sleek bars and predatory businessmen, at least, but I don't think these guys are any safer. I hadn't realized it was possible to feel more out of my element than I do right now.

Ana, on the other hand, looks perfect. With her dress and lips and nails, all crimson and bathed in the red glow coming down from the lights, she looks like the hottest demon I've ever seen—like something in a music video. I can see heads turning as she strides towards the black lacquered bar, and I hurry to keep up with her, tottering in my heels.

"You make a perfect pair."

I nearly leap out of my skin, spinning around to see a tall man in black leather pants and a tight white shirt beneath a leather jacket standing there, his hands shoved casually in his pockets. His hair is very short on top and buzzed at the sides, white blond, and his eyes are startlingly blue.

"What?" I stare at him dumbly. I have to almost shout to be heard above the music.

He nods at Ana. "One dark, one blonde. One in red, one in black. Both beautiful." I hear the hint of an accent in his voice, something rough, but I'm not sure what it is. German? Dutch? Maybe Russian, but it's not clear. Even Ana's accent is thicker than that, and she's spent most of her life here in the States.

"Thank you," I say unsteadily. "But I'm not looking for a date—"

He grins. "Who said anything about a date? But let me buy you a drink."

"No, that's okay." I back up, wanting to be closer to Ana. "I've got it."

"I'll buy you both a drink." There's a gleam in his eyes. "Two such beautiful women shouldn't pay for their own night out."

"That's very kind of you, but I'm sure we're okay."

"I insist." He reaches out to lay his credit card on the bar, and the sleeve of his jacket rides up just above his wrist, revealing the edge of a tattoo. I can't quite see what it is, but it looks like the beginning of an eagle's head.

Ana glances over at him, and I can see that she's annoyed. "We don't need—"

The words die on her lips as she catches a glimpse of his wrist.

Her face goes very pale. "Come on, Sofia," she says, grabbing my hand.

Before I can say anything, she's pulling me into the teeming mass of people on the dance floor, moving through them towards the bar on the far side of the club. I glance back once, catching a glimpse of the man's white-blond hair through the crowd, but I lose sight of him almost immediately as they close around us.

"What's wrong?" I gasp as we finally make it to the other side of the dance floor. "I thought you liked guys like that. Dominant, kind of pushy—"

"Sure." Ana's voice is shaking a little. She turns towards the bar. "Gin and tonic, please, and a double shot of vodka. Top-shelf."

"Ana, what is it?"

"Stay away from him," she says, her voice very low. "If you see him again, go the other way. And anyone else that you see with that tattoo."

I blink at her, confused and scared all at once. "Why?"

"He's Bratva." Ana scans the crowd. "Russian mafia." Her gaze flicks back towards me, and I can see that she's really, truly frightened. "You don't want to be noticed by them."

My stomach flips over. "Shouldn't we just leave, then?"

"No. He noticed you, for some reason. If we leave, they might follow us. Just act normally, and hopefully they'll look for some other prey." Ana smiles brightly, handing me my drink as she tosses back her double shot. "Another, please," she tells the bartender.

She pulls me back out onto the dance floor, moving in time with the beat as she takes the second shot and drops the glass onto a passing tray. I clutch my own drink in one hand, trying not to spill it on anyone as I attempt to carve out my own space amidst the teeming, sweaty bodies. One man in a Matrix-style trench coat and a spiked collar starts moving in my direction, hips gyrating, and I automatically glance towards his wrists. They're both bare, but that doesn't mean I want to let him touch me.

It's impossible *not* to be touched by someone out here, though. The club is packed to the max, and I look around, trying to keep an eye out for the tall blond man. But all I can see are dancing bodies, couples pressed up against walls and pillars making out and grinding against one another, and a few professional dancers gyrating against x-shaped crosses leaning against one wall. There's a black winding stairwell leading up to a second floor, and just off of it, suspended above us, a cage with two barely-dressed female dancers writhing within it. I'm not entirely sure that there's not more than just dancing going on in there.

I can feel the anxious pit in my stomach growing. If we can't leave yet, I at least need to get out of the crowd for a minute. "I'm going to the bathroom!" I yell above the music, leaning close to Ana's ear.

She frowns. "I'll come with you," she says, scanning the crowd for an easy path towards the staircase that leads up to the second floor, and the women's restrooms.

"That's okay! I'll just be a minute—"

"We shouldn't split up." Ana grabs my hand. "Come on."

I can smell the perfume and sweat from the dancers in the cage as we hurry up the staircase, heels clicking against the black lacquered floor as we walk quickly towards the bathrooms. The moment we step inside, I feel my heart rate slow a little. The music is muted in here, the air cool, and I sink down onto one of the black velvet benches, breathing in the scent of clove hand soap and cleaner air.

"You don't actually have to pee, do you?" Ana asks, chewing on her lower lip. "I know it's overwhelming. I'm sorry, I thought it would be fun."

"I know." I lean my head back against the wall. "It's okay."

"Well, I really do have to pee. Just wait here, okay?" She slips into one of the stalls, and I close my eyes briefly. Maybe Ana will come back out, and agree to go home. She can be insistent when she wants to do something, but she's a good friend, and she knows I'm uncomfortable. Maybe enough time has passed since we saw the blond man that—

A heavy pressure descends over my mouth, and the scent of cologne and a man's skin fill my nose.

My eyes fly open. The tall blond man is standing over me, his hand pressed against my lips, and as I try to open it to scream, he smiles coldly and wags his finger in my face. "Don't make a sound," he says in a hushed voice, and now I can hear his accent plainly.

Russian. *Bratva*, I hear Ana's voice say in my head, and a chill runs down my spine. *Mafia*.

"You're going to come with me," he continues, leaning down so that his mouth is very close to my ear. "Quickly. Because if you don't, and your friend steps out of that stall and sees me, I won't have any choice but to shoot her."

My gaze flicks down to his waist. I can see the bulge of a gun beneath his jacket, ruining the lines of it. How did I not see it before?

"Now," he hisses. He grabs my wrist with his other hand, yanking me to my feet and pushing me towards the door, bending my arm behind my back as he keeps his other hand planted firmly over my mouth. "When we walk outside, I'm going to take my hand off of your mouth. You're going to be very silent, or it will be much worse for you."

My heart is pounding in my chest as he pushes me out into the hallway, so hard that it hurts. My throat feels closed off, choked, and I'm not even sure that I *could* scream. But as soon as his hand leaves my mouth, every instinct in my body tells me that's absolutely what I should do.

The music is loud again, pumping through every inch of the club, drowning everything else out. The man sees my face, and leans close again. "No one will hear you. If they do, they'll ignore it, if they don't, I'll kill them and go back and shoot your friend too. Now go."

He shoves me towards the exit. I stumble forward, even more clumsy in the heels. "Hurry," he hisses, and I feel the poke of something in my back. It feels round, like the muzzle of a gun, and my blood runs cold.

The man pushes the exit door open, shoving me out onto the landing at the top of the stairs that lead down to an alley behind the club. The spring air smacks me in the face, warm and fresh and as clean as New York City air ever is, but I can barely breathe. I'm on the verge of tears, but so terrified that I can't even cry. I feel paralyzed with it.

"Let me take my shoes off. I can't go down the stairs—"

"You'll manage. Now go." The man pushes me forward again, and I cling to the railing as I stumble down, the fear of twisting or breaking my ankle adding to the churning terror in my stomach. If I hurt myself, I won't even be able to run if I get a chance. My head swims with the gin and tonics I drank tonight, and I wish fervently that I'd stayed home. That I'd turned Ana down like usual.

If I had, would she be the one where I am now? Or did they seek me out, specifically?

I don't know why anyone would want to kidnap me. Years ago, when I was Giovanni Ferretti's daughter, maybe, but now I'm just a orphan violinist. I only know a little about what my father did, the kind of people that he worked for, but I can't see what that has to do with me now.

The money. I think of the zeroes in my bank account, the deposit that shows up every month. Do they know about that, somehow? Are they kidnapping me so that they can force me to pay my own ransom?

There's a sleek black car idling at the curb. The door opens as we reach it, and the man shoves me towards the car. "Get in," he says coldly, and I balk. Every woman knows that if you get in the car, your chances of rescue drop dramatically.

I feel the weight of the gun at my back again.

"Get in."

I don't want to die. But if they truly want something from *me*, they're not going to shoot me until they get it. So I turn around, swallowing back the fear as I feel the gun poke into my belly.

"If you want the money, you can have it," I say bravely, looking up into the man's cold blue eyes. "But I'm not getting in the car."

He curses under his breath in Russian. "Get in the fucking car."

"No. I won't—"

"Get in the car, or I go back inside and shoot your friend."

"No. If you turn around, I'll run."

The man lets out a long sigh, and looks over my shoulder. I start to turn my head, to see what he's looking at, but before I can I feel a burning sensation in my neck.

"What the—"

It takes only seconds before the world starts to blur. The blond man pushes me backwards into the car, and I fall onto the leather seat next to another man dressed all in black, with the same buzzed hair and blue eyes.

The last thing I see before the world goes black is the needle in his hand, and I know exactly what's happened.

I've been drugged.

LUCA

*T*hirty minutes into the engagement party and I'm already bored out of my mind.

The Rossi family has rented out an vintage bar for the occasion, emptied entirely except for the family and their guests. Caterina is glowing in a white lace dress that goes down to her knees, with a neckline high enough to keep her generous cleavage hidden. She's wearing her mother's ruby jewelry—I remember seeing that same necklace, bracelet and ring on Mrs. Rossi a few years ago at her anniversary party, an equally mind-numbing affair.

The rubies, though, are taking a back seat to the ring that everyone really wants to see, the one on her left finger. I'm pretty proud of it myself, because I helped Franco pick it out. He was a clusterfuck of nerves, freaking out about the prospect of insulting both Caterina and her father with a ring that wasn't good enough, and so I went with him to pick out the ring. The Rossi women wear everything from Cartier to Tiffany to Harry Winston, but for something this important, there's a private jeweler who has worked with the families for generations. He designed the ring and had it ready in a flash—a five carat rose cut diamond that looks as if it's weighing Caterina's hand down, surrounded with a halo of perfectly cut diamonds on a pave platinum band.

I had no idea what any of that meant when the jeweler explained it to me, but apparently it was perfect, because Franco confided in me later that his new fiancée had rewarded him with a blowjob in the back of the limo on the way back from the proposal. "She really liked that fucking ring," he'd told me with a smirk, clapping me on the shoulder. "Thanks, man."

From the way Caterina is beaming at her husband-to-be as she shows off her new jewelry, I'd say she likes *him*, too. I don't know how authentic the expression on her face is, but Franco is young and handsome and on the verge of occupying one of the most powerful seats in the territory, and he just put a seven-carat ring on her finger. She's the envy of every woman in the room right now.

Don Rossi appears at my elbow just as I snag a glass of champagne off of a passing tray, an indulgent expression on his face as he watches his daughter and Franco from our vantage point across the room. "No date tonight?"

"It's a family affair," I say, shrugging. "I wouldn't think it would be appropriate to bring a girl whose name I barely know to an event like this."

"Maybe that's for the best." Rossi frowns. "I've gotten some concerning intelligence recently about the Bratva. They're moving in on our territory, Luca, and they're not being as subtle about it as they used to be. Rumor has it that they've got a card up their sleeve, something that will give them more sway, but I can't figure out what it is. And you know how that makes me feel."

"I do." It's the truth, and I feel bad for anyone who Rossi thinks might have information that they're not giving up. Rossi will turn the streets of Manhattan red with Russian blood before he loses ground to them.

"If they become a danger to us, it's one thing," Rossi continues. "If they become a danger to *her—*"

I look sharply over at him. "Do you have reason to think that they will?"

Rossi shrugged. "They were the ones who killed her father, and yours. It stands to reason that she remains a target. And if she is, you know what that means."

I tense slightly, taking a slow sip of my champagne to hide it. "I do. But I think it's preliminary to say that they're targeting her in any way. And as far as what it means—" I feel the champagne fizz pop on my tongue, the sweet, dry taste of it lingering as I watch Franco and Caterina from across the room. He looks as thrilled as she is, and even though I know their high is from the promise of power rather than love, it makes me yearn the slightest bit, despite myself. I've never looked at anyone like that, and I've never seen anyone look at me in that way, either.

"I like my life as it is," I say casually, still watching the happy couple. And I mean it. I *do* love my life, even without the promise of a wife or a family. I like my penthouse, decorated and arranged as I like it, the bed that is empty when I choose and as full as I want when I desire, the space all to myself. I don't feel lonely there, I feel free. It's the only place I ever truly do feel that way, where the constraints of my responsibilities to the family and the pressures that come with it fall away, and I can be myself, with no one watching me. That space, atop one of the tallest buildings in Manhattan, is my own small private kingdom in a way that no other place could ever be, not even the territory itself once it belongs to me.

"Of course you do," Rossi says indulgently. "You're young, and better-looking than I ever was. But remember, you don't have to change your ways altogether just because you marry. You know that."

I shrug. "A wife lives with you. Intrudes on your peace of mind."

"Does Franco look like his peace of mind is in jeopardy?" Rossi laughs, inclining his head towards them, and I snort.

"They haven't even made it to the honeymoon yet. Give them a year or two."

"I don't disagree with you. My own lovely wife, bless her, tests my patience more than a little. But there's joy to be found in family, too, so long as you have an understanding and loyal wife and devoted children. And there's the promise you made, Luca." Rossi frowns. "I won't say I've never broken a promise. And a promise made without your knowledge or consent—well, there's something to be said about that. But it was a promise made in the eyes of God, and it's up to you to decide what weight that carries, if it comes to pass that you need to make good on it." He pauses, watching his family from across the room. "Just know that whatever choice you make, it won't change your place in this family. You are my heir, Luca, and I've just arranged a marriage for my daughter that will solidify your place and your safety, so much as I can. I think that ought to show you how serious I am about this."

"It does." I finish the champagne, and set the glass on a passing tray, taking another. "And I'm very aware of it. I appreciate all that you've given me."

"But—" Rossi lifts a finger. "If the day comes that Sofia Ferretti is threatened, or worse yet, taken, and you don't wish to fulfill your end of the bargain—" He turns to look at me then, his face very serious. "It will be in my hands then, to decide what to do, so long as I still occupy that seat. And I think you know what my solution to the Ferretti problem is."

Something in my gut clenches at that. I do know, better than I want to. But I'm not ready to accept that I might have to do something about it—not yet.

"Let's take it one step at a time," I say calmly, smiling at him. There's not a single thing on my face that would betray the churning in my gut at the thought of Sofia Ferretti, and everything that could change on account of her. "We don't even know if they're targeting her now. They may have forgotten about her, or written her off. She's nothing but a violinist at Juilliard now—she has no contact with us, besides the money. And we don't know that they know anything about my father's pact with hers."

The look on Rossi's face suggests that he thinks I'm being naïve. But he doesn't say anything else, and after a few minutes takes his leave, going to dance with his wife. I stay on the fringes, though, sipping champagne and watching the festivities. I'm not in a dancing mood.

29

* * *

I DON'T HAVE the chance to indulge my mood until much later that night. When the festivities have wrapped up, I and Franco and Caterina, along with their friends, take off for our own afterparty. Angelica convinces us to go to her favorite bar, a twenties-style speakeasy, and before long we're seated in a half-circle on velvet and leather lounges by a brick wall, drinking cocktails from a secret menu.

The whiskey tastes good after so much champagne, heavy and smoky on my tongue. I glance around the room, and catch the eye of a tall, slender redhead perched by the bar, dressed in a short green velvet minidress.

She gets up almost immediately, striding towards me in heels that emphasize every inch of her mile-long legs, and my mouth goes a little dry as I think of what it might be like to have those wrapped around my waist—or better yet, my head, while I see how many times I can make her come with my tongue.

My favorite thing about Manhattan, by far, is the fact that there are a seemingly endless number of women in this city. I don't think I've ever slept with the same one twice.

The redhead stops in front of me, cocking her head to one side. "I don't think I've ever seen you here before."

I give her my most charming smile, reaching up to loosen my tie. "That's because I've never been." Slowly, I let my eyes rake over her, taking in her narrow waist and small breasts. She's not wearing a bra under her dress—I can see her nipples pressing against the fabric. "You look like Christmas."

Her long eyelashes flutter. "You can unwrap me, if you like."

Very bold. I like women who think they can be in charge. It makes it all the sweeter when they find out that after only a few minutes in my bed, they'll be wet and begging for more.

She smiles at me, inclining her head towards the ornate door at the back of the bar that leads to the ladies' room. "Be right back."

I know that for what it is—an invitation. I hesitate for a moment, wondering if that's really how I want tonight to go. A blowjob or a quick fuck in a bathroom stall, no matter how luxurious, doesn't hold much appeal for me anymore. On the other hand—I wouldn't mind finding out what her full lips feel like around my cock.

Taking another sip of my drink, I decide to wait for her to come back. I like to take my time, and that's best done in my king-sized bed —or maybe on the leather sofa. Better yet, up against the window overlooking the city. *Besides,* I think wryly to myself, finishing the drink, *it's best if she knows who's going to be calling the shots tonight.*

My cell phone buzzes in my pocket, and I reach for it, groaning inwardly. I don't know who would be calling me at this time of night —anyone I might want to talk to is already here. Which means it's probably not going to be someone I want to hear from.

Sure enough, it's Don Rossi.

Fuck.

I stand up, glancing towards the back of the bar to see if the redhead has emerged before mouthing *I have to take this* to Franco, and then stepping outside. All I wanted to do after the last few mind-numbing hours was knock back a few drinks, find the hottest girl in the bar, and take her home so that I could lose myself in the sweet oblivion of a perfect figure and good pussy. The last thing I want to do tonight is put out a fire for my boss.

"Luca, I need you at the warehouse in Chelsea, now. As soon as you can get there. Whatever you're doing or whoever you're with, drop her and get down here."

I stifle a groan. *Can't someone else handle this for one goddamn night?* I'm just about to say exactly that, when Rossi continues, and the words that come out of his mouth send a chill down my spine.

"They have Sofia."

LUCA

The docks smell like fish and garbage. I stride down the dock towards the warehouse, feeling myself tense as I approach it. I can feel the shift in myself, the person that I become when this part of the job requires doing. I don't enjoy torture, but the Bratva has taken too much from me for there to be any true hesitation on my part. I saw my father's body before the funeral. It had to be a closed casket for everyone else. That's how terrible the things that they did to him were.

Tonight it's not even a little bit difficult. All it took were those three words: *they have Sofia.*

I don't care so much about the girl herself. I haven't seen her since she was twelve. But my father died avenging hers. He made a vow, and I'll be damned if I'll let these fucking Russians make my father's—and Sofia's father's—deaths for nothing.

Marrying Sofia Ferretti is the last thing I want to do. But I've never broken a promise yet, and I'm not about to start now.

Inside the warehouse there's a man sitting on a chair, his arms tied behind him. His mouth is already bloody, his eyes swollen and blackening, and I see Rossi standing there with several of his men surrounding the chair. The man has a resigned look on his face, as if he already knows what the end of this is. He knows he's not walking out of here alive. What he says or doesn't say depends on how much pain lies between now and that end.

"Luca." Rossi's voice is dry and cool. "Good to see you."

"I got here as quickly as I could. Who is this?"

One of Rossi's men spits on the floor. "His name is Leo. He's one of the Bratva dogs. But we already knew that."

"We haven't gotten anything else out of him," Rossi says darkly. "Despite the work that my men did on his face. Since this is so personal to you, Luca, I thought perhaps it could use your skill."

I frown, striding towards the chair. The man has distinctly Russian features, his greying blond hair stiffening from dried sweat and blood at his hairline. He lifts his head as I walk towards him, disgust plain on his face.

"So, Leo, is that true?" I squat down in front of him. "Are you Bratva? Do you answer to Viktor Andreyev?"

"Fuck you," he says in his thickly accented voice, spitting on the ground. "And fuck your children, too."

The punch comes before he can see it, my fist connecting with his cheek with a sickening thud and the sound of cracking teeth. Blood trickles from the corner of his mouth—he bit his tongue.

"I don't have any children," I say coolly. "But I can make sure you never do, if you don't talk."

"You're going to kill me. So hurry up and do it. I'm not saying shit." He spits out another mouthful of blood.

"Maybe not," I say conversationally. "Maybe I cut off your balls, and take a few of your fingers, and then let you wander back to your master like a castrated dog. Maybe I let you live that life, instead of mercifully killing you. You don't deserve a kind death, Leo. But you can earn it."

Out of the corner of my eye, I see Rossi's grim, satisfied smile. He called me here for a reason—I'm the best at this game. Better even than him, and he knows it, because he gets too much enjoyment from torture. He doesn't know when to stop, but I will. I'll do just enough to force them to talk, and once they realize that they spill everything

33

they know from the boss's secrets to their grandmother's cookie recipe.

This guy is going to do the same thing. He just doesn't know it yet.

Thirty minutes later, the man is sobbing. His lip is split, two of his teeth are on the concrete, and one of his fingernails is sitting next to it. And I'm still standing in front of him, cool and collected even with his blood and spit on my shirt and jacket, a pair of pliers in my hands.

"Are we going to keep going?" I ask him, smirking. "Or would you like to lose another fingernail? Maybe the tip of a toe. I haven't forgotten about the threat to your balls, either."

The man sneers at me. "You Italians think that you are so untouchable. You think you hold this city in an iron fist. But you can't hold it forever. We're coming for you, for your wives, for your sons and your daughters, for your entire blood-soaked family."

"There's just as much blood on your hands." I click the pliers together, but to the man's credit, he doesn't flinch. There's tear tracks in the blood on his face, but his expression is still defiant. "You've been trying for years to take over, but you can't. This city is ours. You're lucky you have the territory we allow you."

I lean down, fastening the pliers over the man's thumbnail. When he doesn't speak again, I yank.

The scream echoes through the warehouse.

When the man can breathe again, he glares up at me. "We're closer than you know. We're infiltrating your upper echelon, and you don't even know it. And you won't, until it's too late."

I click the pliers together again, and he flinches. "What do you mean by that?"

Rossi clears his throat, and I rephrase, going back to the first question I asked.

"Where is Sofia Ferretti?"

"That name means nothing to me."

I let out a long-suffering sigh, and squat down again, so that I'm eye level with Leo. He stinks of piss—hardly a surprise, after what he's gone through tonight. "See, Leo, that's how I know you're bullshitting me. Because every Bratva man, from Viktor down to your lowest mongrel, knows who Sofia Ferretti is. Now she's gone missing, and what I need to know from you is *where* she is. And if I haven't convinced you already that I'll stop at nothing to find out, perhaps this will help."

Grasping his wrist in one hand, I take the finger that's now short a nail, and yank it backwards.

By the time Leo stops screaming, he's soiled himself again.

I wrinkle my nose with disgust. "Do I need to break another one?"

"I don't know who—"

The heel of my hand comes down hard on one of his balls.

"I'm tired of hearing you scream, Leo," I say loudly, over the noise. "But what I'm more tired of is being lied to. There's a lot of pieces I can take off of you and still leave you alive enough to show us where Sofia is. Save yourself some pain, and tell me now. Because I promise you, I will not let you die until you do."

When the pliers fasten onto another nail, he starts to weep.

"I'll tell you!" he shrieks. "Please, just don't. Not another one, please—"

I stand up, tossing the pliers onto a nearby table. "Good. I was going to move on to your teeth next."

Leo shudders. "I'll give you the address. They're keeping her at a hotel they own with the other girls, the ones who—"

"We know all about Viktor's business, Leo. That's not why we're here tonight." I nod at the man standing next to Rossi, my jaw tense. "Get the address, and gag and tie him. He's coming along with us, just in case he's still lying and we have to take a few more fingernails to get the truth."

I turn on my heel, stalking out into the cool night air. I breathe in, and even the stink of the docks is preferable to being close to the sweating, bleeding, pissing man inside the warehouse.

Don Rossi's footsteps come up behind me, and I turn around. "Well?"

His expression is unreadable. "If she's in that hotel room, and still alive, you know what this means."

"I'll do my duty."

35

"Are you sure about that? There's always a way out, you know. You don't have to marry this girl."

I think of the alternative. Rossi won't leave her alive for the Russians to try to use as leverage again. If I refuse to marry her, Sofia will be nothing more than a loose end that needs tying up. I know Don Rossi very well—he won't flinch at that. I'm all that stands between her and two equally terrible choices: being sold by the Russians, or killed by the man who once employed her father.

The very last thing I want is a wife. But I won't be responsible for breaking my father's promise.

With my lips pressed tightly together, I jerk my head towards the town car, where the bound and gagged Leo is being shoved into the backseat. In the car just ahead of it, a cadre of soldiers armed to the teeth are piling in, ready to take the hotel where Sofia is being held by storm.

"Let's go," I say tightly, not looking at Rossi as I stride towards the car.

Her life is in my hands now. And I know exactly what I plan to do with it.

SOFIA

I wake up in a bed.

The first thought that goes through my head as my eyes blink open is that I feel more comfortable than I would have expected to be. The pillows and duvet feel soft, and the room smells like lavender.

My body, on the other hand, aches throughout every inch.

I try to sit up, pushing myself back against the pillows, and that's when I come fully to my senses as I realize that my hands are bound above my head, tied to the headboard.

Oh my god. Oh my fucking god, I've been kidnapped—

I scream, the sound filling the room as I shriek at the top of my lungs, twisting this way and that as I try to loosen the binding on my hands. As I twist to my right, I see a man sitting in a wing chair near the window, his face slightly amused as he watches me struggle.

"There is no point," he says in a thickly accented voice when I stop screaming for a moment, breathless with shock. "You can scream all you like. Viktor owns this hotel and everyone inside of it. All you will accomplish by screaming is damaging what I'm sure is a lovely voice. And then your sale price will be much lower. You won't like that."

Sale price? My heart pounds in my chest, so hard that it hurts. I glance down at myself, fear licking down my spine and turning my blood to ice, but I'm still dressed.

The man smirks. "No one has touched you, *malyutka*. You're far too valuable for that."

There's a hint of disappointment in his voice, and it sends another shiver through me. "What do you mean, *sale price*? Who is selling me? Where?"

"You are the property of Viktor Andreyev now. Our boss, the *Avtoritet*. As far as where or to who—" the man shrugs. "Whoever offers the highest price, *malyutka*. Maybe a sheik. Maybe some businessman. Who knows?"

"Stop fucking calling me that," I hiss, jerking at the binding on my wrists again. "I'm not your fucking *malyutka*, whatever the fuck that means."

The man stands up suddenly, crossing the room to the bed. I try to flinch away, but he grabs my chin in his hand, not hard enough to bruise, but hard enough to hurt.

"You'll learn to keep that pretty mouth shut until it's needed," he growls, his fingers digging into my cheek. "Or else you'll learn to regret it. The kind of men who buy girls from the Bratva don't tolerate insolence."

I've never known fear like this. I can feel my heart stuttering in my chest, my entire body going cold. It's suffocating. But I still manage to yank my head back, mustering every bit of moisture left in my dry mouth to spit in the man's face.

"They can go fuck themselves, too," I hiss.

He recoils. I brace myself for the slap that I know is coming, but before he can hit me against his better judgement, the door opens.

The man immediately stiffens, retreating backwards. "Mikhail. She spit at me—"

"Sit down." The man who walks in—Mikhail?—is the one from the club. The man with the eagle tattoo, the one who kidnapped me. The fear is momentarily replaced by anger as I jerk forward, struggling again as I glare at him.

"You fucking kidnapped me! Do you know who I am?"

I've never in my life considered using that line. I don't even know if it means anything anymore. But in these, the most terrifying moments of my life, all I can think is that if there's even a possibility that invoking my father's name might save me, I have to try.

But Mikhail only smiles. It curls patronizingly across his face, as if he's looking at someone very stupid. "Of course I know who you are, Sofia Ferretti. That's why you're here."

I stare at him, dumbfounded. "I—"

All of the hope I'd momentarily felt floods out of me, leaving me feeling weak and deflated. That was all I had, my only card to play.

"Is it the money?" I try that tactic again. "Because if it is, you can have it. I don't even want it."

"We know." Mikhail comes to stand closer to the bed, looking down at me. I've never felt so helpless and vulnerable in my life. "This isn't about the money, Sofia."

"Then what?"

"You're bait," he says simply. "You always have been. It just wasn't the right time to dangle you out in front of the man that we know will come for you. But now we have what we need."

"You're wrong," I say, as bravely as I can manage. "No one is coming for me."

The words leave a hollow ache in my chest. But as far as I know, it's true. I have no one left. Ana is my only real friend, and she has no idea where I am. *Ana.* Just the thought of her brings tears to my eyes. She's worried sick by now, probably blaming herself for taking us to that awful club in the first place—

"Oh, I can assure you, someone is." Mikhail checks his watch, a gleaming gold timepiece on his wrist that looks expensive. "And he should be here any—minute."

I hear a crackling, and Mikhail lifts a finger to his ear, as if there's someone talking to him. "Yes. I hear you." He nods to the man on the other side of the bed. "Be ready. The others are outside. They're coming up."

"Who's coming up?" I demand. "What the fuck is going on?"

Mikhail wheels around, slapping me hard across one cheek. "I

39

think that Anton was meant to teach you better manners," he hisses. "For a girl with such good breeding, you have a filthy mouth. I would have thought your father would have taught you better." He smiles coldly as he rises to his feet. "Don't fret, I'm sure the man who buys you will keep your mouth too full for it to say such things."

He leans up then, undoing the binding that holds me to the bed, even though my wrists are still tied together with what feels like plastic, like a zip-tie. I start to struggle the moment he begins to lift me off of the bed, and he slaps me again, hard.

"I don't want to leave marks," Mikhail says, his voice low and threatening. "Viktor will be upset if your price is threatened. But you will be still."

I will not. Ignoring him completely, I writhe in his grip, until he grabs me by the hair and yanks my head back, so hard that tears come to my eyes.

His gaze flits down, landing on the cross at my neck. "What's this?" With his free hand, he touches the necklace, and I all but snarl at him, twisting despite his grip on my hair and trying desperately to bite him.

Mikhail grins. "I should take this from you, I think. No *shlyukha* should have something this pretty."

I instantly stop struggling. I hate myself for it, because I know that's exactly what he wants. But I can't bear to have my mother's necklace taken away. Not even if it means submitting to this awful man, for now.

"No, please," I whisper, hating the whimper in my voice. "Please don't take it."

"If I leave it, you'll be a good girl?" The patronizing tone is back, and Mikhail is grinning down at me. He's playing me like a well-tuned instrument, and he knows it.

"Yes," I whisper, tears leaking from my eyes.

"Good." He drags me across the room then, towards the closet. "You'll stay in here, until we're finished. Less chance of a stray bullet catching you. Don't move," he warns, looking down at my stunned and frightened face. "Don't try to escape. You're a dead woman if you do."

And with that, he closes the door, leaving me in the dark.

* * *

IN THE FIRST few seconds that I spend in the closet, I consider ignoring Mikhail's orders, and trying to escape anyway. My hands are tied, and I can hear that there are still people in the room—whether it's Mikhail or Anton or others, I don't know—but there's always a possibility that I could slip past them. I'm not ready to give up yet.

But then I hear the first gunshot outside the room, and my body turns to ice.

I'd thought I was frightened before. It's nothing compared to what I feel now. I live in New York City—I've definitely heard gunfire before, but never so close. Never so—*personal*. Whatever is happening outside this closet, it's about me. And I don't understand it.

Mikhail said that someone was coming for me. But I don't know who. After my father's funeral, I rarely saw the men in expensive suits. Every now and then, one would come to our apartment. But the visits were fewer and further between as the years passed. The last time I saw one was at the hospital, just before my mother died. I assumed it was someone taking care of the bills, but I'd been too exhausted and grief-stricken to ask questions or care.

I've always wondered if the money had something to do with them. It makes the most sense—but I don't know why, after so long, they would still care. Whatever my father was involved in while he was alive, it has nothing to do with me anymore.

Except apparently, it *does*.

There's another gunshot, and another, and the sound of yelling and cursing in Russian—and Italian. The sound of my father's native language makes me lift my head even as I curl into a tight ball in the corner of the small closet, terrified of a stray bullet piercing the door. The shots are coming faster now, and I feel the room shake as a body hits the wall hard, and too close to my hiding place for comfort.

Whoever has come, they're Italian. Which means they must have known my father.

I press my face against the carpet, tears of fear and confusion streaming down my face. *I don't want to die here, like this,* I think desperately. I don't want to be sold, either, into whatever human trafficking scheme that the Bratva is running. But more than anything, I just want to live. That simple fact has never struck me as clearly as it does now, breathing in the scent of hotel carpet as the sound of gunfire echoes just outside the door.

It seems to go on forever. I've lost all track of time when the room suddenly goes silent, and I feel my stomach knotting as I hold my breath, waiting for more shots.

But they don't come. A second later the door to the closet opens, light flooding in.

I push myself up with my bound hands, blinking as I look up. There's a man standing there, dark-haired instead of blond, his white shirt spattered with blood and a gun in his hand.

My god, he's fucking gorgeous, is the last ridiculous thought that goes through my head as I wobble, tilting dangerously to one side.

And then, as my rescuer looks grimly down at me, I pass out cold.

LUCA

*E*very time I see Sofia Ferretti, she's in tears.

Last time was at her father's funeral, when she was a round-faced, snot-nosed twelve-year-old.

Now she looks entirely different. She's lost the baby fat, and her hair is platinum blonde instead of dark brown—dyed, no doubt. *Something that I'll put a stop to as soon as we're married.* Just like eight years ago, her face is tear-streaked and red, but there's only one, startling thought in my head as I set eyes on Sofia Ferretti all grown up for the first time.

She's beautiful.

"Luca."

Don Rossi's voice cuts into my thoughts. "There's one still alive."

My stomach twists. *I don't want to torture anyone else. I want to get Sofia out of here.* The urgency of the thought startles me. I don't want to care about her. But in this room that smells like gunpowder, blood and death, all I can think is that she shouldn't wake up and see this. The look in her eyes just before she passed out isn't something I'll soon forget. She looked like a terrified animal caught in a trap—which is an apt description for the situation she was in before we arrived.

"I want to get my bride out of here," I say calmly, turning towards Rossi. "I don't want her to see the bodies."

Rossi looks at me curiously. "I thought you didn't give a shit about her."

"I don't." I keep my voice cool. "But I'd rather her first impression of me not be—this." I wave my hand around the room. There's bodies everywhere, blood splattering the walls. Bullet holes in multiple surfaces.

Rossi glances over at the surviving Russian. He has a defiant sneer on his face, and I think I recognize him vaguely, though I wouldn't know his name. One of Viktor's brigadiers, if I remember correctly.

"Bruno can handle him," he says finally. "Get Sofia out of here."

"Thank you." I nod respectfully, mindful despite everything that Rossi is the Don, the head of the family. It could have cost me a great deal to argue with him the way I just did, and I'm not sure why I risked it. So that Sofia could be spared the sight of blood and dead bodies?

Striding towards the closet, I scoop Sofia up into my arms. She feels very light, and her head lolls against my shoulder, her face paper-white and bloodless. I make a mental note to call the doctor who makes house calls for the family on the way back. *If those dogs so much as laid a hand on her—*

As her head tilts in the light, I can see that at least one of them did. Her bottom lip is split, and there's blood dried there and on her chin. A faint bruise is forming on her cheek, and a hot, burning rage rises up in my chest as I walk through the room with Sofia in my arms. I hadn't regretted a single Russian that I killed tonight, but now I'm glad of it. The thought of one of them striking her fills me with an unfamiliar, almost primal rage.

It's an unsettling feeling.

I've made it a point all my life to care only about my job, my position, and my wealth. My father's death taught me a lesson that served me well—everyone in the family lives a life that can end at any time. It's not just the men, either. Our women can be murdered, kidnapped, used as pawns against us. I've seen men brought down, made men who broke the code of silence because they believed the threats against their wives or children.

Loving someone means a loss of control. It means that something can be taken from you, and there's nothing you can do about it. That's not something that fits with the way I've chosen to live my life.

I lay Sofia carefully down in the backseat of the town car, taking a seat across from her. Leaning back as the car pulls out into the late-evening Manhattan traffic, I watch the slight rise and fall of her chest in the tight black dress that she's wearing, study the pale hue of her face, the bow-shaped curve of her rosy lips. There's a faint stain of lipstick around her mouth still, but the color there now is hers, warm and pink and soft. It makes my cock twitch, hardening slightly as I let my gaze drift over her prone body, and I think for a moment of what it might be like to have her as my wife, in my bed.

She's not a child anymore. She's a woman, and a remarkably beautiful one. By tomorrow night, my ring will be on her finger, and before the week is out, she'll be my bride in all ways. Sofia might not know what's coming, but there has never been a woman yet who refused my bed.

I've lost count of how many I've had, and yet the allure of a new body to explore, new lips to taste, has never lost its appeal. I've never wanted to limit myself to one woman, and one of the many privileges of my position and wealth is that I'll never be asked to. Mafia wives know that their husbands aren't faithful. All they ask is discretion, and being gentlemen, we give it to them. But looking at Sofia's face in the passing light, I feel something that I've never felt before—a possessiveness that makes me uncomfortable. A need not just for the pleasure of a woman's body, but for *hers*.

When Don Rossi told me that she'd been taken, the obvious answer had been to go after her. Sofia is too valuable an asset to be left in the hands of the Russians—the choice was always to save her or eliminate her entirely. On the surface, it's easy to tell myself that the carnage I just left behind was part of the job, safeguarding the territory of the Rossi family—the territory that will eventually pass to me.

But deep down, I know the truth.

The dead Bratva in that hotel aren't lying in their own blood because of the need to protect *territory*.

I killed them because they took what was mine.

* * *

DR. CARELLA IS ALREADY WAITING when my driver pulls into the garage. I've never thought much about it before, but for the first time I'm glad that the doctor who makes house calls for Don Rossi, his associates and their families is a woman. Rossi thought that he was being very progressive when he chose her as our personal physician, but in this moment, I don't care about the optics of it. The thought of another man putting his hands on Sofia, examining her, makes me tense all over again.

From now on, the only man who touches her, hell, who even *looks* at her, will be me.

I don't have time to examine these new feelings, and I don't particularly want to either. Instead I simply scoop Sofia out of the backseat of the car, striding towards the private elevator that will take us up to my penthouse with the doctor following in my wake.

She doesn't ask questions. Dr. Carella has kept her job and her life while working so familiarly with the family because she knows the meaning of discretion, and she knows that she's better off with less information, rather than more. So as I lay Sofia down on the bed, she merely gives me a reassuring smile, and says calmly: "Mr. Romano, step out of the room while I examine her, please. I'll come get you in a few minutes when I'm finished."

My immediate reaction is to refuse. The sight of Sofia's delicate body laid out on my black bedspread tightens something deep inside of me. She looks very pale, very fragile, very *breakable.*

It shouldn't excite me as much as it does.

"Mr. Romano," the doctor prods. "Luca."

Her saying my given name is what finally snaps me out of it. "Fine," I growl. "But don't take too long."

I stride out of the room, feeling every muscle in my body tensed.

My hands are clenched at my sides, and I shake them loose, walking briskly towards the floor-to-ceiling glass window on one side of my living room as I try not to think about how Sofia looked in my bed. Every inch of her, from her delicate pale face to her slender body, to the halo of her golden hair around her head, evoked a sleeping angel, a rescued princess, something innocent and pure and lovely.

Which is why you have no business marrying her.

I'm the furthest thing from pure. I've tortured men, I've killed them, I've fucked as many women in this city as I could get my hands on, and up until this very moment, I never had the slightest intention of stopping. In order to keep my city and my territory, I'm going to have to torture and kill even more men, and nothing in me balks at that for even a second. But it's not my seat at the head of this city that I feel compelled to spill blood for in this moment.

It's Sofia.

I've never given a single woman that I've touched a second thought. My relationship with them ended the second that I threw the condom away or watched them swallow my cum. I hadn't expected to give Sofia a second thought either, beyond the day that we exchanged the vows that would protect her and consummated our marriage. Once, after all, is all that's necessary to make it legal. Once would satisfy any lingering curiosity about what kind of woman she's grown up to be.

A few more times, maybe, during the right time of the month, if I decided that I wanted children. But children were never a part of the plan. My seat is meant to go to Franco's son when I die, if Angelica gives him one.

All I can think as I stare down at the city below, this city that belongs to me, is that I want Sofia Ferretti more than once. More than for a night. When I saw her face staring up at me from the floor of that closet, something changed.

Everything changed. And I'll burn this entire city to the ground if I have to, in order to keep Viktor Andreyev from ever taking her from me again.

* * *

WHEN DR. CARELLA COMES OUT, she looks relieved, which in turn calms me a little. I meet her halfway across the room, sinking down onto my leather sofa as she takes the seat across from me.

"Physically, she's fine," the doctor says. "She has some minor bruising on her face and the injury to her lip, as well as some bruising around her wrists, but overall they don't seem to have harmed her. I'll run some blood tests, since she was most likely drugged, and I'd advise you to keep an eye on her once she's conscious again. I didn't see any signs of a concussion, but if she seems ill, it would be wise to call me in case she suffers any adverse effects from the drugs." Dr. Carella pauses. "I didn't see any signs of—abuse, either."

"Meaning?" I want to hear it clearly. *If those dogs violated my fiancée—*

"She wasn't assaulted beyond the bruising that I mentioned. And I'm fairly certain that she's still a virgin, if that matters to you." Dr. Carella's mouth twists downwards when she says that, and I can see plainly on her face exactly what she thinks of that idea.

If she'd mentioned it earlier tonight, I would have said that I didn't give a fuck if Sofia Ferretti was a virgin or if she'd fucked every guy between her apartment and Fifth Avenue. But as with everything else tonight, that seems to have changed.

The thought of another man touching her makes my stomach clench with rage. And the thought of her being a virgin, of me being the first one to see her naked body, to touch her, to slide inside of her and take her for the first time—

I'm hard just thinking about it. The desire that crashes through me is something primal and vicious, and I have to breathe in deeply and force the thought of what I want to do to Sofia's virgin body away, just so that I'm able to stand up and shake the doctor's hand.

"Thank you for coming," I tell her, my voice cool and formal. "I'll call you if I notice anything out of place."

Dr. Carella hesitates.

"Yes?" I can hear my tone harden. "Is there something else?"

I want to be alone with my bride. I'm itching for her to wake up so that I can speak to her and explain the situation, how things will be from here on out. She'll be grateful to me for rescuing her, of course, and then we can discuss the future—our wedding, and what will come after. What will need to be done to ensure her safety, and the safety of everyone that I'm responsible for.

"Her physical injuries were minor," Dr. Carella repeats. "But her emotional and mental state when she wakes up may be—fragile. I'd be cautious of that, Mr. Romano."

"I'll keep that in mind." I stride to the front door that leads out into the hall, opening it wide. "Good night, Dr. Carella."

She presses her lips together thinly, and I can tell that there's more that she wants to say. Wisely, she thinks better of it, and nods, walking out of the apartment without another word.

With the door closed fully behind me, I turn towards the bedroom, my pulse quickening as I think of what's waiting for me there.

It's time to talk to my bride.

SOFIA

*O*nce again, I'm in a bed.

When I come back to consciousness and feel the duvet under my hands, my first thought is that it was all a dream—the gunshots, the rescue, the man who stood in the doorway. A jolt of pure terror rushes through me as I sit up with a jerk, my hair falling around my face as I fight back the urge to scream. *I have to escape, I have to get out of here, I have to--*

And then, slowly, I become aware of my surroundings.

I feel the bedspread under my *hands*—they're no longer tied. I can sit up—I'm not bound to anything. And the room doesn't smell of lavender like the hotel, instead it smells clean, like fresh linens, and faintly smoky like—

Like a man.

The memory of the man in the doorway, blood-spattered and holding a gun, comes back to me. Who was he? Was he the one that Mikhail was talking about, when he'd said that someone would come for me?

I push my hair out of my face, looking around the room where I've found myself. The lights are dim, but I can see some details—I'm sitting

50

in the middle of a massive bed, made up with a sleek black duvet, and a set of neatly arranged pillows in alternating black and white. The entire room is equally elegant and monotone—a blackout blind covers most of one wall, the floor is dark hardwood, and the headboard is black leather. Everything is dark and masculine, and the room reeks of power and money. I'm willing to bet that the iron and wood nightstand to my right cost as much as a month's rent at my apartment, if not more.

Taking a deep breath, I try to slow my racing heartbeat. I'm not in the hotel any longer, which is a good thing. Hopefully I'm out of Mikhail's hands as well, although I don't know whose hands I've fallen into—if they're better or worse, kinder or crueler.

Nothing could be worse than being trafficked, I tell myself. Wherever I am now, it must be an improvement on that fate.

I hope so, at least.

Standing up slowly, I make my way towards the wall where the blinds are drawn. My head swims a little, and I feel unsteady, but I manage to stay upright. Someone removed my shoes—I see the pumps tossed carelessly next to the bed—and the floor feels good under my bare feet, cool and smooth. Something about the sensation grounds me a little, calms me, and I take another deep breath as I reach for the blind to push it back and try to get some idea of where I am.

The blind doesn't move at all, even when I tug on it. Frustrated, I push back one corner to peek around it, and stifle a gasp at what stretches out in front of me.

It's not a window so much as a wall, most of this side of the room taken up by floor-to-ceiling glass that looks out over part of the city. The lights outside stretch out as far as I can see, the buildings that make up the city below scattered out in miniature. *How high up am I?* I think dizzily as I look down over it, and I have to back up for a minute to let the sudden vertigo recede.

"Beautiful, isn't it?"

A deep male voice fills the room, and I spin around too quickly. I feel myself tilt dangerously to one side, but the man strides across the room before I can fall, catching me with broad, strong hands grasping my waist.

I look up into the greenest pair of eyes I've ever seen, and my heart flutters in my chest. His features are shadowed, but I can see the sharp line of his nose, the edge of his high cheekbones, the strong jaw. A strange sensation ripples through my body, and I can feel myself warming under his touch. My heart starts to race again, and I can feel butterflies taking off in my stomach, the tingling spreading throughout me, all the way to my fingertips as I steady myself with my hands against his chest.

And then I glance down, and see the blood on his shirt, crimson stains on white.

I jerk myself out of his grasp, stepping back so quickly that I nearly trip again. He doesn't move to grab me this time, only watches as I sit down on the edge of the bed unsteadily, then crosses to the other side of the room.

"They're electric," he explains, pushing a button on the wall. With a low hum, the blinds begin to pull back, letting the light from the city come into the room, brightening it a little more. "There's an equally stunning view in my living room." He glances over at me, and I see his mouth quirk upwards with amusement at the expression on my face. "It takes some getting used to, I suppose."

I stare at him, uncomprehending. How much money does someone have to have in order to live like this? "How high up are we?" My voice squeaks at the end, and I wish desperately that it hadn't.

"We're on the very top floor," he replies, his mouth still twitching as if he finds my shock funny . "You're in the penthouse. *My* penthouse," he clarifies. "There's a pool on the roof, and a hot tub, if you'd like to see those."

Penthouse? In New York? This man must be a millionaire—a billionaire, *even.* Slowly I get to my feet again, squaring my shoulders and lifting my chin. Whatever is happening here—whatever reason there was for him to be there to pick me up out of that closet, whatever is going on between him and the Bratva, I know for certain that I want no part of it.

I also know that I'm never going to another fucking nightclub in Manhattan again.

"Thank you very much for rescuing me," I begin, with as much dignity as I can muster. "But if you wouldn't mind calling me a cab, I'd like to go home now."

The man chuckles, low and deep. "You're not going anywhere, Sofia."

A chill runs down my spine. "Excuse me?" My voice cracks despite my best efforts, the fear of the last few hours coming back full force. "Who are you? How do you know my name? And what do you mean, *I'm not going anywhere?*"

He presses his hand to the wall again, and the recessed lights in the ceiling brighten, giving me a better view of everything in the room—and of him. I'd hoped in some small part of me, despite the circumstances and the evidence of the blood on his shirt, that he was someone other than the man I'd seen just before I'd passed out. But there's no doubt now that he's the same person.

The man smirks, his mouth twisting up on one side in his handsome face. He's every bit as gorgeous as I'd thought initially, with thick dark hair cut short and expertly styled, sharp features, and a tall, powerful body wrapped in a perfectly tailored suit. If it weren't for the blood, he'd look like any one of the men that I saw in the bars that Ana took me to earlier tonight.

Was that really tonight? It seems like ages ago that I was innocently wandering through Manhattan's hotspots with my best friend. It doesn't even feel as if it happened in the same week, let alone just a few hours before this.

He's still watching me carefully with those intense green eyes, every bit as commanding as the men I saw earlier, the ones that made me so uncomfortable, who reminded me of alpha predators surveying their turf.

Waiting to claim their prey.

I'm not entirely certain that's not what I am to him.

"I'll begin with the first question," he says coolly. "I'm Luca Romano."

Romano. The name rings a distant bell. Closing my eyes, I think back, trying to remember where I might have heard that name before.

Faintly, I remember a tall and handsome man coming to our house for dinner. I can just barely recall my father introducing him to us, and I can hear my father's voice in my head telling us that this was his best friend, a man named *something...Romano.*

There had been someone else there too—his son. A boy older than me, already almost a teenager when they'd come to visit. I can't remember his name now, I can't even remember the first name of my father's friend, but—

My gaze snaps up to the man—to Luca Romano—as the breath leaves my body.

"Your father knew mine," I whisper, my head swimming all over again. I feel dizzy. "Your father was my father's best friend. I remember him coming to our house—" I stare at Luca. I want to say that I can't believe it, but I can. It makes sense now—or at least a little of it does. "You were with him."

"I was. I was at your father's funeral, too. I remember seeing you there on both occasions." Luca replies. He watches me from his spot near the window, as if I'm a frightened animal that might run if he moves too quickly.

"But why—" It still doesn't entirely make sense to me. "Just because our fathers knew each other doesn't explain why you were there tonight. It doesn't explain how you knew where I was—how you know *me.* I don't even remember being told your name before tonight."

Luca smiles, but it doesn't reach his eyes. There's something else in his face, an expression that I can't quite read. "I know you because our fathers made a promise eight years ago, Sofia. A promise that now, on account of the Bratva, I have to keep. A promise that keeps you here, with me."

"What?" I must have heard him wrong. "I'm not staying here."

He lets out a long sigh. "Yes, Sofia, you are. You may as well begin to think of this penthouse as your home. It will be, very soon."

"I don't understand."

Luca takes a step towards me, and then another. I can see the tension in his body, the muscles working in his jaw, and I'm suddenly very aware of how large a man he is. He towers over me by several inches, and I can see the muscles beneath the sleeves of his shirt flex as he crosses his arms over his chest, staring down at me with the imperious look of a man who has already made a decision.

"By the end of the week, Sofia, you will be my wife."

SOFIA

"*A*re you fucking *kidding me?*"

The words explode from my mouth before I can stop them as I back away, intent on edging around him towards the door. "I'm not going to marry you! I don't even *know* you! Why on earth would you think—"

"I know this is a shock," Luca says smoothly, cutting me off. "But it isn't a question, Sofia. I'm not asking you to marry me. I'm telling you that you *will* marry me. You don't have a choice in the matter."

I stare at him, uncomprehending. "Look, like I said before, I appreciate you rescuing me. Those men were awful, and I'm really grateful that you got me out of there. But right now all I want to do is go back to my apartment, let my best friend know that I'm still alive, and then report the fucking *human trafficking ring* that's being run out of a hotel in downtown Manhattan!"

Luca takes a deep breath, and I can see the irritation beginning to spread over his features. "Sofia. You can't leave. Those weren't just any *men*, they were Bratva. Enemies of your father, and mine, and the man that I work for. My enemies, and yours. They won't stop, and they won't leave you alone. There is no going back to your old life."

I hear what he's saying, but it doesn't sink in. I can't believe it—I *won't.* This morning I was just a student at Juilliard, a violinist, an orphan. I wasn't anyone important, or anyone of note, beyond my spot as first chair in my class.

"I don't have enemies," I say, my voice beginning to shake a little. "If they were my father's enemies, fine, but my father is *dead*, Luca! He's been dead for *eight years!* This has nothing to do with me!"

For a second, I almost see a flicker of sympathy in his eyes. "I'm sorry, Sofia. This wasn't my choice either," he admits. "But it has everything to do with you, and me. And they aren't going to stop just because you don't want to be a part of this. You were born into it, just like I was."

I pause, considering. "So you don't *want* to marry me?"

That unreadable expression passes over his face again. "I didn't want to," he says, and his use of the past tense doesn't escape me. "But the choice is made, Sofia. We *will* be married."

"If you don't want to, then don't," I whisper. My heart is pounding so hard that it hurts. "Just let me go."

"I can't do that."

"This isn't my plan for my life!" I snap at him, the anger suddenly returning at his complete and utter intransigence. "I'm supposed to graduate in two months, and leave Manhattan, just like my father wanted me to! I'm going to Paris, and then I'm going to audition for the orchestra in London, and then—"

I stop suddenly, remembering the first thing he said, when he explained how he knew me. "You said there was a promise—that our *fathers* made a promise. What did you mean by that?"

Luca lets out a long breath. "Will you sit down?" He motions to the bed.

Crossing my arms over my chest, I shake my head firmly. "No."

"Fine." His jaw clenches, and I can see the muscles there working as he considers what to say next. "Your mother never told you about it?"

"No." I glare at him. "Just tell me what's going on."

"This has to do with how your father died, Sofia. I'm guessing you don't know the details of that, either?"

I shake my head mutely.

"It's possible that your mother wasn't told much, either. The family that our fathers—and now I—work for, didn't care much for your mother. She was Russian, and so they were suspicious of her. Your father's boss didn't approve of him marrying her."

"I guessed that much." I'd gathered that from the fact that my mother wasn't allowed to speak Russian, even at home, the way my father encouraged her to try to blend in, the way she stayed in the kitchen or in my parents' bedroom whenever the men in suits came to the house. The way the women at the funeral looked at her.

"So it's possible that she was never even told. She was called to the Don's office after your father's death, and questioned about it." Luca pauses. "You don't need to know much about that."

A memory comes back to me then, something that had slipped away in the trauma of the days following my father's death. My mother leaving me with a neighbor, telling me that she'd be back soon —but she'd been upset. I can remember now that she'd looked as if she'd been crying.

If I don't come back, call this number. They'll take her. I remember hearing that whisper, and not understanding it. I remember the sympathetic look on the neighbor's face.

But my mother did come back. She'd had a bruise on her face and a swollen eye, and when I'd asked her about it, she'd smiled and said that she tripped and fell.

I can feel my blood turning to ice as the realization hits me of what really happened that day.

"No," I say coldly, staring at Luca. "They didn't tell her anything. I was just a child, and traumatized, but I remember now. My mother came back with a swollen jaw and a black eye. They thought she had something to do with my father's death, didn't they?"

Luca says nothing. He just stands there impassively, his hands in his pockets as he watches the emotions flicker across my face.

"Didn't they?" I almost scream it, my voice filling the room.

"I don't know," Luca finally says. "I was twelve."

"But you work for him now, you said. The same man my father worked for. What are you, some kind of criminal organization?"

Luca snorts. "We don't talk about what happened back then, Sofia —what happened to your father and mine—very often. What was done is done. I'm sure they determined that your mother had nothing to do with it, or—" he stops then, abruptly.

"Or what?" I feel as if I can't breathe. "What would have happened to her?"

His face is emotionless. I don't know how he can be so calm, while I feel as if my entire world is spinning out of control. "I'm sure you can guess," he says, his voice impassive.

"He would have killed her. That's what you're saying, right? Your boss would have killed her?"

Luca's jaw clenches again. His hands slip out of his pockets as he strides towards me, his entire body tense once again. "Yes, Sofia. Is that what you want to hear? If your mother had been working with the Bratva, if she had betrayed your father, the Don would have had her killed. As well he should have. There are *rules* to this life, Sofia, rules that govern your life, and mine, and everyone who is a part of it! And this marriage is a part of that, too."

I swallow hard, trying desperately not to cry. And then it hits me.

Don. He's called the man that he works for the *Don*, twice now. "You're mafia," I whisper, disbelievingly. "And that means—"

"Your father was, too," Luca says tiredly. "And mine. Sofia, your father was third in command to the Don. He was an important man. The only ones above him were my father, and Don Rossi. And he was my father's best friend. So when the Bratva attacked, and your father knew he was close to death, he did the only thing he could think of to do for his family. He turned to his best friend, and he extracted a promise."

The world seems to slow down around me. "What was it?" I ask again in a whisper, my throat tightening. But I think I already know.

"Your father asked mine to make sure that his family was provided for. That you, in particular, would always be provided for financially, enough to ensure that you would never have to worry about housing or food or necessities and then some."

The money. One huge mystery of my life, cleared up in an instant. "The money was from *you*?"

"Not me, specifically," Luca clarifies. "From the family. But those are bank accounts that I will inherit, once I become the Don."

I feel as if I might pass out. "You?" I croak, taking a step back. "You'll be—"

"Yes. My father was underboss. He died avenging your father, Sofia. And he made sure, before he went after the men who killed his best friend, that I was aware of the promise that he'd made years before—that I was to marry you, if the Bratva ever became a danger to you. If they ever tried to use you to take our family down, or hurt you in any way. Until that day came, however—*if* it came at all—you were to be left alone. The money would be sent anonymously, your tuition and rent paid anonymously, etcetera. Your father hoped that it would never be necessary."

"He used to tell me that he wanted me to leave Manhattan after college. Maybe even to go to college overseas in Europe—" It hits me then, all of it. The plan that I've always had, to go to Europe and play in an orchestra there, the plan that my father planted the seeds of all those years ago—it was to get me away from the life he lived. To keep everything that's begun to happen now from happening at all.

"I shouldn't have gone to that club with Ana," I whisper. I've never regretted something so much in my life.

Once again, I see that flicker of sympathy. "It would probably have happened anyway," Luca admits. "The Bratva isn't known for forgetting about the cards they have to play—and you have always been a card, Sofia. A chess piece in a game that is bigger than you or I. Your father hoped that it wouldn't, but he was being optimistic. In those last moments before his death, I can't blame him. He wanted to believe that his family would be safe, despite everything he knew to the contrary."

I can feel my stomach tightening, and for a second I think that I'm going to be sick. Luca is still between me and the door, but the only thing that I know in this moment is that I'm getting the fuck out of here, one way or another.

"I'm not a card," I say tightly, glaring at him. "I'm not a chess piece. And I'm sure as *hell* not marrying into the mafia!" I can feel my chest heaving now, my breath coming faster. "The people that you work for hurt my mother. My father is dead because he worked for them. And now you tell me that you're going to be the head of this organization one day, and yet I'm supposed to marry you, whether I want to or not?"

I lean towards him, my eyes blazing angrily as I spit the next words into his face.

"Fuck that."

Before Luca can respond, I dart around him, running for the door. I'm still barefoot, but I don't care. I'll replace Ana's shoes, there's no time to stop and grab them, or get them on. I'm not going to stay here another second with this man, who thinks that he can tell me what I'm going to do, who I'm going to marry—that he can change my entire plan for my life in a few minutes because of something that happened years ago.

I'm sorry, papa, I think as I make a break for it, snatching the bedroom door open and careening out into the hallway. *If this is really what you wanted, I'm sorry. But I just can't believe that.*

I don't have time to take in my surroundings. I slip a little on the smooth wood of the hallway floor, steadying myself against the wall before racing for the stairs that lead down to the main floor. I can hear Luca's footsteps behind me, and I'm so terrified that I can hardly breathe. For the second time tonight, all I can think of is that I have to escape.

Luca almost catches up to me, close enough to grab my hand while I'm still on the stairs. He tries to pull me backwards, to turn me around, but I have a death grip on the banister as I yank my hand out of his, lurching forwards.

I'm still dizzy from the drugs that the Russians gave me, and I slip, tumbling down the last few stairs to the floor. The air rushes out of me as I land, and I catch a glimpse of Luca's worried face in the seconds before I manage to scramble to my feet again, ignoring him as I make a break for the front door of the apartment.

Why would he be worried about me? He doesn't even care about me personally. I don't believe for a second, either, that he really cares about a promise made by two dead men, however close he and his father might have been. I'm valuable to him in some way—he did call me a chess piece, after all. That's the only real explanation I can come up with for his insistence that we go through with this.

For a brief second, I think that I'm going to make it. I'm reaching out for the handle of the front door when I feel Luca's strong hands on my waist for the second time tonight, and he drags me backwards, spinning me around to face him.

"No!" I scream, clawing at his face, but he grabs my wrist effortlessly, backing me up towards the door. When I try to slap him with my free hand, he grabs that too, and pushing me back against the door and pinning my hands above my head. His body is nearly touching mine, and I realize that he's breathing hard too, his chest heaving as he looks down at me, his gaze fastened on mine as surely as his hands are fastened around my wrists.

I twist in his grasp, but he's too strong. He's stronger than he looks, even, and I can feel the power in his grip on me, see the way the muscles in his arms flex as he holds me there, like a butterfly under a microscope, fluttering uselessly. I stare up at him, feeling the last bit of fight in me drain away as he watches me. "I won't marry you," I whisper, but I know it's useless. For some reason, nothing I say seems to change his mind, even though he claims he didn't want it either.

He said he didn't *want it*, I recall. And as I look up at him, I wonder what he meant by that.

"You said that you didn't want to marry me." I lick my dry lips, and I see his gaze flick downwards, drifting over my mouth. "Not that you *don't* want to marry me."

Luca is silent for a long moment. "None of that matters, Sofia," he says quietly.

"Why?"

"Because regardless of what I want, or what you want, we *will* be married."

"But—why?" I press again, knowing that I sound for all the world like I'm twelve again, begging for a different response to a question that I don't like the answer to.

"Because," he says simply. "You're mine."

And then he bends his head, my hands still pinned above mine, and his lips come crashing down onto my mouth.

LUCA

*I*rritating. *Stubborn. Infuriating. Foolish. Reckless.*

All of these are adjectives that I could apply to Sofia Romano.

They're also all attributes that I would never choose in a wife.

But when I finally manage to catch my runaway bride with her hand on the doorknob and spin her around and up against the door, that same possessive urge that I felt when I saw her on my bed rushes through me, heating my blood until I feel as if I'm on fire with it.

The only thought in my head is that she's mine. Sofia Ferretti belongs to me.

And I want her.

Her incessant questions, her refusal to fall in line, and her stupid attempt to escape the penthouse should have only pissed me off. They should have made me change my mind, call Don Rossi, and tell him to come and get her and do what he likes.

Because it's very clear that if I marry Sofia Ferretti, she is going to be a pain in my ass, so long as we both shall live.

Instead her delicate wrists in my hands, stretched up over her head, only make me think of what it would be like to tie her to my headboard, strip her naked and tease every inch of her body with my tongue until she begs me to let her come. As I push her against the door and feel her struggle uselessly in my grasp, all I can imagine is how she would feel underneath me, her perfect, slender body writhing as I shove every inch of my aching cock inside of her, making her mine in every possible way.

And then her tongue, dragging over the full shape of her lips, makes it impossible for me to think of anything other than kissing them for the first time.

There's nothing romantic in the image. In that moment, as I hold Sofia Ferretti captive against my front door, I'm not thinking of how to make our first kiss memorable. The only thought in my head is that for some reason, she's made me want her more than I've ever wanted any woman in my entire life. I'm harder than I've ever been in my life, frustratingly, achingly aroused, and all I can think of is that I'm one impulse decision away from picking her up and fucking her against this door, here and now.

But she won't stop asking the same question, over and over: *"Why?"*

So I shut her up in the best way that I and my almost-painful erection can think of.

I kiss her, hard.

The moment that my lips come down onto hers, she stops struggling. For a perfect, blissful moment, she goes absolutely still, and I have a second to realize that her lips are even softer than I'd imagined. Her bottom lip is full and lush, and it fits perfectly against my mouth —so perfectly in fact that I can't help myself from sucking it between mine. I sweep my tongue over her lower lip, sliding it against hers, and for the first time I taste just how sweet Sofia's mouth is. I want to bury my hands into her hair, taste every inch of her, kiss her from her mouth down to her pussy and lick her there until she screams with pleasure. I want to feel those full lips wrapped around me, sliding all the way down as I slide my length into the back of her throat. I want to see that sweet mouth open and waiting as I come all over her tongue.

My cock feels as if it's about to tear its way out of my trousers.

And then she starts to struggle again.

She cries out, writhing in my grasp, and I react without thinking. I push her backwards against the door, letting her feel the hard ridge of my erection against her thigh as I deepen the kiss, letting go of one of her wrists so that I can run my hand down the side of her body, feeling the lush curve of her breast that dips into her perfect waist, over the swell of her hip—

Christ, I want to fuck her.

I feel Sofia's tongue sliding against mine, her head slanting to one side as she starts to respond. *Yes*, I think, satisfaction rushing through me. *All I had to do was kiss you.* No woman has ever refused me, ever resisted the idea of coming to bed with me. There's no reason to think that Sofia would be any different, once she got a taste. I grind my hips against hers, letting her feel how thick my cock is, how eager I am to slide it inside of her, to show her how good it can be if she just accepts that this is the way things are—

And then she bites my lip, hard.

I jerk my head back automatically, running my tongue over the stinging spot where her small sharp teeth sank in, and Sofia takes advantage of the momentary space between us to rear back and slap me hard, right across the face.

"Fuck!" I press my hand to my cheek, grabbing her just in time as she starts to open the door. With my face *and* my cock throbbing now, I manage to get one arm around her waist, picking her up easily as she kicks and writhes in my grasp.

I carry her the few yards across the entrance to the living room, and deposit her inelegantly onto the couch.

Sofia springs up almost immediately, shoving her hair out of her face. Her chest and neck are streaked an angry red now, and her brown eyes are blazing with fury, but she still looks more beautiful than I could have possibly imagined. Her lips are pink and slightly swollen from the kiss, her thick blonde hair tangled around her cheeks, and despite her smudged eye makeup, I'm not sure I've ever seen a more stunning woman.

"Stop looking at me like that," she hisses, glaring at me.

"Like what?" I glare at her. "You're the one who slapped *me*. All I've done is rescue you from Russian sex traffickers, bring you home to my apartment, have you seen by the best doctor in New York City, and offer you a marriage that will keep you safe and cared for as long as you live. And all I get is a bitten lip and a smack across the face."

"Stop looking at me like you're picturing me naked." Sofia lifts her chin. "Because you're never going to."

I can feel my gaze darkening as I step towards her. "See, that's where you're wrong, Sofia," I tell her quietly. "Before a week is out, not only will I have seen you naked, but I'll know every part of your body as intimately as I know my own. You can be sure of that."

The words slip out before I can stop them, and they startle even me. *What happened to one fuck to make it legal, and then never touching her again?* Somehow, over the past few hours, I've managed to forget that Sofia was only ever supposed to be a contractual agreement. Our marriage, much like the monthly deposit to her account, was meant to be a business deal. Signed, sealed, and filed away for safekeeping.

But nothing about what I want to do to her is businesslike. Nothing about the feelings rushing through me, the way I desperately want to toss her back down onto that couch, shove her dress up above her thighs, and thrust myself inside of her is contractual. She's making me feel things that I've never felt for any woman, *want* in a way that I've never allowed myself to want anything.

It has to stop, and now.

I can't allow this woman to unman me. Sofia Ferretti is a duty, a box to check, and she needs to remain exactly that. All of the things that she makes me feel, all of the ways she makes me react, are distractions that I don't need. Emotions that lead to mistakes.

I'm the future Don, the man who is next in line to lead the most powerful criminal organization in the world. A man whose territory is being threatened, whose position and life are in danger.

And it's not just my life, or Sofia's. It's the underbosses, the made men underneath them, everyone who works for Rossi, and me, and now Franco, and the other underbosses and capos. Their lives, and their families lives are at stake. If the Bratva move in on our territory, if they're allowed to start a war, it will be a bloodbath the likes of which hasn't been seen in decades.

Right now it's Don Rossi's responsibility to keep them safe—to keep *all* of them safe—but a large portion of that rests on my shoulders. At some point, all of it will.

That reminder is sobering.

I take a step back from Sofia as I regain control, letting out a long breath as I feel the lust, that overwhelming sense of passion and possessiveness, receding.

"You can fight me all you want on this, Sofia, but it won't change anything. Next Saturday, before man and God, you will become my wife, and this will be settled. We can go over the details of it in the meantime, when you're calmer, but there is no choice. That's final."

She stares at me, wide-eyed and disbelieving. "You have got to be fucking kidding me."

I don't flinch. "You know that I'm not. And what's more, we're going to have to do something about that mouth of yours. Good mafia wives don't talk to their husbands like that."

Sofia jerks backwards, as if I've said something awful. She wraps her arms around herself, shuddering a little as she backs away from me, around to the other side of the couch. "I'm not going to marry you," she whispers. "I won't. You can't force me to say the vows."

I grit my teeth, biting back the words I want to say. "No," I admit. "I can't. But I *can* keep you here until you understand the gravity of the situation, and I will."

"I'll run again. As soon as you leave this room, I swear—"

"Sofia!" For the first time, I raise my voice, and it shocks her into stillness. With two quick strides, I move around the couch to stand in front of her again. "I kept you from leaving the apartment because I don't feel like chasing you all over hell and back. But you are *not* going anywhere. Even if you made it to the elevator, there's a code required to go down after a certain hour. The moment I'm done with this conversation, I will make sure to lock and set the alarm on every exit. And if you somehow managed to get past all of that, I have security all over this building. I'm the only one who lives here. The rest of the units are empty, or devoted to my security teams. Do you understand what I'm saying?"

As I speak, I can see her eyes start to fill with tears as it slowly sinks in. "I am one of the richest men in New York City, Sofia, and second in command to the man who presides over all of it. I have the best security money can buy, out of pure necessity. There are plenty of people who want me dead. And you, too."

Her lower lip quivers. "I hate you," she whispers. "I swear on my father's grave, Luca Romano, I hate you."

I sigh resignedly. "Be that as it may," I tell her flatly. "There's no way out of this, Sofia. At least not one that you would choose."

And then without another word, I turn on my heel and stalk out of the room.

SOFIA

$\mathcal{T}$he moment that Luca walks out of the room, I sink down onto the couch, struggling not to burst into tears.

For all my bravado, I'm terrified. Everything that's happened tonight—the drugging, the kidnapping, waking up in the hotel room only to be stuck in a closet during a shootout, fainting only to wake up in another strange room…and then being told that I have to *marry* this strange man?

It's too much. It overwhelms me, and I press one hand over my mouth, trying desperately to breathe, not to cry, but I can't help it. Too much has happened, too much has changed, and I feel the tears start to drip down my cheeks.

A moment later my face is buried in my hands, my shoulders shaking with deep, wracking sobs that threaten to send me over the edge into hysteria.

Somewhere in the middle of it, I hear a faint *beep*, like a smoke alarm, and look up to see a red light blinking next to the front door. A moment later, there's another, farther off.

Fuck.

He set the alarms, just like he said I would. I'm trapped in this luxurious fortress of a penthouse, with a man who might as well be my jailer. A man who claims I have to marry him—or else.

I don't know what the 'or else' might be, but nothing I've seen or heard tonight makes me think that it would be anything good. I definitely don't think that it would include going back to my old apartment or my old life. And the thought of that terrifies me.

Why would you do this to me, papa? I stifle another sob, the voice in my head that of a sad, frightened twelve year old girl. I feel as if I'm losing him all over again, because the man I knew, the one who spun me in circles and smelled like vanilla tobacco, the one who brought me books and listened to me play the violin even before I was any good at it, wouldn't have done this to me. He wouldn't have forced me into a marriage with a man I don't even know, a man in line to run the same organization that caused his death, that threatened my mother and all but certainly drove her to an early grave.

He would have, if it were the only way to keep you safe, I hear the small voice in my head whisper, but I don't want to believe that. I don't want to believe that there's no other choice. Before tonight, I didn't even know that the Bratva existed. I didn't know any of this—and I can't believe that all this time, this shadowy fate has just been waiting for me. That I've been living out a plan for a life that was never going to exist.

I want to stop crying, to be the strong and resilient woman that I know my father would want me to be, but I can't. I feel betrayed, helpless, completely at a loss as to what to do—and above all, exhausted beyond what my battered body can handle. And so, with tears still streaming down my face, I collapse onto the couch, curling into a ball as I close my eyes tightly.

Maybe when I wake up, this will all have been a terrible dream.

* * *

IT's ALMOST dawn when a hand on my shoulder wakes me up. I see a sliver of the faintly-greying sky outside of the floor-to ceiling window in Luca's living room, and then I sit up with a start, adrenaline flooding my body as I realize with a sinking pit in my stomach that none of it was a dream. I'm still in Luca Romano's penthouse. Everything that happened last night was real.

"Sofia."

I turn sharply at the sound of Ana's voice. She's sitting next to me on the couch, her hands in her lap. Her face looks drawn, tired and pale, and I realize that she was the one who woke me up.

"What are you doing here?" I ask, startled. "How did you--?"

Ana smiles tiredly. "Luca called me."

"Luca—how did he know—"

"Sofia, Luca knows everything and everyone in this city." Ana reaches out, patting my hand gently. "Come on. There's got to be a way to make some coffee, if we can find the kitchen."

I follow her as if in a daze, looking around for any sign of Luca. But he doesn't appear as we make our way into the spacious kitchen, and I let myself relax just a fraction, taking in my surroundings at last without his suffocating presence.

The kitchen is as large as half our apartment, and sparkling clean, as if no one ever actually uses it. *He probably doesn't,* I think grimly. *He probably goes out for every meal, or has a private chef.* No one with this kind of money cooks their own food.

The entire room is as luxurious and elegant as the bedroom that I woke up in last night, after Luca took me out of the hotel room. The counters are all sleek black granite, the floor polished white marbled tile, and the appliances are gleaming steel, shined to a high polish. The cabinets are hardwood, banded with iron, and the island is dark hardwood with a gleaming black granite top as well. *I'm seeing a theme here.*

It only takes a second to glimpse the ridiculously complex and expensive-looking coffeemaker, next to an espresso machine that looks equally expensive and unused. Ana makes a face as she pokes at them, peering at the dials. "I don't know how to use any of this," she admits. "Can't the man just have a fucking Keurig?"

"No," I say tiredly, sinking into a chair. "He's richer than God, apparently." After another few minutes of watching Ana try to figure out the coffeemaker, I sigh. "Ana, please. I don't even want coffee. I just want to go home."

To my shock, I see Ana's eyes fill with tears as she turns to face me.

"You can't," she whispers, and I feel the pit in my stomach turn to ice.

I stand up, almost knocking the chair over in my haste. "Luca keeps saying that!" I exclaim, my hands clenching into fists at my sides. "Why are you saying it too? Did he tell you to say that? Does he have something on you, to make you say that to me?"

"No!" Ana shakes her head, chewing on her lower lip as she dashes away the tears. "Sofia, please listen to me. Just—sit down, okay?"

I don't want to sit down. I want to run out of this apartment, run all the way back to my own safe, warm bedroom, and pull the covers over my head. I want to go back to when I was a child, when I could disappear into my books and my violin and the safe, secure knowledge that my parents loved me, that they would always come home, that I had my whole life stretching out in front of me to be anyone that I wanted.

It was all a lie, I think, and I feel tears clog my throat again. *I was never safe.*

"Sofia, Luca isn't lying to you."

"How do you know?" I try not to yell, but I can hear my voice rising again, choked and panicked. "You've only known *me* for a few years, Ana! You don't know anything about my family, or this promise Luca is claiming our parents made—"

"No," Ana says calmly. She steps forward, gripping the back of one of the chairs. Her tearful blue gaze fixes on mine, and I can see in that moment that she's just as frightened as I am—for me, or for herself, I can't tell. "I don't know anything about that, you're right. He could be lying about all of that. But what he isn't lying about is the danger that you're in from the Bratva."

I feel like I'm going to be sick. Last night, I'd thought that maybe Luca was exaggerating, that he was trying to frighten me into agreeing to the marriage. But now my best friend, the only person I trust in the world, is saying that it's true. That I'm still in danger.

"I'm sorry," Ana whispers. "I shouldn't have taken you to that club last night. Maybe if they'd never seen you—"

I stare at her, still not quite able to believe it. Slowly, I sink back down into the chair across from her, trying to breathe. "Luca said it didn't matter if I'd gone to the club or not. They'd have come for me eventually." I look up at Ana, struggling to hold back tears. "They killed my father. It was the Bratva. I never knew that until last night, and now to find out this way—"

The tears start again, hot and overwhelming, and I bury my face in my hands.

"I'm so sorry, Sofia." I feel Ana's hand on my back, rubbing gently as she comes to stand next to me. She strokes my hair as I sob, making soft soothing noises. "Just get it out. It's okay to cry."

"I don't want to cry," I whisper, sitting back up slowly. "I want to get out of here. I want this to be over."

"I know." Ana sits down again, scooting the chair forward so that she can reach for my hands, holding them in hers as she looks at me. "I lost my father when I was a child too," she says quietly. "I was eight. My mother left Russia after that and brought me here. But I learned very young to fear the Bratva. If they have plans for you, Sofia, you can't escape them. The man who leads them, Viktor, is terrifying. His name is known all throughout Russia. They call him *Ussuri*, the bear. If he has set his sights on you for some reason, whatever that is, you should do whatever you can to escape him. Anything is better than ending up in the hands of the Bratva."

"Even marrying Luca?" My voice cracks. I can feel my world narrowing, the walls closing in around me.

"If what he told me was true, then they took you in order to get to him. Because they knew that he would come for you. You were bait."

You've always been bait. Mikhail's voice fills my head, and I shudder. "I don't understand. He doesn't care about me. I don't believe that he cares that much about an old promise, either—"

"I don't know," Ana admits. "But he called me, Sofia. He asked me to come here and 'talk some sense into you'—his words, not mine. I don't think he would do that if he doesn't care. If he doesn't have some reason to want you safe."

"He cares about his territory," I say bitterly, looking away. "His position. Somehow I threaten that, if the Russians have me."

"If the Bratva take you, your fate will be worse than death," Ana says bluntly. She squeezes my hands gently, and I turn to face her again. Her expression is more serious than I've ever seen it, and it sends a chill down my spine. "I would say that I don't want to frighten you, Sofia, but I do. You're safer then, because you *should* be frightened. If they get their hands on you again, once Viktor has used you to get to Luca and has taken the territory that he wants, he'll sell you. If you're still in good condition by then, and you're lucky, he'll sell you to someone rich and powerful. Someone who hopefully will treat you like any other valuable possession. If you fight enough to make him angry, and wind up damaged, or injured, or even just anger him to the point of wanting to punish you—"

"What?" My voice drops, so low that I can barely hear it. The look in Ana's eyes makes me shiver, despite the warmth of the kitchen.

"I don't really know. There's stories, awful ones. Hunting parties, women sold to brothels, given to groups of his soldiers for sport. Worse things than that. Sofia—it doesn't matter, because you *cannot* let them take you again. And if you try to leave here—"

"What?" I look at her sharply. "What do you know?"

"Ask Luca what happens if he can't convince you to marry him," she says simply. "Sofia, I know this isn't what you wanted. And it hurts me to have to tell you this, because I love you. You're my dearest friend, and all I want in the world is to tell you to refuse him, to run away, that I'll take you back home and everything can go back to normal."

She swallows hard, tears glittering in her eyes, and a long moment of silence stretches out between us. "But I can't. *You* can't. Nothing is going back to the way it was before."

I stare at her for a long moment, not wanting to speak the next words on the tip of my tongue.

"What are you saying?"

Ana squeezes my hands tightly in hers.

"Sofia, you have to marry him."

LUCA

*T*wo things became apparent to me last night.

First, Sofia wasn't going to be convinced of the gravity of the situation merely by my explaining it to her.

And second, I needed to put some distance between her and myself. I hadn't expected for her to have the effect on me that she does, but that doesn't mean that I have to allow it to control me, or my actions. The more space that there is between Sofia Ferretti and I, the better.

Once the Bratva threat is contained, I tell myself, *I'll arrange for her to have her own apartment in one of the other buildings that I own.* Something luxurious and spacious, with plenty of security and amenities, so that she has no reason to complain, but far enough away from me that I can return her to the place in my life that she was meant to occupy—a line item on a budget. A contractual agreement that I'm forced to honor.

I'll pay for anything she wants, I reason, tapping my fingers against my desk. I don't deny that this situation is difficult, that she's undergone more grief and trauma than anyone should have to, and that it's unfair that she's been thrust into this out of no fault of her own. If she

wants shopping trips, vacations, a beach house in the Hamptons
—*anything she wants, once this threat is over.*

As long as I can keep her out of my mind, and most importantly,
out of my heart.

The last thought makes me grimace. It's ridiculous to think that
my heart could be in danger from *any* woman, let alone little orphan
Annie sitting in my kitchen. I glance over at the security feed with a
heavy sigh, wondering how much longer its going to take Anastasia
Ivanova to convince Sofia to come around.

But before last night, you didn't think you'd want her at all. The
thought intrudes uncomfortably, and I do my best to shrug it off,
switching away from the video feed. Anastasia will convince her of
the foolishness of fighting this, the jeweler will come by the apartment with a choice of rings, and within a week the entire matter will
be settled. I'll satisfy myself with one good, long, hard fuck, and then
Sofia can be neatly shelved away with the other fires that I've put out
over the course of my time as underboss.

Calling Anastasia really was a stroke of genius on my part. I'd
known that she was Sofia's roommate, of course—I pay for the apartment, so the fact that Sofia made the odd choice to rent out a room
despite the place being paid for was noted, along with anything else
that needed to be monitored. The fact that her roommate turned out
to be a Russian ballerina with family ties to the Bratva was a concern
—and I recalled Don Rossi briefly discussing whether or not Anastasia Ivanova was one of those potential loose ends that might need to
be neatly tied off.

I'd had that discussion, and my part in convincing Rossi that Anastasia had no intimate knowledge of her father's dealings, ready in case
the girl needed any push to come to the apartment and urge her best
friend to come to her senses. But in the end, Anastasia hadn't needed
any encouragement or threats. Just the mention of the Bratva and a
brief explanation of what had transpired the night before to and with
Sofia had been enough to bring her running.

At least *she* had enough sense to be terrified of them.

Now all that's left is for her to convince Sofia that it's in her own best interest to marry me, without further argument.

I glance at my watch. It's already taken longer than I'd hoped. My phone buzzes on the desk next to me, and I reach for it, grateful for the interruption.

"Mr. Romano?" It's my secretary—*Carmen*, I remind myself.

"Yes?" My tone is even more curt than usual, but I can't help it. The mix of frustrated desire and eagerness to get this whole messy business done and over with has my temper at the boiling point.

"The jeweler said he will be there within an hour, with a selection of appropriate rings."

Within the hour. Anastasia doesn't have long to wrap things up. "Thank you, Carmen," I reply tightly, and I can almost *feel* the pleasure from my remembering her name wafting over the line.

"Will there be anything else, sir?"

I pinch the bridge of my nose, wishing with everything in me that I could call a justice of the peace to the apartment and be done with this whole mess. But the wedding needs to be a spectacle, something to show the Bratva and anyone who might consider helping them that Sofia Ferretti has been removed from the game.

Check and mate.

"Find out who might be available to dress Sofia for the wedding. They need to be able to produce a gown within a week. The ceremony will take place on Saturday, at St. Patrick's. Call the cathedral as well to arrange whatever Father Donahue requires." The last isn't much of a concern, the good Father has enough of a history with our family that he'll do nearly anything that I or Rossi ask of him. And since he was the one who was present when Sofia's father extracted his promise from mine, I expect he'll be even more inclined to hasten the wedding.

"Right away, Mr. Romano."

I hang up the phone, checking my watch again. If this goes on too much longer, I might have to go down to the kitchen myself, and—

A faint, hesitant knock sounds against my office door.

There's no explanation for the knot in my stomach when I hear it. If Sofia still refuses to fall in line—

She won't, I tell myself firmly. And my anxiety is only due to my eagerness to get all of this finished and done with. It has nothing to do with the girl herself.

"Come in."

The heavy mahogany door creaks open, and Sofia steps inside.

Her face is pale and her eyes are red-rimmed, but none of it takes away from her beauty. She looks like a princess trapped in a tower, come to beg for her life, and the irony of it isn't lost on me. Sofia thinks that I'm her jailer, but in truth, I'm the only one standing between her and death.

A knight in somewhat tarnished armor, if you will.

"Is Anastasia still here?"

Sofia flinches at the mention of her friend's name. "No," she says quietly. "She went home."

Good. The girl is brighter than I gave her credit for—she clearly knew when it was time to leave. I can hear the resentment in Sofia's voice when she says *home,* and I hope that's a sign that she's come to accept the fact that she can't return to her former apartment. That this penthouse, and whatever living arrangements I make for her in the future, will be her home going forward.

"She said you called her." Sofia's voice is flat, toneless. She sounds broken, and I know I should be grateful for it. She'll be more manageable this way. But something inside of me revolts against the idea of her losing her spirit despite myself.

It's just another sign that I need to get all of this over with as quickly as possible.

"I did," I confirm. "Clearly you wouldn't listen to me when I tried to explain the gravity of the situation to you. And I understand, in a way—you don't know me." I steeple my fingers in front of me on the desk, watching her from across it. The space between us is good, it helps me to keep this formal. Businesslike. "I assumed that Anastasia might be able to appeal to you in a way that I couldn't. And from the look on your face, I think that I'm correct."

"Don't pretend like you know me that well," Sofia says, a tiny bit of her anger returning. "I want you to answer one thing for me, Mr. Romano. Something that Ana said I should ask you."

So it's Mr. Romano *now.* I narrow my eyes at her. "Yes?"

"She said that I should ask you what would happen if I don't agree to marry you."

Goddamn it. My goodwill towards Anastasia Ivanova evaporates immediately. But if even her friend explaining the threat of the Bratva to her wasn't enough, perhaps this will be. It's all that I have left to convince her.

"I've already told you who my boss is."

"Yes." Sofia doesn't move to step away from the still-open door. It doesn't matter, she wouldn't get far anyway, even if she tried to run again.

"He is not a merciful man, Sofia."

"And you are?" She lifts her chin, glaring at me. "You're keeping me prisoner here."

A surge of frustration verging on anger ripples through me, and I stand up from the desk despite myself, nearly knocking my chair over. "I am keeping you *safe*!" I thunder, my voice carrying out of the office and echoing in the hall, and I see Sofia flinch backwards again. To her credit, she doesn't try to run. "Was your friend not able to convey properly what those men, the Bratva, would have done to you?"

"She said they would have sold me, and she mentioned—worse things," Sofia admits. She swallows hard, and I see her slender throat convulse.

My cock twitches, swelling in the confines of my tailored suit. Just the sight of that makes me think of her throat convulsing around my shaft, the way it would feel while I gripped her hair and thrust myself deeper, fucking her face until—

Goddamn it, Luca, get yourself under control. My reaction to this girl is ridiculous. I consider myself exceptionally virile, but at thirty-one and with half of Manhattan notched in my bedpost, I'd thought my days of uncontrollable erections were behind me. And yet here I am, standing in my office as achingly and inappropriately hard as a teenager who has yet to fuck anything other than his hand.

"You're right," I say calmly. "The Bratva are well known for their treatment of women. Their primary source of income is selling concubines to wealthy men, and sex slaves to all parts of the world. The women who aren't deemed valuable enough for sale are used for sport for their own men."

"Trafficking," Sofia whispers, and I can see the fear in her eyes.

"Not only that, but the women they keep aren't treated much better. Maybe you're thinking that as a daughter of a Russian woman, they might have married you off to someone in their inner circle. Maybe you wouldn't have been sold. But their wives are little more than chattel, too, living in fear and at the whims of their husbands."

"And would that be any different from being married to you?" Sofia lifts her chin defiantly.

I can feel my jaw clench. Slowly and purposefully, I step around the edge of my desk, coming to face her a few feet away. "Our marriage will not be loving, Sofia. I will not be a faithful husband, or a devoted one. But I can promise you this—I will never lay a hand on you in anger. I will never force you into my bed against your will. You will be protected from anything that might harm you, provided for in every way, with every luxury that money can buy. I can't give you romance, or a family of your own, but I will see to it that in whatever way I can make up for that with material things—your home, travel, anything you wish—I will do so. I don't intend to make you unhappy, Sofia. But I do intend to bring this entire matter to a close as quickly as possible."

"You already laid hands on me," Sofia points out. "Last night."

This girl is insufferable. I let out a slow, measured breath. "You were trying to escape."

"Still—"

"Alright!" I grit my teeth. "I won't touch you again, without permission. Is that enough for you?"

"You still haven't answered my question. What happens if I refuse?"

It takes all the effort I can muster not to clench my hands into fists, or shout. But I can't afford to frighten her—at least not when it comes to me.

But I'm done playing games, and dancing around the truth.

"Don Rossi will have you killed," I say simply.

The words have the desired effect. Sofia goes bone-white, and for a second I think she might pass out again. I'm wondering whether my promise not to lay my hands on her again includes keeping her from falling to the floor in a dead faint, but she manages to stay upright, gripping the side of the door to steady herself.

"What do you mean?" she whispers.

"I mean exactly that. You are a loose end, Sofia. A chess piece, a card to play, whatever you want to call it. By marrying you, I am taking you out of play. Off of the board. You will be safe, and the Bratva can no longer use you against us. But if you refuse to marry me, and I let you leave here, they will be able to take you again. Don Rossi will not allow that to be a possibility."

Sofia frowns, her forehead creasing with confusion. "But if you don't want to marry me, how can they use you as bait? Why do I matter, if I don't mean anything to you? Surely a promise between two men who are long dead doesn't mean so much to this Viktor, or to your boss—"

"Sofia!" I grit my teeth, trying to hold my temper. "There are things that you don't need to know, and that I can't tell you. But what I can— what I *am* telling you, is that you actually *do* have a choice. You can agree to marry me, here and now, or I can call Don Rossi and tell him that you refuse. And after that, there is nothing else I can do to save you."

"And will you be the one to kill me, if I say no? Maybe pull out a gun here and shoot me?" Sofia glares at me.

"Not here," I say simply. "And I hope not." It's not something that I can picture Rossi doing, truthfully. He's not the kind to play games, to take Sofia and put a gun in my hand in hopes that she might be convinced to change her mind. He'd simply have her killed, clean and quiet, and wash his hands of the entire mess. In fact, I know that's what he'd prefer. As long as she's alive, even married to me, there are variables. She might try to run again. She might be kidnapped. She might become pregnant, and the baby used against us.

Death is the best guarantee that a potential problem won't come to pass.

But I don't want that to happen. I want to fulfill the promise that was made for me, tuck Sofia somewhere safely away, and put enough security on her that she'll never be in danger. If I'm careful the first night, and never touch her again, there will be no possibility of children. The matter of Sofia Romano will still be handled—and she'll be alive.

"I don't want you dead," I tell her simply. "That's why I'm doing this, Sofia. It's the only way to solve this problem."

"So I'm a problem to you?"

In so many ways.

"Yes," I tell her bluntly. "You have been a problem to be managed since the day you were twelve years old. And you have been managed, without your knowledge, all these years. Now you're simply aware of it."

Something about the coldness in my tone seems to jolt her out of her defiance. "So it's that simple. Marry you, or die."

"Yes."

"How will he do it?"

I blink at her, startled. "I—I don't know."

"Will he come here to take me? Drop me off of a pier? Or will someone break into my bedroom at night?"

"I don't know, Sofia. But it doesn't need to be this way—"

"I'll do it."

"What?" I blink at her, caught off-guard by the sudden change.

Sofia looks at me coolly, her face as impassive as mine was moments ago. "I'll marry you. But I have conditions."

It takes everything in me not to laugh. "*You* have conditions? Haven't I just explained to you that—"

"Yes, I get it. I marry you, or your boss has me killed. Which, like you told me last night, is no choice at all. But that doesn't mean that I can't have some say in how this marriage goes."

This ought to be interesting. "It *does* mean that I don't have to accept," I tell her bluntly. "But go ahead. What are these conditions?"

"I don't want to live with you."

Well, that one is easy enough, at least. "I have every intention of giving you your own residence. You'll have to stay here until we're certain that the Bratva threat is neutralized. But after that I'll allow you to choose your own apartment from among those I own, and you'll be given your own security detail and access to certain bank accounts and credit cards. I told you that I intend to provide for you, Sofia."

She doesn't even blink. "I'll be allowed to see Anastasia still."

"I don't think—"

"You can't force me into a loveless marriage and take away my only friend."

"Your *only friend* is Russian, with a dead Bratva father."

"She's all I have."

I pinch the bridge of my nose, feeling a migraine coming on. "Fine. But only here or at your apartment once you're installed in one, and with heavy supervision. If the two of you go anywhere, it has to be cleared by me, and extra security will go with you."

"Fine." Sofia doesn't look pleased, but at this point, I don't care. This was never supposed to involve *negotiations.* How is it that I can tell my future bride that the alternative to a simple *yes* is death, and yet she is still standing here arguing with me?

"Is there anything else?" I can't keep the sarcasm out of my voice.

"Just one thing." Sofia takes a deep breath. "I meant what I said last night. This will be a marriage of convenience only, Mr. Romano. You will not try to come to my bed, and I will not go to yours. You will not lay a hand on me in any way. You will not ever—" she takes a deep breath, flushing a lovely shade of pink. "—take my virginity. I will remain untouched."

Apparently the doctor was right. And the very mention of her virginity coming from Sofia's lips is enough to make my erection return with an alarming speed. I can't even adjust myself without her noticing, and all I can do is hope that she doesn't glance down, where the evidence of how much I want her is very, very visible. "So it's going to be *Mr. Romano* from here on out, is it?"

Sofia presses her lips tightly together.

Well, two can play that game. "I'm sure you're aware, *Ms. Ferretti*, that a marriage must be consummated in order for it to be legal."

"I think we're a little past blood on the sheets. It is the twenty-first century," Sofia replies sweetly. "You can say whatever you need to in order to satisfy your boss and the Bratva threat, Mr. Romano. Say you fucked me all night long, for all I care. But it won't ever be the truth."

Christ. I'm fairly certain that if I get any harder, my cock is going to burst through the fly of my suit. Hearing Sofia's soft, innocent voice mention me fucking her all night is enough to make me want to forget my promise and bend her over the desk here and now. She's still wearing that ridiculously short, tight dress, and the only thing stopping me is the fragile remainder of my sense of honor—and the lingering desire to enjoy taking her virginity on our wedding night, when I'll have all the time in the world.

All the time I could desire to enjoy my bride once—and only once.

It's the one thing that's been keeping me sane since I saw her yesterday, and realized that for some inexplicable reason, I want to fuck Sofia Ferretti more than I want to breathe.

"I'm not in the habit of lying, Ms. Ferretti." I smile at her. "Besides, you would enjoy it. I'm told that a night with me is quite—pleasurable. I'm in the habit of being a generous lover."

Sofia smiles too, but it doesn't quite reach her eyes. "I'm sure most of the women in Manhattan could attest to that, if I asked them."

"Maybe you should." I shove my hands in my pockets. "Don't tell me that my reluctant bride is jealous."

"Not a bit." Sofia holds firm, her dark brown gaze meeting mine, and she pauses, taking a deep breath. "You say I don't have a choice. Well, I *will* have a choice in this. I'll marry you, since you leave me little option to do otherwise. But I will not sleep with you."

She meets my eyes fearlessly, and for a moment, I can't help but respect her bravery. She believes me, I'm sure of that. But she's refusing to bend regardless.

Despite how desperately I want her, and how frustratingly infuriating all of this is, I feel a flicker of admiration for my future bride, even as she narrows her eyes at me.

"I've made my choice, Mr. Romano. What's yours?"

SOFIA

*M*y heart is galloping in my chest.

I know Luca is telling the truth. If I refuse this marriage, I'm as good as dead.

But I won't walk out of one captivity just to face another. If I have to marry him, I'll do it on my own terms. I won't be his slave any more than I would for the Bratva. I'd die before I let them sell me or use me for sport, and Luca promised that he wouldn't force me into his bed.

So now I get to see just how well that promise holds up.

Still, I don't know what I'll do if he refuses, if he insists that we have to consummate the marriage in order to make it legal. *If it's just once, is that worth my life?*

The problem is, I'm not sure that it would be just once. I felt him last night, when he had me up against the door, and even as innocent as I am, I know the reactions of a man who desires a woman. Luca Romano wanted me, and violently. I'd felt it not just in the hard pressure against my thigh, but in every inch of his body. I'd felt it in the way he'd kissed me.

No one has ever kissed me like that before. And when I bit him, it wasn't just because I wanted him off of me.

It was at least partially because I wasn't sure that I wanted him to stop.

I'm being forced into an arranged marriage with the most gorgeous man I've ever laid eyes on. Everything about Luca is pure, masculine sexuality, poured into a bespoke suit and standing in front of me with the arrogance of a god. And that would be manageable, if he were bad at kissing. Selfish in bed. A terrible lover. Then I could grit my teeth and let him get it over with once and move on with my new life. But I don't think he's any of those things.

That kiss made me fantasize about things I've never even thought about before. The heat of his lips on mine had made me suddenly, achingly wet, so much so that I'd cursed the fact that Ana had convinced me to go out without my underwear, and terrified that he might notice somehow. The feeling of his heavy, muscular body against mine—

Just the thought of it is making me flush with heat all over again, aroused in a way that I've never felt. I should have hated his touch, hated the forceful way that he threw me up against the door, hated everything about his body against mine.

But if I'm being honest with myself, I didn't hate it. And I can't allow that.

I'll marry him if I have to, but I won't allow myself to want him. To give myself to him in any way other than the most basic, legal requirement of signing paperwork.

And in order to ensure that, I have to make sure that he never, ever touches me again.

"Well?" I stare up at him defiantly, making sure that he can't see how terrified I am. How I'm shaking at the thought of him refusing to bend, insisting on taking me to bed, and leaving me with the choice all over again of whether to sleep with him or die.

I can see the frustration on his face, the anger. *He wants me,* I realize, and the thought sends a shiver of desire down my spine despite myself. Which is exactly why I have to keep him out of my bed, and from forcing me into his.

Luca might be the only one who can protect my life, but I'm the only one who can protect my heart. And that starts with protecting my body from *him*.

"Fine," he says, his voice cutting. "You win, Ms. Romano. If you want to stay as pure as the Virgin Mary, be my guest. There'll be no shortage of women offering to warm my bed in your place."

For some reason, that hurts. It shouldn't, but the idea of him looking at another woman the way he's looking at me right now, kissing and touching another woman with the same passion that he displayed last night, makes my chest ache. *You're being an idiot,* I tell myself firmly. Besides, that painful flicker of jealousy is just another reason to deny him. If just the thought of him being with someone else hurts now, how much more would it hurt if I gave him my virginity, if I made him the first and only man that I'd ever take to bed?

He's already made it clear that he has no intention of being faithful to me, or even returning to my bed after the first night. Giving in even once would just make it so much harder in the end. I can't allow myself to want him.

And I absolutely, cannot ever allow myself to care about him.

That last should be easy enough, I think, looking up at the stone-faced man in front of me.

"So you're agreeing to the marriage, then?" Luca looks down at me impassively.

"Yes. As long as—"

"As long as I don't fuck you. I've got it." He smiles coldly at me. "If that's all, Ms. Romano, there's paperwork to sign. Agreement to wed, pre-nuptial agreements, the works. And the jeweler will be here in—" he checks his watch. "Fifteen minutes to provide you with a choice of engagement rings."

I stare at him, momentarily dumbfounded. "Engagement rings?" I squeak, startled out of my sullen defiance. The way he says it is so bland, so contractual, for something that should be so intimate. A sign of a promise between two people who love each other.

But there's not anything resembling love in this room.

"Oh, you like the sound of that?" Luca's smile refuses to meet his eyes. "Women are generally charmed by my money, but I thought you'd be the exception to that, since you were so solidly against the idea."

I clench my teeth, a fresh wave of anger washing over me. "You just caught me by surprise. I didn't think you cared enough to buy me a ring. After all, you're being *forced* into this too."

"I don't care," Luca says bluntly. "But this marriage must appear to be completely real, and completely untouchable. That means we will go through every motion. You will choose an engagement ring, and a wedding dress, and we will have a very large, very public ceremony at St. Patrick's, and a very large, very expensive reception after, as befits my position. You will be a beautiful, happy bride, and I will be a handsome and adoring groom. But most of all, Ms. Romano, you will be *grateful*." He turns then, fixing me with his dark green gaze all over again. "And after that, as soon as I can install you in your own apartment, we will live our lives as separately as possible, except for when it is strictly necessary for us to be seen in public together."

"And you'll forget about me." The statement comes out more pitiful than I'd meant for it to.

Luca smiles tightly. "My dearest wish, *Sofia*, is that we can forget about each other."

TEN MINUTES LATER, I find myself seated at the table in Luca's expansive dining room with stacks of paperwork neatly organized across it, a wizened man who looks older than the antique art on the walls sitting across from me, and a velvet tray with ten different engagement rings in front of me.

They're all large, extravagant, and probably worth more than a year's worth of rent on my apartment. Maybe even more than that. And they're all beautiful.

"If your choice isn't the right size, I can have that fixed and ready for you tomorrow," the jeweler says, glancing between Luca and I. He looks nervous, and I can't blame him. Luca's expression is steely as he stands to the right of me, his arms crossed over his chest as he looks down at the tray of rings.

He's probably adding up how much this is all costing him in his head.

Perversely, it occurs to me to just pick the one that looks as if it costs the most, regardless of my own personal taste. But the one that looks the most expensive is a princess-cut diamond that looks as if it would reach to my knuckle, surrounded by a halo of diamonds and a diamond-encrusted band. It's far gaudier than anything I would ever wear, and I can't bring myself to commit to wearing it forever just to spite Luca. Knowing what I do about him so far, he'll insist that I keep it on my hand no matter what.

It's not as if he plans to even see you all that often, once the Bratva are dealt with though.

I don't know why that thought makes my chest squeeze tightly, as if I'm sad. Luca avoiding me is the best possible outcome. It's not the life I'd hoped for, but at least I won't be dead, and I'll never have to worry about money.

And he'd said I could travel. Even if I can't live in London and play with the orchestra there, I can still go to Paris, maybe—

It's still not your life. It's a life being chosen for you. One that you'll have to get permission for every move you make. No matter how I try to turn it around in my head, nothing can change the fact that everything I've dreamed of, worked for, and hoped for has been taken away in an instant. And even though it isn't Luca who orchestrated this, I can't help but hate him for it. Especially since I can't bring myself to hate my own father, a man who undoubtedly loved me, and who I've never stopped grieving for.

So Luca is the only person left for me to blame this on.

I pick up one of the rings, a round diamond encircled in a halo with a slim platinum band, and slide it onto my finger. It feels heavy and looks odd, taking up so much space on my slender hand. "Don't you have anything smaller?" I ask curiously, and Luca makes a face.

"It wouldn't look right for the wife of the future Don to have a small engagement ring," Luca says flatly, in a tone that brooks no argument.

Of course. Never mind what I would choose. I gingerly set the first ring down, and pick up another, a pear shaped diamond solitaire set on a rose gold pave band that reminds me of Blake Lively's ring. It's less ostentatious than the others, and unique, but the diamond is still huge, covering the entire space between the base of my finger and the first knuckle. *How does anyone wear something like this?*

And then, as I look over the tray of rings with sinking spirits, I notice one that does stand out to me.

It's not as flashy or modern as the other rings, in fact, it looks as if it could be an antique. It's a radiant-cut diamond set in yellow gold, and although it's large—probably still over three carats—it's not nearly as huge as the other center stones. It's flanked by two emerald baguettes, and the band is plain. Nestled next to it is the matching wedding band, a yellow gold eternity ring with the diamonds sunken into it all the way around.

I pick it up, sliding it onto my left hand. It fits perfectly, and my heart beats a little faster in my chest as I stretch out my hand in front of me, looking at the ring. I don't want to love it as much as I do. It's large without being gaudy, beautiful without being overpowering, and the green of the emeralds are the same color as Luca's eyes. For a single moment, as I look at the diamond glittering on my hand, I wish with all my might that things were different. This looks like a ring that should have been chosen for me, a ring that I could pass down to a daughter or for a future son to give to his bride, a family heirloom in the making. A token of love, not wealth.

"Is that the one you want?"

Luca's icy voice cuts through my fantasy, and I feel my stomach drop as I'm brought back to reality. This *is* a token of wealth, nothing more. The ring feels heavy on my hand as I let my palm rest on the table, the sunlight from the window sparkling off of it. This is Luca's way of showing anyone who might threaten him that he owns me. That Sofia Ferretti, daughter of the late Giovanni Ferretti, is his bride. That he takes what he wants, and will do whatever he must to keep it.

I swallow hard. I want to rip the ring off and throw it across the room. Part of me wants to choose one of the others, simply because I *do* want this one, and I shouldn't. I shouldn't want anything that this man chooses to give me. Certainly not something that could hold so much meaning.

But a part of me that I don't want to examine too closely can't bear to take it off.

Instead I hold it up again, smiling pleasantly at Luca as I turn to face him. "Yes," I say simply. "This is the one I want."

"Alright." Luca turns to the jeweler. "That will be all, then. You can send me the bill. And box up the band," he says, indicating the gold ring left in the slot on the tray.

"What about your band, Mr. Romano?"

"Just a plain yellow gold band to match will do. Five millimeters, nothing flashy." Luca gives him a stiff nod. "Have it here by Friday. The ceremony will be Saturday afternoon."

"Very good, Mr. Romano."

The moment the jeweler is gone, Luca takes a seat, pushing the first stack of paperwork towards me.

"Sign," he says curtly.

SOFIA

I can feel the weight of the ring like a brand as I pick up the pen, and I feel sick to my stomach. None of this is normal, or right. There was no proposal, no getting down on one knee, no question to answer. Luca didn't even put the ring on my hand himself. Everything about this is stiff and formal, businesslike.

That's good, though, I tell myself. *The more detached this is, the easier it will be to deal with it.*

I can't help but feel that I'm losing something, though. I'd never been the kind of girl who dreamed about marriage and family, who pictured her wedding day in every detail. I'm still a virgin not because I was saving it for my future husband, but because I simply haven't had the chance to lose it. I've hardly ever dated, and the few dates that I've gone on were with men who were far from being interesting or handsome or fascinating enough to make me want them. I hadn't even really enjoyed the few clumsy kisses that I'd experienced.

Luca's kiss, last night, was the first time I'd ever really felt what it was like to be truly kissed by someone who knew what they were doing. Not a sloppy attempt to smash our mouths together, or the sort of brief, bored kiss a guy gives you when he's hoping you'll hurry up and let him move to the next base. Luca had kissed me as if he wanted my mouth more than he wanted to breathe, as if he were hungry for me. There had been fire and passion in that kiss, and if just one kiss was like that, what would—

I press my lips together tightly as I look at the first page. I can't let myself think about it. Not about Luca's kiss, or the fact that this marriage means giving up any chance at love, ever, or the fact that I'm going to be stuck a virgin for the rest of my life. *At least I'll be alive,* I tell myself, and in the end, that's all there is to it.

"If you're planning to read every page, we're going to be here all day," Luca says dryly.

"Are you suggesting I sign something that I haven't read?"

Luca sighs, a sound that he seems to make around me more often than not. "That document is your agreement to marry me. In it, it states that you will remain married to me until one of us dies, albeit from natural causes or otherwise, and that you will not seek a divorce. If you attempt to separate from me, take up residence in an unapproved place, leave the city, state, or country without my permission, or file for divorce, you state that you understand that I can no longer guarantee your safety, nor will I attempt to safeguard your person in any way."

"That's a lot of fancy words to say that if I try to leave, you'll let me die or have me killed."

Luca's jaw clenches. "*I* will never have you killed, Sofia. It's not my belief that the Bratva pose so great a threat that your death is necessary. But Don Rossi and I have different ideas about some things. And I will not stick my own neck out to protect you if you insist on leaving."

Hmm. I file that tidbit away for safekeeping. Luca has just unwittingly shown me a little of his own hand. So long as Rossi is the head of the Italian mafia, my life is forfeit if I leave Luca. But once Luca is Don—he's just all but told me that he wouldn't have me killed for leaving.

There's still the Bratva to consider, of course. But if I plan carefully enough, and bide my time, it's possible that I might one day be able to be free again.

"It also states that I agree to provide for all your material needs. Your housing, food, utilities, and other necessities will be paid for, and you will be given a monthly clothing and discretionary allowance," Luca continues, not noticing the change in my demeanor. "As my wife, you'll be expected to attend certain events with me. You'll also be expected to perform certain functions—sit on the boards of a few charities, that kind of thing." He pauses. "Are you following all of this?"

"Of course." I smile pleasantly at him.

"As the wife of the future Don, and eventually the wife of the Don himself, you'll be in a position of authority over the other mafia wives. They'll come to you for advice and company." Luca makes a face, then. "I don't know what the hell you'll have to offer them, honestly, but do your best. *Everyone* must believe that this marriage is real, and that involves you playing your part to the fullest."

I wince. I hadn't thought that I'd have to make friends, or be a real part of this "family." I'd assumed that I'd be able to hide away in my apartment, traveling when I could and amusing myself. It had honestly sounded like the only tolerable part of the deal. Now I'm finding out that I'm going to have to preside over this grotesque kingdom with Luca and pretend to like it, and my stomach turns over. I don't want any part of this.

But I still don't have any choice.

"Is there anything else?"

"For that document? Only that you understand that no children will come of this union, or be expected. If you should fall pregnant, the pregnancy will be terminated." Luca smiles tightly. "But since one of *your* conditions is that I don't touch you, I don't think that will be an issue."

"I thought Catholics didn't believe in abortion?"

Luca frowns. "There are—other concerns that take precedence over any religious ones. But that's not your concern. Nor is it something you'll need to worry about." He taps the paper. "That's something else. Father Donahue said that you were baptized, but never confirmed in the church?"

"Um—no. I was baptized as an infant, and took first communion, but my father died before I was confirmed. And my mother only converted for marriage, she grew up Russian Orthodox, so—"

Luca waves his hand, cutting me off. "Father Donahue will expedite that, then."

"But I think there's a process—"

I can see the irritation plainly on Luca's face. "Father Donahue knows the family well, and he knew *your* father well, also. He'll do what we ask." Luca rubs one hand over his mouth, and I see a hint of exhaustion in his eyes. "There's no delaying this, Sofia. The wedding will be Saturday."

"Is there anything else in the document I should know about?"

Luca shakes his head.

"Did you include *my* stipulations?"

"Sofia—" The warning in Luca's voice is clear.

"So the contract has everything you demand, but nothing that I—"

Luca slams one hand down on the table, getting to his feet so quickly that I flinch backwards and almost topple the chair. "My agreeing to your *conditions* is nothing but me being a merciful husband, Sofia. I don't *have* to agree to anything. One phone call, and you are dead! Do you understand me? So instead of insisting that I have all of this typed up again to suit your desires, you're just going to have to trust me." His jaw is clenched as he leans over me, his green eyes blazing. "Or you can tell me that's impossible, and I'll call Don Rossi and let him know the marriage is off. It's your choice, my lovely *bride.*"

He hisses the last word, and I can see in that moment the toll that this is taking on him. I don't feel sorry for him, not even a little bit, but my heart is racing as I look up at his chiseled face, at his green eyes blazing like emeralds, his gaze hard as flint. He reaches out, a hand on either side of the back of my chair, and looms over me.

"I could demand anything I want of you," he murmurs, his voice dropping an octave, low and deep. I feel it shiver over my skin despite myself. "I could demand your body, your submission, every part of you given to me without question, in exchange for your life. But despite the man I am that disgusts you so, despite the blood on my hands, I won't. Do you know why, Sofia?"

"No," I whisper. I'm shaking like a leaf, but my skin is humming with something I've never felt before, some electric sensation traveling over me until it feels as if every hair on my body is standing up. Luca's full lips are hovering over mine, every inch of him rigid with anger, and I know without a doubt that if I reached down, I'd find him as hard as he'd been last night. There's something between us that I don't understand, some chemistry in our undeniable hatred of each other, and a twisted part of me wants to arch upwards, to press my lips against his and wrap my arms around his neck, bringing him down to me until we topple onto the gleaming wooden floor of the dining room together.

Luca stays very still over me, his gaze fixed on mine. "Because I've committed a great many sins in my life, Sofia, many of them mortal. But I've never forced myself on a woman. I've never taken one who didn't want me."

He pushes himself away from my chair then, his jaw still clenched. "And I'm not about to start with my wife."

My hands are shaking. I'm not sure if I can even manage to sign the papers, but Luca shoves them towards me. "Oh," he says coldly. "There is one more thing."

"What?" I try to stop my voice from trembling, but I can't.

"Your hair color. I don't care what it costs, or what a stylist has to do, but that ghastly dye will be out of your hair by Friday, and you'll be as close to your natural color as she can manage. It looks ridiculous on you." He spits the last words out, sitting back down in his chair. "I'll have my secretary send a stylist up tomorrow. And when we're finished here, someone will be coming with a new wardrobe for you, something that doesn't make you look like a whore."

I know that he's being intentionally cruel, undercutting the desire of a few moments ago with anger instead. But it doesn't make the words hurt any less. Nothing he says should hurt me, but it does, nonetheless.

The sooner you can get this over with then, the better. Soon, you'll hardly even have to see him.

Letting out a long breath, I reach for the pen.

* * *

AN HOUR LATER, I'm standing in one of the guest bedrooms in the penthouse, looking at an array of clothing, undergarments, shoes and jewelry scattered across the bed. There's a garment rack with more clothing against the wall. It's the most overwhelming display of wealth I've ever seen in one place, because every single item has a designer tag.

I'm still reeling from the paperwork. In the end, none of it had been anything that I could find a reason to argue about. The part in the marriage agreement about children had bothered me, but as Luca had pointed out, since I was insisting that I would remain a virgin—what was there to worry about? And even *if* I changed my mind, or he changed his and forced the issue, would I really want to have a child with him? Or would I want to take care of *that* particular problem as soon as possible?

I'd never thought it would be something I'd even consider. But the thought of giving Luca a child sends a shudder through me, and not a good one. I can't imagine raising a child in this life—after all, my father had hoped that *I* would escape it for exactly that reason. *All the more reason to stay out of his bed,* I tell myself, running my fingers over a silk shirt. If I don't sleep with him, it's not even a possibility.

The rest of it was just standard prenuptial agreements—nothing that I hadn't expected, and nothing that I took issue with. I don't want Luca's money, or his property. I don't even want this marriage, and he's made it clear that there's no way out. And if I *do* manage to exploit the tiny loophole I think I've found, I won't be stopping to try to take half of his possessions in court.

I'll be running for my life.

"Mr. Romano was very insistent that you should pick anything you like," the prim blonde woman standing off to the side tells me. The bedroom that we're in is more like a hotel suite, with a massive king-sized bed, a wardrobe, dresser, *and* a walk-in closet, and a fireplace with two wing chairs in front of it. I haven't even explored the bathroom yet, but just a glimpse of it told me that it's as big as my entire bedroom in my own apartment.

The memory of my room sends a jolt of sadness through me. I want to go back, but I'll never be able to. I don't even know if I'll be able to convince Luca to get some of my things, or if I should even try. I've taken some pleasure in irritating him and seeing how many of his buttons I can push before he explodes, but his reaction this afternoon told me that I've just about pushed him to the limit. I can't afford to be petty and immature, no matter how much I'd like to be. I'm going to have to learn to play this game his way if I want to survive.

I'm all but certain I've gotten all the concessions out of him that I'm going to manage for a long time.

There's thousands upon thousands of dollars of clothes and shoes and jewelry spread out in front of me, but I can't take any joy in it. *Anastasia would be drooling over this*, I think, running my hand over a long black velvet evening gown. It's beautiful, but all I can think is that this is Luca's way of mollifying me and controlling me all at once, dressing me up like a beautiful doll, to take out when he needs me and put out of sight when he doesn't.

Isn't that what you want, though? I chide myself. If there's no way out of this—and it's clear that there isn't—shouldn't I want as little to do with Luca after our marriage as possible? I look down at the ring on my finger, sparkling brilliantly. A daily reminder of who I'm bound to for the rest of my life. There's no escaping him, even when I'm alone.

The sleek blonde woman remains mostly silent while I try on clothing and pick my way through the items. Luckily, Luca's taste runs similar to mine—simple and elegant—and if the situation were different I might have enjoyed having free rein to choose whatever I like. In the end I wind up with a few pairs of designer jeans, a handful of silk and linen tops and a stack of t-shirts that probably cost more than a t-shirt ever should, some light sundresses and shoes to go with them, ballet flats and heels. There's workout gear too—all branded and expensive, and I grab items without paying much attention. To me, yoga pants are yoga pants, regardless of where they come from. The evening gowns are the hardest to choose—they're a reminder of what Luca told me earlier, that I'll have to attend events and galas with him as his perfect, happy, glowing wife. The epitome of a good and loving marriage.

But I also remember that he'd told me that he'd hoped we'd mostly forget one another, and that makes me think that those might be few and far between. I can only hope that's the case.

I try to avoid the jewelry—I can't even imagine how large of a bill I've racked up this far, and even my petty instinct to spend as much of Luca's money as I can isn't able to overcome the frugality that was instilled in me all my life. "Mr. Romano insists," the blonde woman says, pushing a tray of diamond earrings towards me, and I sigh.

In the end I pick out a few sets—one each in yellow, rose, and white gold—and a pair of small silver hoops. A pretty rose gold cuff bracelet studded with diamonds and a matching cocktail ring catches my eye, but I push them reluctantly away.

"And for the honeymoon?" The woman pulls out another garment rack, this one full of silk and satin and lace, pieces of lingerie both innocent and provocative, and I can feel myself blushing bright red.

"That won't be necessary," I say quickly.

She frowns. "Surely you want something beautiful for your wedding night, at least? Mr. Romano—"

"Mr. Romano has nothing to do with my underwear, I assure you," I tell her firmly. Her expression is thoroughly confused, but I ignore it. I might have to play the happy, satisfied bride for the rest of my life after this, but I refuse to pick out lingerie that I'll never wear, for a groom I'll never sleep with. That's taking the ruse too far.

"I think I'm done," I say firmly. "Tell Mr. Romano, if he asks, that I'm very grateful, but I'm also exhausted. This is it for me, today."

"Very good, Ms. Ferretti."

When the woman and her extensive collection of shopping is gone, I collapse backwards on the bed amidst all the clothing. My entire body aches from the events of yesterday, sleeping briefly curled up on a couch, and tension. I open one eye and see the bathroom door, and despite my stubborn insistence not to enjoy *anything* in this place, I can't help but give in to the idea of a hot bath. My muscles are screaming at me.

The bathroom itself is astonishing. The tiles are heated, something I find out as soon as I step barefoot into the room, and it's as massive as I'd thought it might be. The counter stretches along most of one wall, with double sinks and a huge mirror with recessed lighting all around it. The shower is separate from the tub, with porcelain tiles and rainwater showerheads on either end, and the tub has whirlpool jets. It takes me only a second of opening one of the lacquered black drawers to find sachets of scented bath salts and ampoules of bath oil, and there's literal *candles* underneath the sink. The other drawers are empty, just waiting for someone to fill them with their own things.

Of course there's nothing personal here, I think dryly, as I turn the bathwater on. Luca doesn't seem like the kind of guy who calls a girl for a second date, or lets them leave a toothbrush or lipstick behind. Everything about this guest suite is carefully curated, undoubtedly by someone else, for any guest he might have. And I'm sure the girls don't stay in here. They probably don't even stay the night. *He probably fucks them and just calls a cab, and they thank him for it.*

I'm not quite sure why I feel so bitter about it. Truthfully, I should be grateful. The busier he is in his own bed, the less trouble I'll have keeping him out of mine. And I don't believe for a second that Luca is a man who lacks for female company, even if he hadn't bragged about it. But the same way that my skin feels as if it's electrified every time he looms over me, the thought of another woman in his bed makes my stomach feel queasy with anxiety.

Jealousy. It's a strange emotion to feel over the man who is essentially my captor. *It's just because you're marrying him,* I tell myself, sliding into the vanilla-scented bathwater and stifling a groan of pleasure as the hot water closes over my body. *You just feel obligated to be jealous of other women in your husband's bed. But that was never going to change. All you can do is stay out of it yourself, and look the other way.*

Luca had made it clear that he expected to be allowed to do whatever he wanted. *Was my father like that?* For the first time, I allow myself to wonder about his marriage to my mother. I can't believe that he was ever unfaithful to her. I remember the way he looked at her, the way they would sneak kisses when they thought I wasn't looking, the way he always touched her waist when he passed her even after years of marriage. I know that he loved her. But fidelity? Now I'm not so sure.

It's clear that my father lived a life that I never knew about. That much I'd always been aware of—but I'd never imagined *this*. And I'd never have thought he'd be capable of promising me to a man like Luca. *Did he know what the alternative would be, if I refused? Did he know I'd be backed into a corner like this? And if he did, was the promise made because he was afraid of Rossi killing me?*

I close my eyes, sinking deeper into the bath. There's so much that I don't know, so many questions left unanswered, and Luca doesn't seem inclined to give me any of those answers. I know that he's hoping I'll be meek and quiet after our wedding, that I'll stop fighting him and asking questions.

But I've spent my whole life being meek and quiet, trying to stay out of sight, and it didn't work. It only got me here, forced into a marriage I don't want, my entire life wiped away in one night.

I press my lips together, breathing in the vanilla scent of the water.

It might just be time to try something new.

LUCA

*T*he paperwork is signed. The ring is on Sofia's finger. Carmen has all of her instructions to set the wheels in motion for the ceremony and reception on Saturday. Father Donahue has reluctantly agreed to see Sofia for her confirmation, despite how "irregular it all is."

I should feel satisfied. Content, even, that the matter has been handled despite Sofia's reticence, and that everything is falling into place.

Instead, as I sit in the back of my town car being driven to an appointment with Don Rossi, I feel more agitated than ever.

I was supposed to be the one in control of all of this. The one calling the shots, telling Sofia how things were going to go. And yet somehow, my lovely bride-to-be managed to make me feel that in the end, despite all the paperwork and all the demands and restrictions I've placed on her, that she has the upper hand.

Surely I don't feel this way just because she's told me I can't fuck her?

I've never been hung up on any particular woman before. I lost my own virginity at fifteen, and I've been happily fucking my way through Manhattan ever since, first through the freshman girls at my private high school, and then once I graduated, well—I've been fucking my way through the rest of the city. Never once have I given any of them a second thought, except for a pair of blonde twins who are to this day the only women I've ever called twice.

In my defense, that was the first time I'd ever had my cock sucked by two women at once.

Maybe it's just that you don't like being told what you can and can't have.

That's as good a guess as any. But all I know is that I need to get over it. I *can* have just about any woman I want, so why is it rattling me so much that this one girl is stubbornly refusing to bend?

I know where I'd like to bend her—right over my knee the next time she opens her mouth to argue with me.

The thought comes out of nowhere—hell, I don't think I've even ever *done* that with a woman before. I've tied a fair few of them up to my bed, blindfolded a couple—and there was that one threesome that involved some chocolate and hot wax—but other than that my sexual exploits have remained largely vanilla. Most women are turned on enough by my good looks and money to not need much else to get them wet.

But something about Sofia makes me want to do things to her that I've never even dreamed of doing. She makes me lose control of my emotions in a way that's entirely unfamiliar to me, and she makes me harder than I've ever been in my life.

All of those individually are excellent reasons to stay as far away from her as I can. Together, they tell me that she's a ticking bomb waiting to go off, blowing my carefully constructed life to pieces.

The day that I can put her in her own apartment and get her out of mine can't come fast enough.

Both Franco and Don Rossi are waiting for me in his office, and Franco gets up the minute I walk through the door, a shit-eating grin on his face. "Luca!" he greets me enthusiastically, clapping me on the shoulder as I stride towards the desk. "And here I thought I was going to be the first one to get married."

"Don't rub it in," I growl, sinking into one of the leather chairs in front of Rossi. "The Ferretti girl has already taken five years off my life, and it's not even lunchtime."

"Sounds exciting." Franco winks at me. "Caterina—"

Rossi clears his throat, shooting Franco a look that tells him that he probably shouldn't let whatever remark he was about to make regarding the Don's daughter out of his mouth.

Franco flushes to the roots of his red hair, sinking into the chair next to me without another word.

I glance over at my friend. He's always been the more extroverted of the two of us, likely because he's had to overcome a lot in order to hold any position in the family. His father was a made man under Rossi, not someone of high rank, but someone well-trusted enough that Franco and I grew up together. But thanks to Franco's red hair, pale freckled skin, and green eyes even brighter than mine, a lot of rumors and gossip dogged his childhood. He was born roughly nine months after the head of the Boston Irish family, along with a handful of his men, came to visit. I was barely out of the oven then, but everyone's heard the story of how Franco's black-haired, dark-eyed father took one look at his new son and demanded a paternity test.

The results came back that Franco, despite his unusual coloring, was as Italian as a good Bolognese. But still, the rumors persisted, and grade school started out miserably for Franco. He spent a decent amount of it being bullied, beaten up, having his lunch stolen, and hearing his mother called a "shamrock-loving whore" before he made it to seventh grade and managed to befriend me.

I honestly don't remember what we bonded over. It might have been baseball cards, or it could have been a shared appreciation for the fact that Angie Greco was the first girl in our class to develop breasts. But once we became friends, there was no chance that anyone was laying a finger on him.

It earned me his loyalty, which has paid for itself in spades over the years—and now Franco has been rewarded handsomely with the Don's daughter, and the place at my right hand when I inherit Rossi's seat. It's all worked out very well for him, and I know that he's grateful.

These are the kinds of alliances that have to be made. It's how our families have done things for centuries, how we've kept the Irish and the Russians from taking over, how we've held our place through the mob wars over the decades. We've lost battles, but in the end, we won the war. And for now, there's peace.

But the Bratva are threatening that.

"It sounds as if my solution might have been easier," Rossi says dryly. "I hope that the girl isn't going to cause undue trouble, Luca."

"She'll be fine," I reply quickly. Almost too quickly—I see the suspicion on Rossi's face. "The rock weighing down her finger and the shopping spree that I had delivered to the penthouse should have made her more pliable by now."

"You'll spoil the girl," Rossi warns. "Don't let her think that she has the upper hand. She needs to know that you're in control, Luca. That you hold the power of life and death over her. It's the only way to be sure that she'll comply."

"She's very aware," I tell him firmly. *If only he knew,* I think, forcing myself not to shift uncomfortably in my chair. If Rossi knew that Sofia had already managed to set her own conditions—

He'd think I'm pussy-whipped. And maybe I am. By a pussy that I won't even get to taste, let alone fuck.

Just the thought is enough to make my cock twitch rebelliously in my pants. But I meant what I said to Sofia. I've never forced myself on a woman—I've never even considered it. There are things that not even I can justify. So no matter how much I want Sofia, her precious virginity will remain untouched. There's no question about that. All that's left for me is to figure out how to get her out of my head.

But if I ever find out that anyone other than me has touched her—
I'll kill him.

The girl has doomed herself to a life of celibacy. And if playing the nun ever gets to be too frustrating—well, I'll be right there to ease the burden. For one night only, of course.

But what a fucking night it would be.

Rossi clears his throat again, and I realize that I've been lost in my thoughts for too long. "I'm sorry," I say quickly. "It was a long night."

Franco cackles at that, but Rossi ignores him studiously, a faint expression of annoyance passing over his face. "I simply asked if you wish anyone besides myself and Franco to come up the morning after your wedding to witness the bridal bed. Seeing as how Sofia has no parents to vouch for her—"

"That won't be necessary," I say smoothly. I knew this issue would come up, after Sofia's insistence on a chaste marriage, but I'm prepared.

"Tradition insists—"

"I'm well aware of tradition."

"Then you know that we need proof of consummation. Of Sofia's—"

"Sofia isn't a virgin." I speak the lie with absolute assurance, even knowing what it could cost me if Don Rossi ever discovered that I lied to him. The subject of the lie wouldn't even matter that much—only the act of it.

Even as I say it, I know I must have truly lost my mind.

Why am I willing to put so much on the line for this girl? She should mean nothing to me. Our impending marriage is born of nothing but a father's desperate plea for his daughter, and my father's weakness in the face of friendship. *I* didn't make the promise. I was never consulted about any of this. And yet not only have I agreed to wed the girl, but I've just lied to the most powerful man in not only the North American continent, but half of Europe as well. A man who trades in life and death like they're penny stocks, who scruples at almost nothing in his own quest to maintain the dynasty that he's built. If his only child had been born a son, I'd never be elevated past underboss. Worse, I might have been demoted in favor of that fictional heir's own choice for his right hand. Sent off to be a capo in Philadelphia, or something equally cringeworthy.

Instead, Rossi chose me as his heir, and I've just told him a bare-faced lie.

And why? I could have insisted that Sofia go to bed with me on our wedding night. I can tell myself that I'd conceded because of my fear that she'd refuse the marriage and wind up dead, but I don't for a second truly believe that Sofia wouldn't have traded her virginity for her life.

The truth that I don't want to admit to myself is that I gave in because from the moment I caught her trying to run out of the apartment, I knew I didn't want to take her unwillingly. I didn't want to fuck her while she laid there cold and compliant, doing her duty the one time.

No, if I ever take Sofia Ferretti to bed, I want the hellcat that I had pinned up against my front door. I want the woman who declared passionately to me that I'll never see her naked, dripping wet underneath me while she begs for my cock. I want her aching for it, desperate, ready to take me in her body in any way that I'll give it to her. I want her pleading for me to let her come.

I want to wring every ounce of pleasure that I can out of her perfect body, until she's addicted to what I can do to her. And then I want to get my revenge for the way she's made me feel these past twenty-four hours—and no doubt will continue to make me feel until I can get her the hell out of my penthouse—and never touch her again.

No matter how much she begs me to.

Just the thought of it has me rock-hard all over again.

"It certainly is a struggle to keep you present today, Luca," Rossi says dryly. "Is the thought of your bride's lack of innocence that distracting?"

I sit up straighter, willing my stubborn erection away. Luckily I'm sitting down, and it's not overly obvious, but still—

"It's not important to me," I say flatly. *Another lie.*

Rossi looks unconvinced. "And she told you this? You trust her?"

I snort. "Of course not." *At least that's the truth.* "I had Dr. Carella come and examine her after I took her out of the hotel room. The doctor confirmed to me that there was no sign that she was untouched."

Another lie. I'll have to make certain that Dr. Carella is thoroughly aware of what her answer should be, if Don Rossi ever thinks to check with her regarding the state of Sofia's virginity when I brought her back to my apartment.

Rossi looks thoughtful. "Was it the Russians?"

I can see the wheels turning in his head, and I know exactly what he's thinking. I owe Rossi a great deal—my position, my wealth, my power—but for the first time, I'm truly sickened by him. He's not concerned in the slightest for Sofia, or what might have happened to her. But if any Bratva man *had* violated Giovanni's daughter, that would be cause to wipe the stain of them from the face of the continent.

Rossi is trying to avoid a war, on the face of it. But deep down, I know he would welcome the excuse to cut a bloody swath through them all.

"No." My tone is curt and firm. "She wasn't harmed physically, beyond some superficial bruising to her face and wrists. There were some lingering effects from the drugs, but she wasn't—assaulted."

Rossi looks mildly disappointed, and I have the sudden, violent urge to lunge forward and punch the expression off of his face.

The thought startles me. I've often been a violent man, but never an impulsive one. It's part of what has made me such an excellent asset to the Rossi family. I'll do what needs to be done, but always with a cool head and no emotion behind it. The fact that my gut is churning with disgust at the knowledge that Rossi would gladly exploit Sofia's potential abuse is just further proof that I need to put some distance between myself and her. I've always known that he was willing to order her killed if need be—so why does this surprise me?

"A shame," Franco says cheerfully. "It's been a while since you've gotten to be the first one in, eh?"

I glare at him. "I'll leave that to you," I tell him sharply, ignoring Don Rossi's expression at the reference to his daughter. "Proof of consummation won't be necessary," I continue, turning back to face Rossi.

He frowns. "This marriage needs to be legal," Rossi cautions. "There can be no question that Sofia Ferretti is your wife in all ways."

I smile blandly at him. "Of course," I say simply, my expression giving away nothing. "Have you ever known me not to take a woman to bed, if I have the opportunity to get her there?"

SOFIA

I'm waiting for Luca when he returns to the penthouse.

His look of surprise is almost satisfying enough when he sees me standing by the window in the living room, wearing a knee-length red sleeveless dress and nude Louboutin pumps, a pair of yellow gold diamond studs in my ears to match the ring on my finger and a diamond cuff on my wrist. I don't have any makeup or anything to style my hair with here, but I did find a hairbrush in one of the drawers, and there's enough product left in it from last night that it still falls in slight waves around my face.

"It's still blonde," I say, allowing a hint of apology into my voice as I push a curl away from my cheek and look across the room at him. "But I'm sure the stylist you're sending will take care of that in the next few days."

It's incredibly gratifying to see Luca speechless, even if it only lasts a few seconds. Then I see his expression go carefully blank, and he strides into the room, his hands shoved carelessly into his pockets. It reminds me of the way he stood across from me in his bedroom last night, and a small shiver runs down my spine.

"I see you enjoyed your shopping trip."

"Is it a shopping trip, if I don't leave the house?"

"I'd hate to know how much it would have cost otherwise, if it wasn't."

Luca and I face off on opposite sides of the window, the vast city stretching out underneath us. Looking at him in the soft light, it's easy to see why so many women have swooned over him—why he expected me to do the same. I've never seen a more handsome man. Everything about him is perfection, from the chiseled lines of his face to the cut and swoop of his dark hair, to the expert tailoring of his suit. Every inch of him screams wealth, power, and control, and it both terrifies me and intrigues me all at once.

Mostly I want to know why he's going to such lengths to keep me safe. Is it the possibility of breaking me? The gratification of owning a wife the way he owns everything else? Something darker? I can't believe that this is all because of a promise that he didn't even make.

"Why did you bother dressing up for me?" Luca's voice is dangerously soft. His eyes linger on my face for a moment, and then boldly sweep downwards over the rest of my body, reminding me that even if he can't touch, I can't stop him from looking at me—the wife he bought today.

And in five days, I'll be his wife in the eyes of man and God—in word, if not in deed.

"Who said it was for you?" I look up at him, lifting my chin and meeting his eyes. "Can't a girl wear a pretty dress for herself?"

Luca shrugs. "I don't pay much attention to the things women do to amuse themselves."

"No, I suppose you don't. Only what they can do to amuse *you*."

His gaze darkens, and he takes a step towards me. "Are you planning to amuse me tonight, Sofia?"

I pretend to look shocked. "We're not even married yet, *Mr. Romano*. Surely you wouldn't expect—"

"You'd be surprised what I might expect." His voice drops an octave, and he takes another step. He's too close to me now, closer than I'd planned to allow him. My heart flutters in my chest despite myself—this wasn't what I'd planned. "And call me Luca. Mr. Romano was my father. Husbands and wives should call each other by their given names."

"That wasn't in the contract." My voice sounds breathier than I meant for it to. Silently, I curse the fact that he seems to affect me like this every time he's near. How am I supposed to gain the upper hand in this situation when just being within touching distance of him makes my hands tingle and my palms sweat, my stomach tying itself in knots just from the scent of his cologne?

He smells like salt and lemons, but not the cleaning-product scent of cheap citrus fragrance. Luca's cologne smells rich and expensive, like saltwater and lemon trees and sugar, like dessert with an edge, like drinking limoncello on a sailboat while the sea breeze tousles your hair. I take a deep breath, and I realize as my skin flushes with embarrassment that I'm breathing him in.

I can't help it. I've never been so close to a man like Luca, never spent so much time around any man who looks like him, who commands others the way he does, who truly believes that the world was designed especially for his pleasure. And in five days, I'm supposed to marry him.

"How do you know?" His mouth twitches slightly, as if he wants to laugh. "You didn't read it."

"Because you told me what was in it!" My voice rises, and Luca's mouth does quirk upwards then.

"And you believed me?" His voice is deep and rich, drifting over me like smoke. "You're very naïve, Sofia."

I swallow hard. "How do you think I ended up in that club?"

Luca's gaze slides over my face. "By listening to the wrong people."

"And I should listen to you?"

"You'd be safer if you did."

I tense, stepping back and breathing in deeply again. A few inches further away from him and the air is mine again, smelling blandly of furniture polish and woodsy air freshener. "Ana didn't mean any harm," I say defensively. "She had no idea what would happen."

"I'm sure," Luca says dryly. "If I'd thought she meant you harm—"

He trails off, and I can feel my eyes widen slightly. "What? What would you have done?"

Luca ignores the question, changing gears as smoothly as a Ferrari. "You still haven't told me why you're so dressed up. I saw the invoice from your shopping, you did pick out some more casual clothing."

"I ordered us dinner."

That look of surprise crosses his face again, only to be quickly smoothed away. "I planned to have dinner in my office. I have plenty of work to do—"

"We're getting married in five days, Luca."

He looks at me curiously. I'm not sure if it was my admission out loud that I'm going to marry him, or my use of his name, but for once Luca doesn't look as if he's already thought of what he's going to say next.

"We should talk," I say simply. "I know that you want us to avoid each other as much as possible, and believe me, I'm fine with that. But we have to go out in public occasionally, like you said. And that public will expect us to behave like a happily married couple."

"And?" I can see the irritation in Luca's face. "If you have a point, Sofia, hurry up and make it."

"Happily married couples know things about each other. Their favorite foods. Favorite colors. What they like to do on the weekends."

Luca frowns. "I'm partial to wild mushroom ravioli with cream sauce and a good red to go with it, I don't have a favorite color, and—" he leans closer to me, as if to tell me a secret. "On the weekends, I like to go out and find the most beautiful woman I can, bring her home, and then fuck her until she screams my name."

I know he's trying to shock me, to get me to back down. Instead I look up at him, keeping my face smooth and blank. "Don't you have anything more creative than that?"

Luca purses his lips. "You're right," he says finally. "Sometimes I bring home two. If it's an exceptionally good weekend, maybe even three."

"No one can satisfy three women at the same time."

"You're right about that, too." Luca's smile spreads across his face.

"But two of them can entertain each other while I'm fucking the other. And then I move on to the next." He's still too close, looming over me in the light from the window. "Can you imagine that, Sofia? Three beautiful women in bed with me, all of us naked, tangled up in each other. Have you ever heard two women come at the same time? It's like music. And the scent—" he breathes in, closing his eyes, and then straightens, grinning down at me as if telling me a joke that he knows I don't understand.

"No, of course you can't imagine that," he says coolly. "And if you keep clinging to your innocence, Sofia, you never will."

"I don't have any interest in sharing your bed with other women," I snap, before I can think that sentence all the way through. But Luca grabs onto it immediately, his smile almost mocking now.

"So you *do* have an interest in my bed."

"No, I—" I try to backtrack, quickly. "I don't have any interest in what happens there at all."

I've never told such a barefaced lie. Just the thought of Luca naked and tangled in the sheets of that massive bed makes my heart race. The thought of what his body might look like under that carefully tailored suit sends a shiver down my spine, and for a moment I can't speak. I never thought anyone could make me feel something like this —the kind of breathless wanting that I've seen in movies or read about in books. I never thought it was real.

But right now, I think that if he tried to touch me, I might not be able to tell him no.

And I've only been here for a day. How am I going to manage until he gives me my own apartment?

Remember why you're here. What he's done to you. What he wants from you.

Luca has made it plain that he doesn't plan to be a real husband to me in any way. What he wants is to fuck me once and toss me aside like any of his other women, and I refuse to be treated so callously. But anything else is out of the question. He isn't going to love me. And I shouldn't want him to.

I've never felt so confused.

"Are we done here?" Luca looks down at me, his face expressionless once again. "Or do you have any other inane questions to ask me? How I like my steak, maybe? Who my eighth grade history teacher was? Some other trivia that I suppose married couples know about each other, in whatever world you live in?"

"I grew up in the same world as you," I say defensively, crossing my arms over my chest. "Until my father died—"

Luca's face hardens then, and he takes a step back. "No," he says coldly. "You did not. *Your* father shielded you from the worst of what he did. *Your* father did all he could to make sure that you would never be a part of any of this. But I was the son of Rossi's underboss, the eldest Romano son, and my life has *never* been anything like yours, Sofia." His gaze has that steely edge again as he looks down at me, and I'm reminded of the way he behaved in the dining room earlier, when I signed the papers.

It should terrify me. Everything about this man should. But the feeling in my stomach when I remember his hands on either side of my chair and his mouth hovering above mine has nothing to do with fear.

"When it comes to my world, Sofia," he says, his voice icy, "you are nothing but a child. Don't make the mistake of thinking that we're the same. We're not."

And then, before I can say another word, he turns on his heel and stalks out of the room.

I'm BACK in my room before I remember about the dinner that I ordered. It's probably still on the dinner table, getting colder by the minute, but I can't bring myself to go back out—especially with the possibility that I might run into Luca.

Even as unfamiliar as the bedroom is, I wish I could just hide away in here until the wedding. *What was I thinking, trying to get to know him, as if he's anything other than a heartless criminal who takes what he wants and gives nothing back?* I'd thought that if I could draw some kind of humanity out of him, get some insight into who he is, that maybe we could come to some kind of understanding. But instead, I was just left feeling overwhelmed again, small and helpless in the face of his wealth and power and raw masculinity.

But I'm not helpless. If I have to put on a show every time I have to appear in public on my "husband's" arm, if I have to give vague answers to hide how little I really know about him, fine. Once I've settled into my own apartment, I can do my best to forget about him, just like he said. We can forget about each other. The ridiculous jealousy I feel, the way my knees turn to water and my blood heats every time he's near me, all of that will fade away.

I just can't pretend that there's anything special about me, that the way he seems to focus on trying to seduce me every time we're near each other is anything other than what he does to every woman. The difference is that I won't be fooled by it.

A knock at the door jolts me out of my thoughts, and I stiffen, hesitating. If it's Luca, the last thing I want is to talk to him again. But all I hear is a metallic *clank*, and then the sound of footsteps walking off down the hall.

After a moment's debate with myself, I get up and walk to the door, gingerly opening it. To my surprise, I see a covered silver tray outside on the floor, like something a hotel might leave for room service, and no one waiting outside.

Quickly, I pick it up and shut the door again. When I set it down on the bed and take off the cover, I see my portion of the meal I'd ordered—a lamb chop and garlic potatoes on an etched white china dish, and a salad in a crystal bowl with a miniature silver pitcher filled with vinaigrette.

For a moment, I just stare at it. *Did Luca drop this off for me?* The thought of Luca going to the dining room, parceling out my portion of dinner and serving it up in this ridiculously elegant—if completely on brand—way seems entirely out of character. It must have been some member of the staff that he almost certainly has—except I haven't actually *seen* any staff. No housekeeper, or cook, or maid.

They're probably just very good at staying out of sight. It's impossible that Luca did this for me. It doesn't fit with anything I've seen from him. It would imply that he actually cares, that he has a heart, which he's already gone to great lengths to show me isn't true.

But as I pick at the food, my appetite completely gone, I can't help but wonder if there's another side to this man that I'm about to marry —that I hardly even know.

SOFIA

I wake up the next morning overwhelmed by sadness, my chest aching and on the verge of tears. I'd dreamed that I was back in my old apartment, sitting in the living room with Anastasia watching trashy reality tv while we drank wine and ate popcorn. Instead, when I open my eyes I'm in this new, strange bed, in this huge and impersonal room, and I miss my old home and old life so much that all I want to do is curl up into a ball and cry.

Instead I resolutely get up, and walk over to the dresser to fish out a pair of jeans and one of the light, sleeveless tops that I picked out. As I slip my feet into a pair of buttery-soft leather flats, I glance over at the row of velvet boxes on the nightstand, all containing my new jewelry.

Am I supposed to put on diamond earrings to go down to breakfast? Everything about this life that Luca lives is so unfamiliar. I walk over to the window and push back the curtains—the ones in the guest room are normal drapes over a more normal sized, if still large window—and hold up my left hand to the light. The huge diamond sparkles in the sunlight, and I frown, realizing that I hadn't thought to take it off last night before I went to bed.

I don't want to examine that too closely. I tell myself that it was

120

just an oversight, that I was too confused by the appearance of dinner in my room to think about it, or that I didn't want to slip up and forget to put it back on this morning. Anything other than the possibility that I might already be getting used to the weight of it on my hand, that I might actually *like* wearing it. That I might think it's beautiful.

Turning away from the window, I grab the pair of silver hoops that I'd picked out yesterday, and pull my hair into a bun atop my head. I have no doubt that the stylist Luca mentioned is probably going to show up today, so there's no point in trying to do much else with it.

I head down the staircase, trying not to think about how just two nights ago, I tried to make a break for freedom down these steps, how it ended with Luca pinning me up against his front door, making me feel things that I've never felt in my entire life. *If this were a movie, I know exactly how that would have ended.* It would have ended with that stupidly short dress up around my hips, and Luca claiming his prize as the first man to ever be inside of me, while I gasped and moaned and begged for more, completely giving myself over to him.

But this isn't a movie. It's not a story of any kind, it's my *life*. A life that has been, without my knowledge, promised and bartered away years ago. And if I give in to Luca, I'll lose the last thing that I have power over.

It's true that a night with him would be something beyond anything I've ever dreamed, that it would be worlds away from what I'd always expected my first time would be—clumsy, probably a little painful, and almost certainly not living up to the hype. Even Ana, once she'd figured out that I'd never slept with anyone, had warned me not to expect too much from the first time. "It gets better later on," had been her exact words, if I remember correctly.

But with Luca, it wouldn't be clumsy. It might not even be painful. And it would *definitely* exceed anything I'd heard about—regarding the first time, or probably any other time.

It would also be only once. Loveless. Passion without substance. Pleasure without any meaning.

If I'd been someone who had had plenty of casual sex before, if I weren't so naïve and innocent when it came to what went on between two people in the bedroom, maybe I could have enjoyed what Luca could offer me, and then written it off as an experience. Taken from him as much as he would take from me, and then shut myself off.

But that isn't the case, and now it never will be. Luca would take something from me that he can't give me any equivalent of. Pleasure isn't enough to make up for allowing him so close to me, allowing him to take something that, even if it never held any deep meaning for me before, suddenly feels like the last thing of my own that I'm allowed to possess.

I'm so deep in thought that I don't notice at first as I walk into the kitchen that Luca is sitting at the table. He's behind a newspaper, and as soon as he hears my footsteps he lays it down, his handsome face looking more peaceful in the early morning light.

In fact he almost looks—normal. As normal as a man who is sitting at his ridiculously expensive kitchen table in a suit can, anyway. But he's holding a newspaper, and has a cup of coffee in front of him—black as his soul, of course—and there's a plate of eggs and sausage in front of him, as of yet untouched.

"Sausage is bad for your heart," I tell him as I head to the fridge, trying to seem as unaffected as possible by finding him in the kitchen. It is *his* house, after all—I can't imagine this place ever feeling like home to me. But I hadn't thought that he'd be in here at ten o'clock in the morning—in fact, I was fairly sure he'd probably never set foot in this particular room at all.

"It's good that I don't have one then," Luca says, smirking.

He just made a joke. My cold, calculating, second-in-command to the head of the Italian Mafia fiancé just made a *joke.* At the breakfast table. In broad daylight. As if us meeting each other here were an ordinary thing.

I feel as if I'm getting whiplash.

I manage to hide the expression on my face, opening the refrigerator and finding a yogurt and a pressed juice. The yogurt is in a *glass jar* of all things, and the juice looks like one of those seven-dollar-a-bottle types you find at a Whole Foods. The kind of thing that Ana always used to bemoan not being able to afford, that the rich ballerinas at Juilliard lived off of. They apparently were always talking about their juice fasts and wheat grass shots and whatever else they used to stay stick thin and permanently hungry.

But I'm getting married in five days, and although a small, petty part of me wants to show up looking my absolute worst, I'm not entirely without vanity. I'm only ever going to get one wedding day, and I'd like to feel beautiful, even if I can't stand the sight of my groom.

The problem though, isn't that you can't stand the sight of him. It's that you can, even though he's a heartless monster and you shouldn't want him in any possible capacity.

Gritting my teeth, I walk over to the table, plopping down in one of the chairs with the determination to act as normally as possible. If Luca doesn't want to eat breakfast with me, he can leave.

Luca glances over his paper again, and wrinkles his nose. "Well, I suppose I should be glad that you're mindful of your figure at least. Designers don't typically like to dress a girl over a size four."

"Well, I'm right at their limit then," I say pleasantly, scooping up a spoonful of blueberry yogurt. "Maybe I should have had some sausage after all."

He doesn't take the bait. "The stylist will be here in an hour," he says, checking his watch. "Apparently dealing with your disastrous hair will take some time, so your appointment to choose your wedding dress has been postponed until late afternoon. But I expect it to all be done by the end of the day, since you have your meeting with Father Donahue tomorrow." Luca sets his paper down, stabbing one of the sausages with a fork. "Friday night is the rehearsal, and by Saturday night, this entire matter will be settled and over with." He pops a bite into his mouth, and chews thoughtfully, watching me from across the table. "Carmen will email you the itinerary for the week, with all of your appointments, just in case you forget."

It's on the tip of my tongue to point out that I don't have my phone any longer, or any access to a computer, but instead I take that moment to blurt out what's been on my mind since last night, even though I know I should have come up with a plan for asking him, some way to manipulate Luca into saying yes. But at this point, I'm so drained that I can't do anything except let the request spill out while Luca looks at me from the other end of the table.

"I want Ana to come with me today, to help me pick my dress," I say, the words stumbling over each other. "And I want her at the wedding, too."

Luca looks at me as if I've lost my mind. "I've already told you how I feel about your Russian friend," he says flatly.

"She's my—"

"Yes. I know. Your only friend. She also has old ties to the Bratva, and—"

"You agreed that I could see her!" The words burst out of my mouth, petulant and angry like the child he accused me of being last night, but I can't help it. He's taken so much away from me already, and I'm terrified that he'll take this last thing, that the only person I have left in the world to love and who loves me will be gone forever.

Luca's jaw tenses, and I can see that he's on the verge of snapping again. He sets his fork down, carefully placing his palms on the table. "I agreed to that *after* the threat was contained—"

"You're forcing me to get married. You're forcing me to do this all alone—"

"No one is forcing you to do anything." Luca looks at me coolly. "You're welcome to call the wedding off."

"And then I die." I bite off every word, my hatred of him from yesterday returning full force. *I can't believe that I started to warm up to him, just because of a ring and him possibly leaving me dinner.* I clench my jaw, staring at him with as much anger as I can muster. *Fuck him, even if he did bring that dinner up with his own two hands.* I'm not a dog, to love my new owner just because he might have fed me.

Luca shrugs. "It's still a choice."

"Maybe in your world."

His face darkens. "Yes. In my world. Which you are now a part of, Sofia, whether you like it or not."

"Well I don't like it!" I hear my voice rising, but I can't stop myself. "My family is dead, Luca. My father is dead. My mother is dead. I *know* I've said it before, but Ana *is* my only friend! I know you don't give a shit about what I want, or how I feel, but can't you for one second pull your head out of your own ass and realize that I might want *one* person that I love there to help me choose my fucking wedding dress? To be there when I get *married? One person* to be there for me?"

I'm breathless by the time I finish, and I realize too late that I was yelling, that I just literally cursed and screamed at the man who has the power of life and death over me. I don't believe for one second that the document I signed yesterday, hell, that even my fucking marriage license will save me if Luca gets tired of dealing with me. This man, and everyone like him and around him, is above the law.

If he saves me, it's because he's choosing to. Which begs the question all over again—*why?*

I expect him to lose control again, to yell back, to threaten me. But instead he takes a deep breath, the muscles in his jaw working as he looks at me with that same hard expression on his face.

"I'll allow your friend to come and help you choose your dress today," he says finally. "And she can attend the wedding."

My mouth drops open. Even with the clear anger in his expression, this isn't what I'd expected.

"But." Luca raises a hand, indicating that I shouldn't speak until he's finished. It doesn't matter—I couldn't have anyway. I'm too shocked. "Caterina will come with you today as well, so that it's not only you and Anastasia. And Anastasia may not come to the reception. There's too many people there who might take offense to it, and I think she would be—uncomfortable."

I definitely don't think that he cares about Ana's feelings. But I'm too dumbstruck that he's actually given in to argue about that. The fact that he's going to allow her to come to the penthouse today, and that she'll be at the ceremony, is far more than I'd expected him to bend on.

"Thank you," I whisper. I should still be angry with him about so many things, and I am, but in this particular moment I'm more grateful than anything else.

"Don't mistake this for anything other than me having better things to do than argue with you every time I see you, Sofia," Luca says warningly. "And I've already told you what I think of your mouth. The kind of woman I would marry wouldn't curse like that. Or scream at her husband across the breakfast table.

You're not my husband yet, I want to retort, but I bite it back. I don't want to risk him going back on agreeing to let Ana come over today. Instead I just nod. "I'm sorry," I say contritely, but I can see from Luca's expression that he doesn't totally buy it. In fact, he doesn't look entirely happy that I've apologized.

"Who is Caterina?" I ask quickly, trying to change the subject.

Luca's face smooths instantly. "Don Rossi's daughter," he says, taking another bite of his breakfast as calmly as if we didn't just have a shouting match across the table. "She was recently engaged to my closest friend, Franco Bianchi, who will be my underboss when I take Rossi's seat." He pauses, looking up at me. "Try not to judge her based on your feelings about her father. She's actually quite a nice girl. She might have some good advice for you about—managing all of this."

It's a rare admission from him that all of this might be difficult for me, and I can feel myself softening towards him again, just a little. *Maybe that's why he's doing it. So that you'll trust him. So that you won't be on your guard.*

Regardless of his power or wealth or status, when it comes right down to it, Luca Romano is a criminal. A man who is willing to hurt or kill others to achieve his own ends. What do I know about him, really? What do I know about the things he might have done?

I can't afford to let my guard down. Not even for a minute. No matter what he does for me.

"I'll keep that in mind," I say tightly. "Thank you for letting Ana come."

Luca says nothing as I get up from the table, clutching my unopened bottle of juice. But as I head out of the kitchen, intending to go back to my room and call Ana, I can feel his eyes on me.

I need to be very, very careful.

SOFIA

I don't have any way to call Ana—my phone and anything else that was in that little clutch that I took with me the night I was kidnapped is long gone—but I assume that Luca will delegate the particular task of letting her know about the conversation to someone. Probably whoever "Carmen" is—I'm guessing his secretary.

Ana shows up partway through my hair appointment. The stylist, a tall blonde woman named Brigit, took one look at my hair and made a face that told me that we'd be struggling with it for a long time—it's apparently, in her words, "difficult to salvage," thanks to all the bleaching kits and box dye I've used on it over the years. I haven't bothered to get a haircut in probably eight or nine months, so several inches of it are lying on the floor now, leaving it just below my shoulders. It feels lighter already, but I've been sitting with some concoction on my hair meant to strip the old dye for nearly an hour, and I'm completely and utterly over it.

The only thing that could cheer me up is my best friend coming through the door, which is exactly what happens in that moment.

"Sofia!" Ana grins at me, gingerly giving me a hug despite Brigit's glare. "I can't believe Luca agreed to let me come."

"Me either," I admit, uncomfortably shifting in my chair. I open my mouth to say something else, but then someone else comes through the bedroom door—a tall brunette who I can only guess must be Caterina Rossi.

She's gorgeous—tall, with a slender hourglass figure, long brown wavy hair, and dark eyes in her perfectly shaped, olive-skinned face. With high cheekbones, feathery lashes that are almost definitely due to extensions, and full pouty lips, she could have been a model.

No wonder Luca's friend agreed to marry her, I think dryly. I can't help but wonder what *she* thinks of the match—if her fiancé is as handsome as Luca, and as much of a manipulative asshole.

"Hi," she says pleasantly, holding out her hand once she's close enough. "I'm Caterina. Luca asked me to come and keep you company."

No, he asked you to come keep an eye on me and make sure I'm not plotting anything with my best friend. I force a smile onto her face, shaking her hand limply. "Sofia."

"It's nice to meet you." To her credit, she does look as if she's trying to be friendly. "I've heard a lot about you."

"You have?" I blink at her. I can't imagine Luca taking time out of his day to gossip with this woman about his upcoming marriage. And then I remember—of course. She's Don Rossi's daughter, the same man who wanted to have me killed.

"My father mentioned you," Caterina says, perching delicately on the edge of the tub. "And Franco told me that you'd agreed to marry Luca."

I can't help but wonder how much she knows. My gaze flicks down to her left hand—there's a diamond there that looks nearly twice the size of mine, surrounded by a halo, on a band so encrusted that it looks as if it was dipped in diamond dust. She wears it as casually as if it's nothing, but then again, to her it probably is. She probably expected nothing less from her fiancé. Everything about her is as polished and cultured as Luca is, from her perfectly styled hair and lightly-made up face, to her designer skinny jeans and stylish light blue blouse. She has diamond studs in her ears and Louboutins on her feet, and I'm reminded suddenly of this morning, when I wondered if

I was supposed to wear my diamond jewelry down to grab breakfast out of the fridge.

Luca probably thought I looked like a child who doesn't know how to dress. It still rankles that he called me a child last night. And I'm not about to change everything about myself for a fiancé who plans to neatly tuck me away and forget about me like an old t-shirt as soon as he can. I've never been the kind of person who wears diamonds to breakfast, and I'm not about to start.

"We're leaving to pick out my wedding dress after this," I say neutrally as Brigit tilts my head back, washing the concoction she slathered onto it earlier out. The combination of the warm water and her fingers against my scalp feel good, but I can't relax. I'm too on edge from Caterina's presence, and the knowledge that anything I say wrong might find its way back to Luca—or worse, Don Rossi.

Ana reaches out and squeezes my hand. "You're going to be a beautiful bride."

"Picking out your dress is the best part." Caterina beams at me, but I can see a hint of discomfort under it, as if she knows that no one actually wants her here. "I can't wait to go shopping for mine. My mother—"

She trails off, as if realizing what she's said. Ana stares daggers at her, and she licks her lips quickly, knotting her hands in her lap. "I'm sorry, Sofia," she says quietly. "I know both of your parents are gone. That must be hard—not having your mother here."

"Can I talk to you outside?" Ana stands up, and I can see the tension in her shoulders. "Give Sofia a minute."

Caterina looks unhappy, but stands up, glancing at me before following Ana out into the bedroom.

I lean forward as Brigit starts to paint dye onto my hair, trying to hear what they're talking about. Ana closed the door as she left, but I can still hear murmurs.

"You don't know Sofia," I hear Ana say coldly. "You shouldn't even be here."

"I'm just trying to help." There's a note of defensiveness in Caterina's voice. "Luca asked me to be here—"

"Sofia is being forced into this marriage, by him *and* your father. Do you really think she wants that reminder? Today, when she's being prepped like a Barbie doll?"

"I didn't get to pick my husband either," Caterina says quietly. "I can offer her some insight into what that's like—"

"Your life wasn't in danger if you said no."

"I still didn't have a choice, either way." There's a steely edge to Caterina's voice now that reminds me of Luca, but oddly it makes me like her more. She's holding her own, at least, and Ana's not an easy person to argue with when she's angry.

"You don't belong here."

"Neither do you, little ballerina," Caterina says softly, so low that I can barely make out the words. "You owe Luca your life too, just like Sofia does."

There's a long moment of silence in the bedroom. My heart thuds in my chest, squeezing painfully. I had no idea about any of this, and I strain to hear as much as I can.

"What do you mean?" I hear Ana whisper, her voice choked. "You can't tell me that you know what's going on in your awful family. No one in the mob tells women anything, it doesn't matter what kind. Italian, Russian, Irish—they all treat women like toys."

"I'll ignore the insult to my family," Caterina replies calmly, her voice hushed too. "But I've learned how to listen, Anastasia. I hear things. And I know that my father wasn't happy that a girl with Bratva ties, no matter how distant now, had moved in with Sofia Ferretti."

"So what? He was going to have me killed?"

"Probably." Caterina's voice is flat. "That's his solution, usually, so far as I can tell from what I've overheard. Luca was the one who insisted that you meant no harm, that your father was long dead and that you weren't of any interest to the Bratva any longer."

It takes all of my effort not to react. I'm not surprised that Rossi wanted to get rid of Ana, as much as it makes me hate him more than ever—but *Luca* saved her? Luca disagreed with his boss over a Russian girl he hardly knew? It, like the plate left outside of my door last night, doesn't fit with the cold and heartless man that he's made himself out to be.

"We women, in this world, don't have choices." Caterina's voice drifts through the door again, firm and cool. "It's up to us to find ways to make the best of it. I always knew I wouldn't get to choose my husband. I knew that I wouldn't get to choose who I slept with for the first time. Someone would be picked for me, and I'm glad that it was someone young and handsome, and not some old capo that my father wanted to elevate. Franco will think that he has the last word in our family, but I will find a way to be my own person still, and a way to make sure that my life is at least something resembling what I want it to be. And I can help Sofia learn to do that too, in a way that you can't." She pauses, and when she speaks again, I can hear sympathy in her voice. "You're her best friend, Ana. I'm not trying to take your place. But Luca doesn't trust you. The closer I am to Sofia, the easier it will be for you to be, too. I really do want to help."

"Why would I believe that?"

"Because, Anastasia, none of us as women are safe in this world. Not even I'm safe. My father, and Luca, and Franco are all that stand between me and the Russians, or the Irish. They're all that stand in front of Sofia. They can protect you too, if you're someone that they can trust. You can help Sofia better by letting me in than you ever can by fighting me."

"Sofia doesn't deserve any of this—"

"None of us do. But when my father is gone, I'll be the wife of the second most powerful man in the family, and Sofia will be the wife of the first. Don't you see the power there? Franco is enamored with me. I can make him believe that some things that I want are his own ideas, if I'm careful, and learn how to play him. Sofia can do the same with Luca."

"I don't believe that anyone can do that with Luca."

There's another long pause. "Maybe not," Caterina admits. "But it's better than the alternative."

The bathroom door opens, and I lean back in my chair, trying not to look as if I've been listening in. Caterina's face is very smooth, giving away nothing, and I can see that Ana is doing her best to look happy, and not as if they were just arguing outside.

Brigit steps out, leaving me with my hair plastered atop my head with dye, and Caterina carefully sits on the edge of the tub again. "I know you probably don't want me here, Sofia," she says quietly. "I know you didn't invite me. And I know that this is very hard. I don't know everything about the situation—but I do know that you aren't choosing any of this." She pauses, glancing nervously at Ana, and I can tell that she feels out of her depth. "I didn't choose to marry Franco, either. But I plan to make sure that I'm more than just another mafia wife. And I can help you too, Sofia."

"I appreciate it." I can't quite look her in the eye. "But I don't want help being more. I don't want to be anything in this family. I just want to get this over with, and then disappear until Luca needs to pull me out to parade me around some charity event or something."

"You're going to have to—"

"That's fine, Sofia," Ana says quickly, cutting Caterina off with a sharp glare. "Luca can force you to marry him, but he can't make you play a part that you don't want to."

Her words are meant to soothe me, but as I look over at Caterina, I can tell from her face that not a single word of it is true.

Luca can force me to do a great many things. I might not want to have to learn to play this game, but I'm quickly learning that I have no other choice.

* * *

TWO MORE AWKWARD hours pass before my hair is finished being dyed, highlighted, curled and styled. But I have to admit, when I turn and look at my reflection in the bathroom mirror after Brigit has cleaned everything up, that it suits me a million times better than the blonde ever did. She dyed my base color as close to my natural roots as she could, a deep chocolate brown that looks even richer than my actual color. It's highlighted with soft, thin pieces balayaged throughout in shades of honey and caramel, so subtle that they're only noticeable when the light catches them. Curled, my hair brushes just below my shoulders, and it looks healthier than it has in a long time, accentuating my cheekbones and making my skin glow even without makeup.

I hate to admit that it looks so much better, that I actually think I look pretty—but I do.

The doorbell rings, startling me, and Catarina gracefully stands up from her spot on the edge of the tub. "That's probably the driver, letting us know he's here." She gives me a quick, hesitant smile. "I'll let him know that we'll be down in a few minutes."

She strides out, leaving me alone with Ana, and my stomach tightens with nerves. "I don't know if I can do this," I whisper, turning towards her. "How am I supposed to pick out a dress for a wedding that I don't even want?"

"I know," Ana says, reaching out to squeeze my hand. "But I'll be with you the whole way. And Caterina too, I suppose." She rolls her eyes, and I stifle a laugh.

"I think she means well." I frown, looking out in the direction that she left. "I don't know. I don't think I should trust her, right? She's one of them."

Ana shrugs. "I would say that you shouldn't trust anyone. None of them have your best interests at heart, Sofia. Certainly not Luca—and I wouldn't think that the Don's daughter does, either. This isn't your world, regardless of what your father used to do. Be careful." Her fingers lace through mine, and I'm more grateful than I ever have been for anything that she's here with me today. "I'll be here for you as long as I can. Longer than that, if I can find a way to manage it."

My stomach flips over again at that. Luca could stop me from seeing her at any time, isolate me away from the one person I have left. The thought of how lonely that would be makes me feel sick.

"Come on," Ana says gently. "This is hard, but it's not the worst, I promise. I know this isn't how you pictured picking out your wedding dress, but we'll try to make it as fun as we can."

"That's the thing," I tell her as we walk out. "I never really pictured it. I never imagined getting married. And yet—here I am."

Leaving the apartment is strange. Just two nights ago I was trying to flee, and here I am, walking out of the front door and to the elevator as if I'm free to do what I like.

Of course—I'm not. The driver is waiting with Caterina at the elevator, and he punches in the code to go down, yet another reminder that I couldn't leave on my own if I wanted to. Caterina casts me a sympathetic glance as we walk in, but I don't quite meet her eyes.

There's a sleek black car waiting for us in the garage, and the driver opens the door, letting me slide in first. Ana slips in next to me, and Caterina opts to sit across from us. The car is barely moving when she slides open a panel, revealing—to my complete and utter surprise—a bottle of champagne and glasses.

"How did you know that would be there?" I blurt out, staring at her. The minute the words are out of my mouth I wish I could take them back—the last thing I want is to look foolish or stupid in front of this elegantly dressed, perfectly polished woman.

I expect her to say something cutting or mocking, the way Luca probably would, but instead she just smiles. "Just one of the perks," Caterina says, laughing softly as she pops the cork and starts to pour a glass for each of us. "There's always some kind of alcohol in these cars. And mixers too—do you want some orange juice in yours?"

For a second, all I can do is keep staring, dumbfounded by all of it. "Sure," I manage, trying to regain my composure. *This is ridiculous. All of it. How am I asking for a mimosa in a car on the way to a bridal salon I could never, in my entire life, afford to shop at before?*

Except I could have afforded it. No matter how much I want to try to forget about the money that's appeared in my account every month for the last three years, I can't. No matter how much I want to pretend that I've been just another struggling student, that I would have made my own way in the world after graduation, it's a lie. I've never had to struggle, and I never would have, even if the Bratva hadn't come for me. My father made sure that I was provided for, and Luca followed through on that promise—has continued to, to the very letter of it. As much as I want to cast him as the villain, and say that I'm not a part of any of this—I am.

I have been since I was born. I've just been living with one foot in and one foot out without even realizing it. But when it comes to money and privilege, no matter how much I want to deny it, I have more in common with Caterina than I do my best friend. I've just been running from it this entire time.

The champagne is dry and sweet on my tongue, but I can't shake the bitter taste that my thoughts leave behind. "I don't want to be a part of this family," I whisper desperately to Ana, low enough that Caterina can't hear. "I wanted to escape. That's all I ever wanted. And that's what my father wanted for me too, I know it is."

"You're not like them," Ana replies, equally hushed. "You never will be. Don't worry about it, Sof. You won't lose yourself."

The sound of the childish, familiar nickname and the way she cut immediately to the core of my fears soothes me, just a little. I'm terrified that if I allow myself to enjoy even a little bit of what's being handed to me in preparation for this wedding, whether it's the new clothes or a luxurious bath or my newly styled hair, it's giving in. Saying that I want this. That if I let myself drink the Kool-Aid, even just a little, I'll lose everything that makes me *me*, and become just another pawn in this awful world of mobs and mafia.

The car slows to a stop, and outside of the tinted window I can see the sign for Kleinfeld's. "We're here," Caterina says, and once again I see the sympathy in her eyes. I don't want her pity—but the logical part of me, the part that knows I can't fight this forever, says that I'm better off with her as my friend than my enemy.

The door opens, and I take a deep breath. *You can do this,* I tell myself.

I step out of the car, and into the sunlight.

LUCA

I have my own appointment with Father Donahue this afternoon, and I'm dreading it. I already know that he's going to chastise me for the way I'm handling the situation—and he's probably the only man in all of New York, hell, the only one in the fucking *world* who could get away with chastising any one of us.

But more than that, I know my feelings for Sofia are far from pure. So far, in fact, that I'll be surprised if I don't catch on fire the minute I walk into the church.

The nave of the church is empty when I walk in, except for the balding, black-robed priest sitting on the front pew. Father Donahue stands when I walk in, one eyebrow raised as he sees me walking towards him.

"No matter how many times I see you, Luca, it's always startling not to see the little boy I remember." He grips my hand when I extend it, covering our grasped hands with his other as he looks up at me. He's grown bent over the years, what hair he has left grey, but his dark eyes are still sharp and piercing as ever.

"I'm not a child anymore," I say curtly, taking a seat next to him in the pew. "And I'm not interested in a lecture today, Father."

"I'm sure you're not," he says wryly, sitting down gingerly once again. "But you know what I think about all of this."

"Actually, I don't. But I'm sure you're about to tell me."

"I was the one that witnessed the vow between Giovanni Ferretti and your father all those years ago, Luca. I know as well as you do what Giovanni wanted for his daughter. But he extracted that promise because he saw no other way of keeping her safe."

"And I'm marrying her because there's no other way of keeping her safe." My voice is flat, completely without emotion. "I'm not sure what it is that you think I should be doing."

"No other way?" Father Donahue tilts his head, looking at me with those sharp, keen eyes. "Nowhere that you could send her, no way to keep her safe in that fortress you live in, other than to make her your bride? Force her into your bed?"

The last part stings. "I may not live a life of celibacy like you, Father, but I've never forced a woman. I don't intend to start with my new bride."

"So Sofia is willing?"

"Sofia and I have come to—an arrangement." It's all I can say without revealing that I've made concessions to my future wife that Rossi would lose his head over. A priest is supposed to be able to be trusted with secrets, but Rossi has ways of getting secrets from men that could gain him the nuclear codes, if he wanted them.

Father Donahue looks unconvinced. "I can't imagine that Sofia is pleased with any part of your 'arrangements.' And this wedding is taking place faster than I can condone. Even Sofia's confirmation—"

"I can't keep her safe otherwise," I say sharply, cutting him off. "I know you think that I should be able to find a way, but there isn't one, Father. Rossi's solution is to have her killed. Easy, neat, no fuss. Then the Bratva wouldn't be able to get their hands on her, and I wouldn't be wrestling with a reluctant bride. One person fighting me on this is enough, Father, I don't need you to stand in my way too."

"I've already agreed to perform the marriage, on the basis of my friendship with both your father and hers, if nothing else," Father Donahue says quietly. "I've been loyal to the Rossi family for many decades, Luca, ever since I was spared in the Irish purge, and the Italians took the city again. I was left alone with my church and my faith and my place here, and I have not forgotten it. But there are some sins that I cannot absolve, Luca. You know that as well as I do. You haven't left the confessional with absolution in many years."

"I know." The words come out hard and biting. "It's the life I lead, Father. I've never had any choice in the matter. You know that."

Father Donahue shrugs. "There is always a choice." He pauses, looking at me thoughtfully. "I wonder, if Giovanni knew the kind of man you would grow up to be, if he would have promised his daughter to you?"

The words sting unexpectedly. "I've tried to do my best within the confines of the life I was born into," I say tightly. "I've never hurt a man beyond what was necessary to find out what I needed to know. I've never killed someone out of anger—in fact, I've never laid a hand on anyone, man or woman, out of anything but necessity."

"Yes. Business." Father Donahue shakes his head. "It's a difficult life you lead, Luca. So many ways that you have to justify the blood on your hands, so many codes and rules to make sure that you can sleep at night."

"I sleep just fine," I say stiffly. "Often with a woman on either side of me. But you wouldn't know anything about that, would you, Father?"

The priest smiles. "No. I wouldn't. But I would not trade lives with you for all the pleasure and all the luxury in the world, my son. I think one day you may understand why." He takes a deep breath, looking across the nave at the altar, the crucifix, and the unlit lantern behind it. His gaze turns back to mine, and he holds it for a long moment, until I want to shift uncomfortably in my seat. I don't, but I can't help but feel that he's looking into my very soul, that he can see something there that even I can't.

"For Sofia Ferretti's sake," he says softly, "I hope you do."

He stands, looking down at me, and something in his face makes my chest tighten. I've never been afraid of anything, but there's some knowledge in his expression, almost a foreshadowing that sends a tremor of what I imagine is fear through me.

"I'll bless your wedding and perform it, for Giovanni," Father Donahue says, in that same quiet voice. "And I'll turn my face away from all that you and the Rossi family does, as I have for decades. But if ever the day comes that you wish to truly atone, Luca Romano, you know where I am."

He turns to walk past the pews then, disappearing into the dark, cavernous arches of the nave. And I sit there for a long moment, the weight of everything I've ever done suddenly falling heavy on my shoulders, all at once.

* * *

I GO BACK to the penthouse afterwards, instead of my office. I don't know why, exactly, except that I know Sofia won't be there, and I want the peace that it offers while it's empty.

But when I walk through the front door, the silence feels almost oppressive.

Almost—lonely.

There's no reason for me to miss her. No reason for me to wonder how her appointment is going—for a *wedding dress*, of all things, why on Earth would I give a shit about that—to wonder if I'll see her when she comes back or if she'll just lock herself in her room after the way the conversation went down last night.

No reason for me to almost regret that I hadn't taken her up on her offer of dinner last night.

I've never regretted anything I've done. There's no room for it in my life. There's too many things that I *could* regret if I allowed it, too much blood, too much death. If I allowed myself even an ounce of regret, even a second, it could swallow me whole. Paralyze me, make me incapable of action without questioning my decisions first.

And in this life, that's a death sentence.

I walk up the stairs, but instead of going in the direction of my room, I find myself turning down the hall, walking past the guest rooms, all the way down to the one that I designated for Sofia. It's no coincidence that it's the room furthest from mine. I didn't want her close, didn't want the temptation of knowing she was only a door or two away. I wanted there to be as much time as possible for me to talk myself out of it, if I ever found myself heading towards her bedroom.

The fact that she somehow has so much sway over me, that I would even *need* to safeguard myself against her, is more unsettling than anything I've ever seen or done in my life. No woman has ever made me feel as if I might lose control, as if I might not be able to stop myself from being overwhelmed by desire. I always, *always* have the upper hand when it comes to women. Even in bed, even in the very height of passion, I always know what I'm doing. There's always intent. I've never lost myself in pleasure.

On the surface, almost nothing about the room has changed. The bed is neatly made, there's no personal possessions scattered about—all of Sofia's things are still back at her apartment. It's all clean and tidy, but as I stand in the middle of the room, something about it *feels* different. When I breathe in, I can smell the scent of shampoo and detergent and cleaning products, the faint hint of whatever the stylist used on her hair still lingering, but there's something else there too. I can smell her in the air, that soft powdery sweetness of her skin that I inhaled when I held her up against my front door, and I'm suddenly hard all over again.

Achingly, throbbing, rock-hard, standing in the middle of my fiancée's bedroom.

I feel like a fucking pervert.

The closet door is hanging open, and I walk over to it, noticing something lying on the floor. When I pick it up, I realize it's the tiny black dress that she was wearing the night that I rescued her from the Russians. Just the sight of it brings back the memory of seeing her lying in my bed, of feeling her soft curves pressed up against me as I held her up against my door. It brings back the memory of her lips on mine, of one single, searing kiss that told me that for some inexplicable reason, when it comes to Sofia Ferretti—

I'm the only one who is well and truly fucked.

I clench my fist, wadding the dress up in my hand, and without thinking bring it up to my nose. It smells like her, like the sweet floral perfume that she'd had on, like that soft powdery scent of her skin. My cock throbs angrily, the memory of breathing that scent in as I pinned her wrists above her head flooding over me, and I feel momentarily unhinged.

Out of control.

Overwhelmed with lust like I've never felt before.

Before I've realized what I'm doing, my hand is inside my suit trousers, wrapping itself around the aching length of my cock and yanking it out into the open air, stroking feverishly as I breathe in Sofia's scent. All I can think about is what else might have happened that night if she'd given in, if she hadn't bitten me, if she hadn't stopped me. I can imagine myself picking her up, shoving that tiny black dress up her thighs and pulling her panties aside, sliding my fingers into her to feel how wet she must have been before shoving myself into her as deeply as I could, letting her feel what it was like to have a man inside of her for the first time.

My fantasies spin out of control as my hand speeds up, feverishly stroking myself as I imagine carrying her upstairs, bending her over my knee with that dress shoved up above her pert little ass, bringing my palm down on it again and again as she writhes in my lap, squirming against my hardening cock until she learns her lesson not to run, not to deny me. I imagine pushing her down to her knees between my legs, watching her open those full lips for my cock. I can feel my groin tightening as I imagine pushing myself into her mouth, feeling the warm, hot pressure of it as I teach her how I like to be sucked, watching that soft pink tongue slide down the length of me until I've had enough, until I'm ready to bend her over the bed and shove myself inside of her at last, looking at her reddened cheeks, still stinging from my palm, a reminder that she's mine, mine...*mine*.

"Fuck!" I moan aloud as I feel my cock throb in my fist, my hips thrusting forward as I squeeze the head of it in my palm, feeling myself come in a hot rush into my hand as I stand there in the doorway of the closet shuddering, my muscles rigid with the intense pleasure of the sudden, violent orgasm.

And then, as the last shuddering, hot drops spill into my palm, reality comes back like a slap in the face.

What the fuck?

What the hell is wrong with me?

Even with as active of a sex life as I have, I've jerked myself off plenty of times. Sometimes the mood just hits and there's no time to make a booty call, sometimes you just need the clarity of a good, quick stroke. But never, since the day I discovered what my cock could do, have I ever stood in a woman's closet and stroked myself to a climax while breathing in the scent of her perfume from her fucking *dress*.

It's a step up from her panties, I suppose, but still.

What the fuck is she doing to me?

I'm not a teenage boy, to lust over the idea of fucking a girl—any girl. All it would take is a phone call, and any number of my one night stands would trample each other to be the first one in my bed if I were feeling horny on a Sunday afternoon. And for fuck's sake, I just came from *church*.

There is no reason, not a single one, for me to be standing and clutching my wilting cock in my hand, sticky with my own cum, fantasizing like a lonely seventeen-year-old about the one girl who refused me. Who turned me down.

Who told *me* that I wasn't allowed to touch her.

Me.

"Fuck." I mutter the word aloud again, this time with an entirely different inflection as I drop Sofia's dress back onto the floor, striding to the bathroom as quickly as I can to clean up.

I don't know how Sofia's gotten into my head. Worse yet, I don't know how to get her out.

But I'm going to have to figure out a way, and fast.

Because this has gone too far.

SOFIA

*K*leinfeld's is empty when we walk inside.

Okay, not *empty*, empty. There's plenty of staff, salespeople and their helpers, not to mention Ana and Caterina, and the apparent *army* of security that was sent along with us. I hadn't had any idea when I'd gotten into the car that once I got out, no less than a dozen armed bodyguards were coming with me. They're scattered around the main sales floor now, looking tall, muscular and menacing in their black suits and earpieces, and I feel ridiculous. Everything about this is insane.

Including the fact that Kleinfeld's has, apparently, been closed to the public while I'm here.

"Are we seriously the only ones shopping?" I hiss at Caterina, who seems most likely to know what the hell is going on. "How—*why?*"

"Safety," she says simply. "If you asked Luca directly, he'd probably give you some trite answer about how he wanted you to have an uninterrupted shopping experience, or some made-up excuse like that. But the truth is that if there's no one else allowed here, then it will be very obvious if someone is who is not supposed to be. And in the event that someone did try to harm you, the public wouldn't be in danger."

I stare at her. "Is this normal?" I manage. "Is Luca going to clear out a store every time I want to go shopping?"

"Once the Bratva threat is managed?" Caterina shrugs. "Probably not. But who knows?"

"Did they do this for you?" I wave a hand around the empty salon.

"I haven't gone shopping for my dress yet. But when I do, no. I'll have a private appointment at whichever designer I choose, but the shop won't be closed."

"Why not?" I look at her curiously. "You're Rossi's daughter."

Caterina's mouth twitches upwards into a small smirk. "My life isn't in danger," she says. "No one is trying to kill or kidnap *me*. I suppose it does come with certain—perks."

Despite myself, a tiny squeak of laughter slips out. Caterina glances over at me, meeting my eyes, and I can see the humor in hers. For the first time, I feel myself starting to like her, just a tiny bit.

"Don't go having hysterics on me," she says with a small grin. "Your appointment is about to start."

The woman who approaches us is dressed neatly in a black skirt suit, her slightly greying hair twisted up behind her head. "Good afternoon, Miss Ferretti," she greets me, her voice formal and polite. "I'm Jennifer. Mr. Romano's office called to tell us you'd be coming. We were told that there's no budget, so I suppose we'll simply start with what kind of dress you could see yourself wearing?"

No budget. Of course. Luca is clearly sparing no expense on this entire charade, and I can't help but wonder what he would do for a woman he actually loved. Is all of this just to keep up appearances, a show of wealth that has nothing to do with me? Or is he, on some level, trying to make up for all of this by letting me blow as much money as I'd like on the trappings of a dream wedding?"

Not that anyone has consulted me about the wedding itself. But still—

You know better. This is all just to show the Russians how much power they have, how much money to burn, showing that they can throw it away on a wedding to a woman that Luca doesn't even want. I can't allow this to go to my head, no matter how dazzling it might get.

"Miss Ferretti?"

The woman is still waiting for me to give her an answer about the style of dress, and I quite frankly don't have a single idea what to tell her. I know this salon is famous, but I've never watched the show about it, I've never Googled wedding dress designers or scrolled through pages of them on my phone, daydreaming about what I would pick one day. I've never made a wedding Pinterest board.

I, quite frankly, have never spared a thought for my theoretical wedding.

My post-graduation trip to Paris, on the other hand—

"Why don't we start with a few different styles," Caterina says quickly, stepping forward. "Maybe one of each silhouette?"

Ana shoots her a dirty look, but I feel relieved. "Thank you," I say quietly when Jennifer steps away, leaving us alone with the champagne that another tall and elegant saleslady brings us, and Caterina gives me a small smile.

"I told you I wanted to help," she says quietly, and then backs up, letting me have some space with Ana.

"I don't know what to pick," I whisper to Ana nervously. "I have no idea—am I supposed to pick what *I* like? What I think Luca would like? What I think his boss would like?"

"Well, you're getting married in the cathedral, so we can start there," Ana says calmly. "Nothing off the shoulder, nothing see through, nothing super low cut. And from there—" she shrugs.

"If you can't find anything you like because all of this feels too awful and weird, then pick something you think Luca would like. Or, god forbid, ask Caterina what Don Rossi would approve of," Ana adds, giving a faux shudder.

"If you do find something you like," she continues, "then choose that. And fuck what Luca wants."

I feel a small smile tugging at the corners of my mouth, despite my nerves. "Fuck what Luca wants," I agree, and both of us start to giggle.

For a moment, I feel okay again, almost free. Despite the eerily empty salon and obnoxious amount of security and the impending need to choose a dress for my sham of a wedding, having Ana here with me, making me giggle over what feels like a tiny but necessary rebellion, makes me feel almost whole again for the first time in days.

Jennifer appears again a moment later, motioning for me to follow her back to the dressing room, and I cast a nervous glance in Ana's direction.

"It's fine," she says reassuringly. "I'll wait out here with Caterina, and I promise I'll be nice."

I can feel the nerves fluttering through me all over again, twisting my stomach in knots until I feel like I might be sick, but I follow Jennifer back anyway, all the way to the spacious dressing room that is already half full of lace and silk and puffy skirts.

"I'm getting married at St. Patrick's," I tell her quickly, remembering what Ana said. "So it has to be appropriate for that."

"Ah." Jennifer quickly sweeps away two of the dresses. "These won't work then. I'll be right back."

I look at myself in the mirror as I wait for her. I almost don't recognize myself. It's not just the designer clothes, or the new hairstyle and color, but something else. My face looks drawn and pale, my entire body somehow more fragile, as if the stress of all of this is already wearing me down. I look like a frightened child, and I hate it. I don't want to be a shrinking violet. But I also don't want to be a part of this world that I've been thrust into.

Is there something in between? How do I play this game without losing myself in it?

The door opens, and Jennifer walks back in with two new dresses. "Alright, let's get you into the first one," she says cheerily, pulling a frothy confection of a dress off of a hanger.

I feel more vulnerable than ever as I strip out of my jeans and top, laying them neatly on a chair and leaving me in just the bra and panties that were part of what I'd chosen from the mountains of clothing brought to the penthouse yesterday. Like the designer outfit I'd worn today, my underwear is staggeringly different from the usual simple cotton bra and panties I typically wear—there was nothing like that in the options I'd been given. Instead I'm wearing light pink lace, and the effect is startling when I look in the mirror. I'm reasonably fit, slender with what I think are nice curves, but I never pay much attention to them. In the gilded mirror of the dressing room, lit up and wrapped in lace, I look—sexy.

I wonder what Luca would think, if he saw me like this.

The thought horrifies me. I shouldn't even consider it, shouldn't wonder for even a second what the man who is practically my jailer would think of me in lace underwear. But the curiosity lingers as I step into the first dress, no matter how hard I try to push it away.

Jennifer zips up the back, deftly hooking the first few faux buttons as she pins the back of it to fit me. "You look lovely," she declares, but I'm not so sure.

I look like a cupcake, frankly. The dress is completely lace from the waist up with a satin lining beneath it, long-sleeved with a sweetheart neckline. The waist has a grosgrain ribbon bow, and from there the skirt froths out in layers and layers of tulle, until I look like nothing so much as the topper on a music box.

"I—don't think this is it."

"Well, show the others, at least," Jennifer says enthusiastically, and I wince.

"Alright," I agree weakly.

Ana's face confirms what I'm feeling as I walk out—she looks as if she's trying desperately not to laugh. Caterina's expression is more demure, but even her mouth is twitching as I walk up onto the platform and turn to face them.

"Well, what do you think?"

"I hate it," Ana says decisively.

"It's—not that flattering," Caterina adds hesitantly. "Maybe try the next one?"

"Yes," I agree fervently.

The next dress isn't much better, though. This one is strapless—Jennifer assures me that there are capelets and toppers that can cover up my sleeves so I don't scandalize the priest—and the skirt reminds me of a prom gown, with tiered pickups and tiny rhinestones. Even Caterina has to clap her hand over her mouth to hide her reaction when I walk out, and Ana shakes her head violently.

"It's hideous," she says, looking at Jennifer. "Don't you have anything that won't make her look like a Barbie doll?"

"Maybe something classic," Caterina adds. "Elegant."

The next dress is better. It's a plain white gown in a heavy satin, with floaty cap sleeves and a fitted bodice that flares out into a trumpet skirt. Caterina beams when I walk out, and even Ana grudgingly admits that it's beautiful.

"It might be a little plain," I say hesitantly, turning this way and that in the mirror. I feel guilty even suggesting that I might have opinion on a dress that I shouldn't even want to wear, but looking at myself in this one, I feel the first glimmer of what it might be like to be a bride. To want to look beautiful on my wedding day.

"Maybe something with a little lace?" Ana suggests. "Nothing over the top, but something to make it a little more interesting."

The next dress Jennifer pulls out *has* lace, but it's a ballgown, with a lace half-sleeved bodice and a full satin skirt big enough to hide another person in. I'm on the verge of just picking the one that was alright, when she brings out one last dress.

Like the ring on my finger, I hate to admit how much I love it once it's on me. It's spaghetti straps, with a sweetheart neckline that dips a little deeper than some, but not so much as to be dramatic. But the part I love the most is the fabric.

It's a soft, off-white chiffon, lined so that my skin doesn't show through the lace and applique, but the lining is a soft champagne color that makes you wonder, just a little. The entire dress is covered in a bold leaf and floral applique, covering the bust entirely and feathering out from the waist down into large leaves that scatter over the loose, flowing skirt.

It's soft and ethereal and beautiful, and I feel like a princess.

I feel *perfect*.

Caterina audibly gasps when I walk out. Ana's eyes go round, and she gets up to stand next to me as I step up onto the little platform. "It's beautiful," she says softly. "You look beautiful, Sofia."

"We can add soft chiffon sleeves for the ceremony," Jennifer adds, "and they can be removed after for the reception." She disappears for a moment and then comes back, slipping a comb into my hair with a long, floor-length veil attached. "There. Now you look like a bride."

I can feel my throat tightening as I look in the mirror, a dozen emotions flooding me at once. I'm both happy and sad that my mother isn't here—happy because she would be horrified at the entire situation, sad because I would give anything for her to be able to see me in what I'm certain will be my wedding dress. I think of my father, who I won't ever be able to have walk me down the aisle—but if he were here, I wouldn't *be* walking down any aisle. He wouldn't give me away to a man like Luca if he were alive.

I'm only standing here in this beautiful dress because my parents are dead. Because no one can protect me anymore except for a heartless, mercurial criminal who is poised to run the very same organization that took my parents away from me. And as I look in the mirror, I'm horrified that I can find any joy at all in the dress that I'm going to wear to marry that man.

And yet—I can't help but think that I do look beautiful. That if I'd chosen to get married, this is the dress I would pick.

I turn around and see Caterina watching me, and to my surprise, I can tell that her eyes are a little misty. *Why?* I can't help but wonder. *Why does Rossi's daughter care anything about me?* "You are going to make the most lovely bride," she says, smiling at me. "Even lovelier than me."

"I don't know about that," I say wryly, glancing back in the mirror. I can't imagine ever being as polished or glamorous as Caterina is, or Ana. Even now, standing next to me, Ana looks graceful and rosy, pale and pink as a porcelain doll in the skinny jeans and cropped tank that she's wearing, her nearly concave stomach on display, her silky blonde hair cascading everywhere. She's the perfect picture of a ballerina, elegant in her every movement, and I've always felt slightly clumsy and graceless next to her.

But now, in this dress, I look like a princess. I look like a girl who could marry someone like Luca Romano.

And I don't know why that sends a flicker of excitement across my skin.

"This is the one," I tell Jennifer quickly, stepping down off the platform. "I'll take the veil, too."

"Very good," she says, her face glowing, and I'm sure that she's already calculating her commission off of whatever ridiculous price tag is on this gown.

When I'm safely out of it, pulling my jeans back on as I look at it hanging in the clear garment bag, waiting to be taken to the alterations department for the quickest work they've probably ever done, I feel that knotting in my stomach again.

Four days.

Four days until I'm Luca Romano's wife.

SOFIA

ednesday, two days before the rehearsal, is my meeting with Father Donahue. I dress as conservatively as possible, throwing a light spring-weight cardigan over my t-shirt, and touching the cross at my throat as I meet the driver at the elevator. I haven't been to a church since my mother's funeral, and I'm almost shaking with nerves. I can't imagine what this priest will be like, a supposed man of God who still does the bidding of the mafia.

Once I'm in the cool darkness of the car, I lean my head back against the leather, trying to calm down. The last few days haven't been the blur that I expected them to be, instead, they've dragged. I haven't seen Luca, he seems to have made a point since that last morning that I saw him at breakfast to be gone when I wake up, and to not come home until I'm settled in my room for the night. As a result, I've been left to wander through the penthouse alone, trying to find anything I can to distract myself from my impending nuptials.

But it's impossible to do. It's not that there's nothing to occupy me —the penthouse has a legitimate theater room, with a screen the size of an actual movie theater's, soft reclining chairs, and a library of every movie or television show I could want to watch and every streaming service available. There's a gym in the building, which I haven't been able to access due to the code-locked elevator but probably could get someone to escort me to if I asked, and a rooftop pool, which I *have* been able to access.

I guess Luca trusts me not to jump off of the roof, or drown myself. Or maybe he's just hoping I will before the wedding.

That's where I spent the majority of the last two days, stretching and working out on one of the mats that I found stashed in the cubbies on one side of the roof—along with towels and sunscreen and anything else I could need. There's even a self-serve wet bar up there, but I stuck to laying out on one of the lounge chairs in my new bikini and swimming in the pool sober. The last thing I needed was to get drunk and make a stupid decision, like trying to run away again.

I've determined that the best course of action is to play along. Of course, that's been easy when I haven't even seen Luca the last few days. Without him there to push my buttons or ignite the strange feelings that always seem to flood over me whenever he's around, making me lose my temper or my better judgement, I've been able to actually think through my situation.

And I've also seen what my life will be like married to him, but without him anywhere around.

It's not *that* bad. Sure, I don't think he's going to put me up in a penthouse of my very own, but I have no doubt that whatever apartment he gives me is going to be stupidly luxurious and expensive. It's not the life I planned for myself, not even close, but it's far from torture. It's better than looking over my shoulder every time I walk down the street, wondering when one of Rossi's goons is going to pull me into an alley and finish me off with a silencer to the back of the head. And I'd be stupid to say otherwise.

So my best bet is to grit my teeth, get on with it, and behave as if I've accepted all of this until the day comes that Luca is in charge. And then, with Rossi and his hard-on for my death gone, I can plot my escape.

And all the while, I think with the tinies bit of satisfaction, *I'll know that Luca is probably furious as hell that I'm the one woman in Manhattan who won't fall into his bed.*

I've never been inside St. Patrick's before. I cross myself habitually as I walk inside, the habit sticking despite years away from church, and walk into the nave. It arches high overhead, the architecture taking my breath away as I walk down the central aisle, and I think about what it will be like on Saturday to take this same walk in that dress, with Luca waiting at the end of it for me. I can't help but wonder how he'll look at me, if his expression will be cold and hard the way I'm already used to, or if he'll pretend to be an overjoyed groom.

I'd rather he just be honest, but I'm sure he'll play his role to perfection. And he'll expect the same from me.

A tall, balding man in black clothing and a white collar who I can only assume is Father Donahue steps out as I make it to the front of the church, and smiles at me. His expression is welcoming, and I feel myself relax just a fraction as I step forward to shake his hand.

"Miss Ferretti." He pauses. "Can I call you Sofia?"

I'm taken aback for a moment by his warm, friendly tone. I'd expected someone colder, harsher even, but he seems kind. Kinder than I would expect, for someone in Rossi's pocket.

"Of course," I manage.

"I'm sure you've guessed that I'm Father Donahue. I'm glad you're here, Sofia." His voice still has an Irish accent, not thick, but still rich around the edges.

"I thought the Italians hated the Irish," I blurt out, and then immediately flush pink. "I'm sorry, I don't know why I said that. It was rude."

"No, it's a fair question. Sit," he instructs, gesturing towards the front pew. I quickly obey, with my face still burning.

"I was a young priest here when the Rossi family flushed the Irish out for good," Father Donahue says calmly. "I have your father to thank for my place, in fact. He convinced Vittorio Rossi that I had nothing to do with either side, and that I should be left here for exactly that reason. 'A good priest has no loyalty to sides or families, only God,' I think were his exact words. " He smiles at me, his eyes crinkling. "Does that sound like your father to you, Sofia?"

"I don't know," I admit. "I didn't know anything about this side of him. The father that I knew—" I bite my lower lip hard, feeling my throat tighten with emotion. "He was kind. Fun. Funny. He picked me up every time he walked in the front door, brought me books, always listened to me. I can't square that with—with the person that I'm being told he was. With someone who could hurt and kill people. With a member of the *mafia*." To my horror, I feel tears starting to well up.

I won't cry, I tell myself fiercely. *Not in front of this man, this priest that I don't even know.* But I can feel the tears coming, and I don't know how to stop them. I haven't talked to anyone about my father in so long.

There's sympathy in Father Donahue's eyes when he looks at me. "Your father was a good man, Sofia," he says quietly. "Sometimes good men do the wrong thing, but at their core, they're still good."

"How well did you know him?"

"Very well. He was conflicted, Sofia. He saw his place at Rossi's side as a way to temper the violent urges of a power-hungry man, to keep Rossi in check. Rossi trusted your father a great deal—the only man he trusted more was Luca's father, Marco. And your father and Marco were as close as brothers."

"I remember Luca's father, a little," I say softly. "He came to our house at least once."

"Your father tried to keep his two lives as separate as he could—his family and his job. But for a man at the Don's left hand, it's difficult. And he married a Russian woman. It made a great many people in Rossi's circle question him. I'm not sure Rossi ever fully forgave him for putting him in the delicate situation of defending him and his marriage."

"He loved my mother," I say defensively, wrapping my arms around myself.

"Of course. I married them, I would know." Father Donahue smiles. "But love is the downfall of a great many people, Sofia. After all, it was Marco's love for your father and their friendship that led to his death. And your father's love for you is why you're sitting here, now, in front of me. Instead of continuing your studies like you should be."

I shift uncomfortably. "How do you know so much about me?"

"Your father talked about you often, in the confessional. He told me about your love for reading, for the violin, how talented you were. The dreams he had for you. His greatest fear was that the life he'd chosen, long before you were even a thought, would somehow come back to harm you. He loved you and your mother more than anything in this world, Sofia. He would have done anything to keep you safe. And he did."

"You know about the promise?"

"Of course." Father Donahue looks at me, his face unreadable. "I was there when it was made. I witnessed it. Giovanni came to me in the middle of the night, bleeding and on the edge of death. He asked me to call Marco to the church."

I stare at him. "What do you mean? He didn't go to the hospital?"

"He knew he was going to die," Father Donahue says gently. He reaches out then, touching my hand lightly. "This is hard to hear, Sofia. But you should know the truth about what happened. Maybe it will—make this easier, in some way."

I doubt that. But still, I listen quietly, waiting to hear about the night my father died.

"He wouldn't hear of me calling an ambulance. He said he knew the wound was going to kill him, and he only wanted to make a last confession, and receive last rites. But he wanted something more—he wanted a promise from his only true friend. And he wanted it made on sacred ground, with a priest there to witness it. He wanted it to be inviolable."

"Providing for me and my mother," I say softly. "And this marriage."

"Yes." Father Donahue pauses, and I can see him considering what to say next. "But there's more to the promise of marriage than Luca might have led you to think, Sofia. I don't know what his father told him about the vow, or his part in keeping it. But Giovanni was clear that it was meant to be a last resort, if there were no other means of keeping you safe. If it turned out to be marriage, or your death."

"Luca says that's the choice. That Rossi will kill me, tie up a 'loose end', if I don't marry him."

"I believe that's true," Father Donahue says carefully. "I know Don Rossi well, and he's a cruel man, without much moral fabric. He prefers easy solutions to complex ones."

"So why are you loyal to him?" I blurt out. "Why help them?"

"Because Rossi is one man out of hundreds," Father Donahue replies, his voice calm and even. "Rossi is power-hungry. He demands absolute obedience and absolute loyalty. Everyone is afraid of him. If he replaced me with a priest of his choosing, there would be no moral compass in these walls any longer. But when his men come to me for confession, I don't give them absolution without counsel. I don't wipe away their sins in an instant in order to mollify Rossi's whims. I tell his men to be careful. To consider the orders they follow. To think of their immortal souls before they torture and maim and kill, before they start a war over another man's power and greed." He shrugs. "I don't want to fall prey to pride, but I'd like to think that I have made a difference, during my time here."

"And what? You think I should try to make a difference too?" I narrow my eyes at him, feeling the urge to be angry and combative rising up. It's easier than the grief I feel thinking about my father bleeding to death inches from where I'm sitting now, asking for his best friend, giving up any chance at surviving his wounds in order to extract a promise on holy ground. An unbreakable vow.

Like the one I'm meant to make on Saturday. A vow that is supposed to last a lifetime, to a man that I would do almost anything to escape.

"No," Father Donahue says quietly. "I think you should do your best to survive, Sofia, as your father wanted you to. You should do what you must."

"And what if I don't want to?" I can feel the lump in my throat rising. "What if it's unbearable?"

"Luca is not the man I hoped he would grow up to be," Father

Donahue admits. "He is a hard man, and prideful, and arrogant at times, and cold. But the world he is in shaped him to be that way, and I don't think that he's truly an evil man. I think there is some good in him—there's just been no one to bring it out."

"And I should be that person?" I demand, narrowing my eyes again. "I don't *want* to be his therapy, Father. I don't want to fix him. I hate him." The last words come out childish and petulant, but I don't care. "I'm not about to sacrifice my self-worth on the altar of fixing a man."

Father Donahue's eyes crinkle around the edges, and his mouth twitches in a real smile. "I see so much of Giovanni in you," he says with a laugh. "You are your father's daughter, through and through, and he would be proud of you. No, Sofia," he continues. "You are not responsible for Luca's behavior. You should never take that on yourself. I'm only saying that what seems like cruelty may be his defenses —defenses against the world around him, against what he perceives as weakness, against you. I don't think he means to be cruel, if he is. And I have some small hope for him still."

"So that's it?" I look at him helplessly, and I realize in that moment that I was hoping for an out. Some way to escape my impending marriage. "I just marry Luca on Saturday—and give up everything *I've* ever wanted?"

"For now, yes." Father Donahue hesitates, and then turns to face me fully, reaching for my hands. His are cool and dry, aged and weathered, but I can feel the strength in them. "I've agreed to this wedding because for now, it seems to be the best way to preserve the vow that your father asked Marco Romano to make. But—" he lifts a finger, his eyes narrowing. "Your father, above all, wished for you to be happy, Sofia. And he wished more than anything for you to escape this life, and everything in it. So if the day comes that your life is not in danger, and you are unhappy in your marriage and wish to leave it, I want you to come to me, Sofia." His voice lowers as he speaks, until it's barely a whisper.

"I loved your father dearly, and I owed him a great many things. I vowed, too, to look after you. And so I repeat that vow now, Sofia, in the presence of the Lord and the Holy Mother, in memory of your father, that I will do all I can to protect you, and keep you safe. If there comes a day when you wish to leave Luca, all you need to do is walk through those doors, and I will find a way." He pauses, letting go of my hands. "But for now, this is the best path forward that I can see."

For a moment I can't breathe, hope springing up inside of me for the first time since I woke up in Luca's room. The tiny loophole that I found seems bigger now, more possible, and the looming threat of Saturday wanes a little with this new information.

I just have to wait until Don Rossi dies. With the immediate threat to my life lifted, I can run to Father Donahue. He'll help me escape. And I can put all of this behind me.

My marriage is no longer a life sentence. Only a temporary one.

Father Donahue smiles kindly at me, standing up slowly. "Come, Sofia," he says, his voice deep and calming. "It's not the ceremony we usually have, but it's time for your confirmation. And then you can go."

He doesn't say "back home," and I know why. Luca's penthouse will never be my home, and neither will whatever apartment Luca chooses to give me.

I don't know, in the end, where my home will be. But I feel hopeful that I'll have one of my own, one day.

Standing up slowly, I follow Father Donahue to the altar, breathing in the scent of incense in the vast room.

In three days, I'll take my marriage vows. I'll do the unthinkable, and stand in front of Luca, in this church, and lie.

Because I have no intention of keeping them.

LUCA

J hadn't thought that there could be anything I wanted to do less than go to one of the formal parties that the Rossi family throws from time to time, like the Don's anniversary party or Catalina's engagement.

But now I've found a new one to dread.

My own wedding rehearsal.

I've managed to avoid Sofia entirely since the afternoon I found myself jerking off standing in her closet, clutching her dress like a deranged, lovesick boy. That was the wake-up call that let me know I needed to put some serious space between the two of us, and I proceeded to do exactly that.

There's just one problem left.

I haven't fucked anyone in a week.

That same night, I went out to my favorite whiskey bar and took my usual spot near the window, waiting to find the perfect woman to take home and use to fuck every single thought of Sofia out of my head.

I waited. And waited. And waited some more.

And for the first time since I was old enough to go out to a bar, hell, since *before* I was legally supposed to be drinking in bars—it's amazing what being rich allows you to do at eighteen—I went home alone.

I, Luca Romano, legendary Manhattan playboy, went home alone.

And jerked off again, in the shower, thinking about the hot water and my expensive soap dripping off of Sofia Ferretti's luscious tits.

Okay, fine, I'd told myself, waking up the next morning. I'd just found the rare night—the *only* night—in which there hadn't been a single woman out who was my type. Never mind that my type is between eighteen and thirty and breathing—I just hadn't found anyone to pique my interest.

Nothing wrong with that. Everyone has an off night.

But I didn't bring anyone home that next night, either.

This morning makes almost a week running that I've pleasured myself every single day, multiple times most days, unable to find a woman that makes me want to turn on my trademark charm and sweep her into my bed. Instead I've come home and fantasized about all of the filthy, dirty, *insanely* pleasurable things that I want to do to Sofia and her prized innocence. How I want to rip it away from her like that stupidly short black dress, and make her beg for me until she's breathless with it. How I want to teach her how it feels to have every inch of her body touched and kissed and stroked, how it feels to come over and over again until I lose all control and cover her in my cum, marking her as mine once and for all--

And just like that, I'm rock-hard in the back of the car, a mile away from the church where I'm getting married.

At this rate, it's going to be impossible for me not to wind up erect during the ceremony just from the sight of her.

I can't understand it. A week ago, I would have laughed until I pissed myself at the idea that there could be a woman anywhere, in the entire world, that could make me celibate. That could keep me from fucking anyone and everyone that I please. And yet, since I carried Sofia out of that hotel room, I haven't seen a single woman that can make me forget about her.

Not a single one that makes me want anyone else.

I want Sofia. I want her in every single way that a man can want a woman, and apparently I want her so desperately that I can't get a hard-on for anyone else. Part of the reason I haven't brought anyone home is on account of the fact that I couldn't bear the humiliation if I couldn't get it up for another woman.

I should *want* to fuck someone else. I should want to take another woman to bed and fuck her so soundly that Sofia would hear the moans all the way down the hall, and realize the utter foolishness of holding out on me. I should bend another woman over in front of Sofia's goddamn door and let her hear the sound of me slamming balls deep into literally *anyone* that isn't her.

But I haven't, and at this point, I'm starting to think that I won't.

So what the fuck are you going to do? Stay celibate forever? Sofia and I are at a stand-off, and once I banish her to her own apartment, I can't imagine the situation is going to improve. Maybe having her out of sight will successfully get her out of my mind—but I'm not sure that I can bet on that anymore.

I'm not sure of anything. And I could strangle her for shattering my peace of mind so thoroughly.

I'm going to see her in less than twenty minutes, and I couldn't be less ready.

There's only a few people at the rehearsal—Don Rossi and his wife Giulia, Franco and Caterina, and of course Father Donahue. The rehearsal dinner will be a different matter altogether, with several of the higher-ranking members of the family there.

I walk down the aisle towards the altar, feeling as if my tie is choking me. I want out of here more than I want to breathe—I want to flee this church, get on the first plane to Amsterdam, and lose myself in the filthiest fucking sex imaginable. Maybe crossing an ocean would mean enough space between Sofia and I that I could stop thinking about her.

Probably not.

What the fuck does she want? I think as I stand at the altar with Franco next to me, Don Rossi and his wife sitting in the first pew, and Caterina striding down the aisle to go meet Sofia and bring her in.

Does she want love? Fidelity? Is this just a way of punishing me for forcing her into this?

Surely she doesn't want me to be a real husband to her—faithful, loving, all of that bullshit. Even if I were capable of it, I don't know what reason she would have for wanting that. In her eyes, I'm just the man she's being forced to marry. Not the man who rescued her, the man who saved her from being sold or worse—just her jailer. Her unwanted husband.

But I've felt, in those moments that we were alone together, that a part of her wants me physically. I felt it in the brief moment that she gave into my kiss, in the way she reacts every time we fight, in the way I see her skin flush and her chest heave. She's fighting desire, too.

So why not just give in?

I've got to stop thinking about it, or I'm never going to get through tonight.

The doors open, and the music starts. *Canon in D*, the traditional wedding music, and I stand up a little straighter. "Here comes the bride," Franco says with a laugh, nudging me playfully. "Shame you won't be the first, but damn if you weren't lucky enough to get a hot piece of ass."

I feel myself tense, and for the first time, I find myself wanting to punch my best friend. *A good right hook to the jaw ought to teach him not to talk about my fiancée that way,* I think, gritting my teeth.

But we've been talking that way about women all our lives. For fuck's sake, he gave me the gritty details of the blowjob Caterina gave him in the back of the limo after he put the ring on her finger, right down to how he was sure she'd done it before, because she took it all the way down her throat, and knew to swallow. I should have just elbowed him back, and made a comment about what, exactly, I plan to do to that ass tomorrow night.

Instead, I want to punch him for even mentioning that he's looked at Sofia.

As the music fills the room, Caterina comes through the doors, walking slowly down the aisle just as she will tomorrow. I glance sideways at Franco, and see that his eyes are locked on his own fiancée, his face so full of lust that I'm surprised he hasn't managed to fuck her already. "I can't wait to plow that virgin field," he says longingly under his breath, his eyes greedily undressing her as she walks towards us. "The Don's daughter. My god, Luca, you're a good fucking friend."

"You earned it," I tell him quietly. And I mean it. He's earned everything he's gotten and more over the years, standing steadfastly by my side through everything we've done. I couldn't ask for a better friend.

But right now, watching him eye-fuck his future bride, knowing that he's going to get to take her to bed on their wedding night, I've never been so jealous.

How the fuck did I get myself into this?

Not for the first time, I wish that I'd told Sofia that her conditions could go straight to hell. But I agreed to them, promised to honor that agreement, and I can't go back on it now.

No matter how desperately I wish I could. At this point, I'd almost take having her even if it meant she laid there like a cold fish. Hell, maybe that would be better. It might cure me of my insane desire for her if she turned out to be awful in bed.

"There she is," Franco hisses, and I look towards the doors, feeling a sudden tightness in my chest that's wholly unfamiliar to me.

Sofia walks through the doors, and that feeling only intensifies. She looks beautiful, wearing a light pink lace dress with a ribbon belt and half-sleeves. It clings to her curves without being too sexy for the cathedral, and I feel my mouth go dry as I look at her long legs in the high heels that she's wearing—undoubtedly ones that she purchased on my dime during her little shopping spree.

All I want in the world, in that moment, is to have those legs wrapped around me. *I'd spend any amount of money,* I think fervently, as I watch her walk towards me, struggling mightily to keep my desire under control and not embarrass myself in the middle of church. *I'd buy her anything. Promise her anything. Just to get inside of her once.*

The worst part of it is that I can't figure out how on Earth this one inexperienced, virgin girl has managed to undo me so completely. *She probably doesn't even know what to do. I'd have to teach her everything.* But I don't even care. Ever since I pinned her up against that door, the thought of being the first man to make Sofia Ferretti whimper and moan and beg, the first man inside of her, has reduced me to this.

A man who is completely hung up on one woman. The kind of man I swore I'd never be.

The sooner you get this over with, the sooner you can start to forget about her.

The problem is, I'm not sure I want to anymore.

Sofia stops at the foot of the steps leading up to the altar. "Is anyone giving you away?" Father Donahue asks, and I'm temporarily distracted from my inappropriate, lustful musings by the look on Sofia's face.

It actually cools my desire, briefly. The grief that fills her eyes is sharp and immediate, plain to anyone who is actually looking. She looks years younger in that moment, as if she's been transported back to the day that she was a twelve-year-old girl who just lost her father, as it hits her all over again that he'll never walk her down the aisle.

If he were here to walk her down the aisle, she wouldn't be marrying me. And we'd all be better off for it.

"I can give her away tomorrow," Don Rossi speaks up, leaning forward.

"No." Sofia's voice rings out, surprisingly strong. I feel Franco tense next to me, and we both look towards the Don, wondering how he'll take the rejection—especially considering his feelings about Sofia. I can see his face redden slightly, and I feel my pulse speed up. In that moment, I realize that I'm prepared to defend her against his anger—yet another reaction I don't understand.

"Thank you," Sofia continues politely, her face completely neutral. "But my father, it seems, already gave me away once. So I'll walk myself down the aisle tomorrow." Her gaze flicks to me, and I see a hint of steel in it.

My little fiancée has found her backbone.

It shouldn't turn me on. But like everything else about her, it unfortunately does.

"Whatever you prefer." Don Rossi leans back in the pew, his expression still irritated, but he seems willing to let her insolence go. I let out the breath that I hadn't realized I'd been holding, and glance over at Father Donahue, who looks slightly uncomfortable.

"Very well," he says, gesturing to Sofia. "Step up here then, and take Luca's hands. Luca, on the day, her veil will stay down until it's time for you to kiss her after the vows."

I half expect her to argue. But instead she reaches out, settling her hands in mine, and I feel a shiver run down my spine. Her hands are small and soft and warm, fitting perfectly in my broad palms, and I have to fight the urge to pull her towards me, gather her into my arms, and kiss her as thoroughly as I know how.

Tomorrow, she'll be my wife. I should be able to kiss her whenever I want.

Instead, tomorrow will be the next, and only time.

I only half hear the vows that Father Donahue tells us we'll be repeating. I can't take my eyes off of Sofia's face. She's wearing very little makeup, enough that I can see the rosy flush of her skin peeking out through it, the few soft freckles on her cheeks. My eyes flick down to her full lips, and all I can think about is the fact that I'll get to kiss her again tomorrow. For the first time since the night I had her up against the door, I'll have her lips against mine.

"You'd better not bite me tomorrow," I murmur under my breath, looking at her as Father Donahue finishes telling us our vows.

Sofia smiles brightly for his sake, but I can see the challenge in her eyes. "I wouldn't dream of it," she says sweetly, squeezing my hands. "My groom? On my wedding day? I would never."

Father Donahue pauses, looking at us suspiciously. "This is where you'll kiss your bride, Luca—*tomorrow*," he adds pointedly.

Sofia's smile is still plastered onto her face. As Father Donahue continues speaking, she looks up into my eyes and speaks through clenched teeth, her gaze fixed on mine. "Make it a good one tomorrow," she says, her voice low and full of all the resentment that I know she must feel for me, down to her core.

"Because after that kiss," she continues sweetly, her gaze still wide-eyed and holding mine. "You'll never touch me again."

SOFIA

*J*f I'd thought the rehearsal would be nearly impossible to get through, the dinner afterwards is even worse. The restaurant that's been rented out for the occasion is beautiful, an elegant five-star Italian place owned by a friend of the Rossi family, but I'm completely overwhelmed. The banquet room that we're using is full of the Rossi's, their extended family, Luca's remaining extended family, and their friends—and no one at all who knows me. I feel like I stick out, the girl who appeared out of nowhere to marry their prince, and as if everyone knows there's something up.

The questions don't make it any easier, the: "where were you hiding her?" and "why haven't we met her before?" I just smile prettily while Luca comes up with bland answers for why no one has even heard a hint of him dating anyone before this, and try to remember names. But I can't. I can feel my pulse pounding in my throat as I'm introduced to person after person, and I realize suddenly that if there's this many people at the *rehearsal dinner*, there's going to be so many more at the wedding itself, and the reception.

I feel like I'm going to have a panic attack. My throat closes over as Luca introduces me to someone's grand-uncle while barely even bothering to glance at me, and I have a second to choke out a passable "nice to meet you," before I excuse myself in a hurry. Luca is probably going to think I'm being rude, and he'll probably be angry with me, but I can only imagine how much ruder it would be if I just fainted in the middle of our rehearsal dinner.

It's not a lie, either. I feel dizzy and clammy, and I escape to the ladies' room as quickly as I can, splashing cold water on my face before retreating into one of the stalls and hoping that no one comes to find me anytime soon.

But when I step out, I see Caterina leaning against the sink counter, toying with a lipstick with a sympathetic look on her face.

I tense up, waiting for a comment about how I'm being missed out there, or how I shouldn't be hiding out in the bathroom during my own rehearsal dinner. But instead she just gives me a sympathetic, soft smile. "Are you okay?"

How do I even answer that? The obvious answer is, of course, no. Absolutely not. I couldn't be further from *okay.*

"It's alright to be overwhelmed," she continues, watching me as I touch up my own makeup in the mirror. "I was born into this family, and I'm still overwhelmed by it sometimes. There's a lot of them, and they're so loud. So—*much.*" She shrugs. "They're my family, but I don't always love everything about them."

It's all I can do not to snap at her. There's any number of things I could think of to say, from *I don't want your pity,* to *I don't care how you feel,* or *at least you aren't being forced into a marriage with a man you actively despise.*

Of course, the last one is rapidly becoming a case of my protesting too much. Just having Luca's hands wrapped around mine at the rehearsal was enough to make my skin heat and my heart race, and thinking about him kissing me tomorrow made me come face to face with the uncomfortable truth that a part of me—a very *small* part—is actually looking forward to the kiss.

Because I have to kiss him tomorrow. Kissing him tomorrow isn't admitting that deep down, I'm curious, or that deep down, I'm attracted to him, or that deep down, a part of me wants to give in and say *fuck my conditions, take me to bed.* I don't have a choice—and that very small part of me is glad about that. Glad that I don't have to wrestle with whether to let him or not.

Instead of saying any of those things, I turn to her, shoving my own lipstick back into my clutch. "You said you didn't choose to marry Franco," I said tightly, trying to keep my emotions under control. "That you could understand how I feel."

"I didn't choose to marry him," Caterina says calmly. "I was— informed that I'm going to marry him, on account of the fact that he'll be Luca's underboss, when Luca takes my father's seat."

"I see the way you look at him, though. You don't hate him."

"No, I don't." Caterina pauses, setting her clutch down as she turns to face me. "I'm lucky, I know. He's handsome, and young, and we get along. I wouldn't say we're the best of friends, but we enjoy spending time together. I won't mind going to bed with him on our wedding night, and I won't mind being his wife. It could have been much worse."

I just stare at her. I can't wrap my head around how she can be so calm about it, how she can behave like *any* of this is fucking *normal.* "How can you say all of that—like *that*? You're talking about an *arranged marriage*? How can you be so okay with it—how can you say it's anything like what I'm going through, when you're clearly okay with it?"

There's a long pause between us, my outburst hanging in the air. Caterina takes a deep breath, pressing her lips together for a moment before she speaks.

"I'm not okay with it," she says softly. "Deep down, I'm not. I had things I dreamed of—things that had nothing to do with being a mafia wife. But this is the life I was born into, and I always knew it would be this way. I was never going to be able to choose my own husband, never going to be anything except a wife and a mother to a high-ranking man in the family. All I can do is make the best of it. Perhaps I'll love Franco, perhaps not. But it will be a decent marriage." She stops, looking at me with that same sympathetic expression. "Yours could be the same, if you'd allow it."

For a moment, I feel completely unable to form a complete

169

thought. I want to scream at her, to throw something, but deep down I know that she's right. I was born into this life too—I was just given a brief window of time where I didn't realize what my fate would be. The only real difference between Caterina and I is that I insist on fighting it.

And for the first time, I see that she's trapped too, more so than I realized. She might be more accepting of it than I am, but that doesn't mean that she isn't a prisoner in this world too.

"What did you want to do?" I manage to ask, when I feel like I can breathe again. I can't imagine what she'll say she dreamed of being, this perfectly polished woman in front of me, an absolute vision of the ideal mafia wife. Everything I know Luca wants me to be.

Caterina just looks at me, and I realize that she's wondering if I'm mocking her. She almost looks hurt.

"I really want to know," I say quietly.

She doesn't say anything, and I'm about to give up, just walk out and find my way back to the hall, when she speaks up. Her voice is soft and sweet and quiet, and I can hear the hint of sadness in it. The longing for what might have been.

"I always loved art, and children," she says simply. "I wanted to be an elementary school teacher. Somewhere that I could make a difference. But that was never going to happen."

That sadness is written all across her face as she speaks. "I went to college for it, you know," she says with a short laugh. "I always knew that it was pointless, that my father was just indulging my mother by letting me get a degree at all. I wasn't allowed to move out, and I had a strict curfew. My virginity had to be protected, of course—I'm too valuable of an asset."

There's a tinge of bitterness in her voice that shocks me. I've never seen anything outwardly rebellious about her. But for the first time, I see a hint of rebellion in her eyes. I can't help but admire her a little— she got a degree in something she knew she would never use, just to prove that she could.

"I should go," I say softly.

"Yeah." Caterina picks up her clutch. "They'll be missing us before too long. Don't worry, I'll be out in a few minutes."

As I walk out of the ladies' room, I almost feel as if I might have a friend here—or at least the start of one. And I know that I'll need all the friends I can get. Still, I can't bring myself to trust her entirely. She's still a Rossi, the Don's daughter—and one of them.

I'm supposed to go back to the party. But as I step out into the hallway, I can't bring myself to keep going back towards the banquet room where everyone is gathered. I can't bring myself to face Luca, or deal with being introduced to more people whose names I don't know, I need to be alone, to breathe, to get away from all of this—

Against my better judgement, I find myself walking away from the party, my pace picking up more and more with every step. *I'm not running away,* I tell myself. *Just getting some air. Just going outside.* I hurry towards the glass doors at the front of the restaurant, the faint chatter from the room at the back where the party is fading even more as I shove the doors open and burst out into the cool spring air.

I breathe in, sucking in huge gulps of it, realizing how on the verge of a panic attack I really was. It's hitting me now full force—*I'm getting married tomorrow*—and I want to scream. I'm going to be legally bound to a man I hardly know and don't even like, a man who has been both cruel and kind to me in turns, and although I have some small hope of finding a way out eventually—there's no guarantee.

This could be my forever. And that knowledge suddenly feels suffocating.

I don't mean to walk away from the restaurant. My feet just carry me a few steps, and a few more, until I'm at the far end of a bar a little further down the street, leaning up against the brick wall with my eyes closed and my breath coming in small, quick pants as I try to calm down.

It's going to be okay, I tell myself, repeating Caterina's assurance from earlier in my head. *This won't be so bad. It could be worse—you could be dead.*

Somehow that doesn't make me feel much better, though—that my only options are marrying Luca or death.

He's the prince of the Italian mafia, heir to the throne, and I can't say he isn't charming. But a Prince Charming? He's anything but that.

All fairytales have a dark side.

My throat closes over as I remember my father handing me the book of Grimm's fairytales, speaking those exact words to me. He must have known, somehow, that the darkness would eventually come for me. That I would have to make an impossible choice.

I should go back inside, before someone comes looking for me. Before Luca or anyone else who sees me out here gets the wrong idea. But I can't bring myself to move. The cool air, the traffic passing by and the scents and sounds of the city all help to ground me, make me feel just a little less afraid. This city has been my home all my life, but I've never felt more lost than this past week.

There's people passing by on the sidewalk, but one set of footsteps comes closer, growing louder until they stop very close to me.

"Sofia."

It's Luca's voice. It's cold and angry, and my heart drops into my stomach at the sound of it.

Fuck.

"Didn't I tell you what would happen if you tried to run away?"

My eyes fly open. "No," I say quickly, turning to face him. "I wasn't —I just needed some air. I wasn't going anywhere—"

"Then why are you a block and a half away from Vitto's, over here like you're waiting on someone? Maybe you're waiting for Ana to come get you and sweep you away? Or to catch a cab?" His face is like granite, hard and set in cold lines that make me feel like I want to throw up. He looks furious. "I told you what would happen if you tried to leave."

"I'm not, I swear—"

"Come on." Luca's hand darts out, grasping my elbow. "We're leaving, now. I've already made our excuses to everyone else."

"Wait—where are we going?" I dig my heels in as he starts to pull me away from the building. "Where are you taking me?" I have sudden visions of bloody basements and cold warehouses on the docks, wherever he and men like him do the awful things that they do. Is he really going to have me killed because I went for a short walk?"

Luca turns to me, his face silhouetted in the streetlight. Even his eyes look dark, angry and full of seething frustration.

"We're going home," he says coldly. And then he pulls me forward, towards the curb where his driver is waiting.

LUCA

I can't remember the last time I was so furious with anyone. Sofia doesn't seem to grasp how frail of a thread her life hangs by. How I'm the only one keeping that thread intact—how much Don Rossi would like an excuse to call this whole expensive mess off, and just have her killed.

A bullet is cheaper than a wedding ring. And a divorce will cost her life.

That was the last thing he'd said to me, in that meeting when I'd lied to him about Sofia's virginity. And now I've had it with her. I've spent the last week rescuing her, protecting her, lying for her and walking into a marriage I don't want for her, and now she's got me so messed up that I can't even get a good casual fuck to unwind. My balls and my brain are both boiling over with frustration, and now I have to deal with her disappearing in the middle of our fucking *rehearsal dinner*, with all of my and Don Rossi's families there, with the highest ranking members in attendance, leading to questions about where my beautiful bride-to-be has gone and embarrassing me in front of everyone.

She's going to learn tonight how to behave. How a proper mafia wife acts in public. How much danger she's really in.

Sofia doesn't speak a word for the entire ride back to my apartment. She stays on the far side of the limo, her arms wrapped around herself, and frankly I don't care. I've tried giving her space, I've tried catering to her emotions as much as I can manage, and now she needs to understand, once and for all, that everything she knew before is over.

Her life depends on it. And I can't have the Don believing that I can't control my wife.

"Out." I say coldly the minute the car pulls into the parking garage. I don't even wait for my driver to come around and open the door. I open it myself, waiting on Sofia as she looks up at me with a hint of defiance still in her lovely dark eyes.

"Luca, I—"

"Out!" I can feel the thread of my control beginning to fray.

She scrambles out of the car, paling slightly as she waits for me to stride ahead towards the elevator.

Contrary to what I'm sure she believes, I don't enjoy raising my voice. I don't like the idea of my wife being afraid of me. Truthfully, I'm not sure what emotions I would like for her to have towards me—ambivalent obedience, maybe. If we could get to that by the end of the night, I'd be tempted to start singing a hallelujah chorus.

The elevator ride up is in silence as well. Sofia doesn't speak a single word until we step into the penthouse and the lights come up softly in the living room.

"You promised," she says accusatorially.

I cross my arms, facing her with the last shred of my patience. "Promised what exactly, Sofia?"

"You promised not to lay a hand on me again!" She chews on her lower lip, her eyes widening. "You lied to me."

"*You* promised not to try to run away. Not to leave. To obey me—"

"I never promised to obey!"

"Well, you're going to tonight. You're going to learn, Sofia, that *I* am in control here. Not you."

She glares up at me, her eyes still spitting some of that fire I'm coming to know so well. It turns me on more than I want to admit.

"Are you going to walk to the bedroom, or am I going to have to carry you?"

Her eyes go even wider in her delicate face. "You promised—" she splutters, and I smile coldly at her.

"You've broken part of your agreement already, Sofia. And don't bothering telling me again that you weren't running away. Maybe you hadn't planned on it, and maybe you didn't even mean to, but some part of you was trying to get away."

"I was overwhelmed, and—"

"I don't care." My voice is as flat and toneless as I can manage. "And I asked you a question."

The last thing I want is for her to see how she's affecting me. How much I want her right now, how ridiculously, stupidly arousing her defiance is. The last fucking thing in the world that I need right now is for Sofia to know she has that kind of upper hand.

"I'm not going to your bedroom." She bites off each word as if it were its own sentence, glaring at me despite her obvious uncertainty as to what's going to happen next.

I smile coolly at her. "Don't worry. You won't have to."

She blinks at me, as if she's not quite sure what I mean, and before she can open her mouth to hurl some other statement at me I cross the space between us, throwing all sense of restraint to the wind. I reach out for my lovely, stubborn, reckless, *infuriating* fiancée and grab her by her upper arms, hauling her against me and kissing her with all the force and passion that I can't put into tomorrow's kiss at the altar.

And God, it feels so fucking good. Her body bows against mine for just a moment, before her thoughts have a chance to catch up, and her lips are so soft. They sink into mine, full and warm, and the instant I pull her against me my cock is hard as hell, my erection raging within the confines of my suit as I fight the urge to take her right here and now.

My hand slides up into her hair, yanking the pins free that hold it up, and her now-brunette curls come loose around her face in a tumble of soft perfumed hair that makes me groan against her mouth as I feel it slipping through my fingers. I slide my tongue over her lips, prying her mouth open as I grip the back of her head, wanting to taste her, to feel the warmth of her tongue against mine, to breathe her in—

"Fuck!" I jerk backwards as I feel the sharp pain of her teeth sinking into my lip again, and I glare down at her, seething with pent-up anger and arousal.

She doesn't slap me again, at least. But she stares up at me with those defiant eyes, somehow more beautiful than ever with her lips slightly swollen and pink from my kiss, her soft brown hair tumbling around her face, and in that moment I can't remember ever wanting to possess anything more.

Sofia is mine. My wife. My bride. Mine.

My arm goes around her waist, still holding her against me. She's not struggling, but I can feel how tense she is—with fear or anger or desire, or possibly all three. "You promised," she hisses again, and I look down at her, my mouth twitching with amusement.

"I'm not going to fuck you tonight, Sofia. Your precious virginity is safe. After all, even if I planned to take it, I wouldn't deny myself the pleasure of doing that on our wedding night. I'm not even going to give myself the enjoyment of stripping you naked so that I can see what I've bought before tomorrow."

"You haven't *bought* me!" She squirms in my arms, trying to hit my chest, but she's too close to me for it to be effective. Her fists barely do more than bounce against my hard, muscled pecs, and I chuckle deep in my throat as I watch her writhe in my grasp.

"Oh, but I have, Sofia. And I don't mean that ridiculously expensive ring on your finger, or the thousands of dollars of new clothes hanging in your room, or the fancy party being thrown tomorrow night to celebrate a wedding that neither of us really wants. I gave you your *life*. And yet you have the absolute *audacity* to embarrass me in front of everyone tonight!"

"I didn't mean to—" her lips part, and I want nothing more than to kiss them again.

"You have to mean everything you do in this life, Sofia. There is no room for mistakes, no room for *I just didn't think.*"

"I didn't ask for any of this!"

"Neither did I." I stare down at her, my own chest heaving with frustration. I reach down, my hand sliding over her waist and down her hip, bunching in the lace of her dress there. "You can argue all you like that I don't own you, Sofia, but all it would take is one phone call, and you'd be as good as dead. You'd spend your last few days looking over your shoulder until the bullet finally came. You'd end your life in a cold wet alley, or in your kitchen, or maybe in this very living room, if Don Rossi wasn't patient."

My hand slips under the fabric of her dress, and for the first time I feel the warm smoothness of her thigh, the firm silkiness of her skin. She gasps softly, and I feel my cock throb with need at even that tiny hint of desire.

"Some part of you knows it, Sofia. Your body knows it, even if you keep denying it."

I trail my fingertips up her inner thigh, repressing a groan at the heat that I can feel there, radiating over my hand.

"And by the end of tonight, there will be no doubt."

"What do you mean?"

Her voice is a tiny whisper, curling in the air between us like smoke.

"I mean this, Sofia." My hand slides up her inner thigh, feeling the soft curve of it that fits into my palm. Her body jerks against me when my fingertips press against the silk of her panties, and my arm tightens around her. I can feel how wet she is even through the fabric. "You want me. You're telling me that I don't own you, that you don't want any of this, but this tells a different story. What will I find if I slip my fingers under here, hmm?" I stroke my fingertips over the space between her thighs, and to my delight, she makes a small sound that's almost a whimper.

I'm so fucking hard that it hurts. But tonight isn't about my need to come, or how much I want to sink myself into the heat that I can feel burning against my fingers right now. It's not about bringing Sofia pleasure, either.

It's about making her understand her new reality, and her place in it.

"Nothing," she whispers, squirming in my grasp. "Luca, please—"

"Please, what?" I smile down at her. I can feel her heartbeat against my chest, fluttering like a caged bird. I raise my voice a little, mimicking her breathy tone. "Please, Luca, slide your fingers inside my panties? Please, Luca, I'm so wet, I need to come?"

"No!" Her face flushes bright red, but my fingers are already at the edge, slipping beneath the silk. "That's not what I mean, Luca, please, I —" She gasps as I brush over the crease of her inner thigh, edging towards that soft, wet flesh that I'm aching to touch. "No one's ever—"

"I know," I murmur, my voice dropping an octave, hoarse with desire. "I know how inexperienced you are, Sofia. How I'll be the first to touch you in every way. It only makes me want to possess you more, to show you how completely and utterly you'll belong to me, once you give in."

"I won't—"

"No?" My fingers slide over the soft outer folds of her pussy, and I feel her quiver in my arms. "You're so wet that I can feel it here, too. And here—"

Sofia cries out in shock and surprise as I slip my fingers between her folds, and I have to grit my teeth against the shock of lust that runs through my own body at the feeling of her wet heat, my cock straining against my pants. I can't stop myself from pushing it against her thigh, a wave of satisfaction filling me as I see her eyes widen when she feels the thick ridge of it. "You'll beg me for it one day," I growl down at her, my fingers sliding up through the slick heat between her legs until I find her small, throbbing clit. "You'll beg for my cock instead of my fingers. But tonight, you're going to beg me for something else."

"What? I—"

I yank my fingers away from her, spinning her around. With one swift movement, I push her forward over the side of the leather couch, her hands going out to catch herself as I bend her over the arm.

She starts squirming immediately, but I keep my hand on her lower back, holding her in place as I yank up the skirt of her dress.

"You said you weren't going to—" Her fingers scratch at the leather, trying to push herself up, but I have her pinned down.

"I said I wasn't going to fuck you, and I meant it." It takes me all of a second to pull her panties down around her thighs, and the sight of Sofia bent over my couch, the silky fabric twisted around her thighs as her bare ass and the soft pouty lips of her pussy are bared to me for the first time is enough to make me feel like I might lose control altogether.

"Luca!"

"Lie still, or I'll tie you up," I warn her. I reach out with my right hand, the left still pinning her down with the skirt of her dress bunched in my fist, and run one finger down the crease between her thighs, gleaming wet with her arousal. "There's so many things I could do to you that don't involve my cock, Sofia. It could be my tongue here instead, tasting you, licking you until you writhe and beg and moan, teasing you until you're desperate to come. Do you know how many times I can make a woman come with my tongue, Sofia?"

She shakes her head mutely, refusing to turn and look at me.

"I've lost track." I slide my finger down. "I could make you come, though, Sofia, over and over again. I could leave you breathless and exhausted before I ever get to the point of my cock being inside of you. And by the time I was ready to fuck you, you'd be begging for it."

"Never," she whispers. "I'll never beg you for anything."

"No?" I step between her legs, nudging them apart with my knee as I press my fingertip against her clit. I'm rewarded immediately with her soft gasp and whine, and I can feel her throbbing against my finger. "Have you ever been this wet before? Have you touched yourself, maybe, and felt this?"

"I've never done that, I—"

"Don't lie to me." I pull my finger away immediately. "That's another rule, Sofia. You can't run, and you can't lie. I'll know if you do."

She'd never in a million years admit it, but I can see her back arch when I pull my hand away, her thighs spreading just a little as she feels the loss of my touch.

"Everyone masturbates, Sofia," I murmur, returning my hand to her wet, swollen pussy. I cup her in my hand for a moment, letting my middle finger sink between her folds as I press the tip to her clit again. "I know you've touched yourself here. I know you've made yourself come. Maybe you even fantasized about something like this, about a man who would make you give in to all the desires that you're afraid to admit to. All the things you've wondered about but were too afraid to find out for yourself."

"I never, I didn't want—" She writhes under the pressure of my hand on her back again, but I can feel her pushing back into my touch, wanting more.

"But you do." I slide my hand under her dress, stroking her lower back as I start to rub her clit in slow circles, enjoying the feeling of it throbbing under my touch. "The evidence of it is all over my hand, Sofia. It's dripping down your thighs, you want it so badly. You want me to make you come with my fingers, with my tongue, even with my cock, although you think you'd *never* admit that. But we'll start with fingers, tonight."

Her head drops forwards, her breath coming in small, mewling gasps as I increase my speed, my palm pressed against the heat of her skin. Carefully, I take my left hand off of her back for a moment, ready to capture her again if she tries to move, but I can see that she's losing herself in the pleasure of my fingers already. I yank down my zipper, groaning aloud with relief as my aching cock springs free, and I see Sofia stiffen at the sound, arching backwards as if she's going to try to escape again.

"Don't you dare," I hiss, my fingers going very still against her clit as I pin her down with my hand again. "I told you not to lie to me, and I won't lie to you, Sofia. I'm not going to fuck you. But I *will* show you that you belong to me. All of you, from your lovely face down to this perfect pussy."

She whimpers at that, slumping forward over the couch as my fingers start to move again, and her legs spread open despite herself.

"Luca," she gasps, but the sound of my name on her lips is different now, pleading instead of accusing.

"Are you going to beg, Sofia?" I lean forward, the head of my cock brushing against her inner thigh. I grit my teeth against the sensation, made so much stronger by a week without any pleasure other than my hand, and I feel my balls tighten as I stroke her clit faster, moving my finger in small quick circles as Sofia starts to moan.

"No!" she manages breathlessly. "I won't—beg—you—for anything, I—"

"Not even this?" I tug at her clit gently between two fingers, slowing down my movements. "Not even an orgasm? I can make you come so hard, Sofia. Just from this. You can't even imagine what I could do with my mouth, with my—"

"God, Luca!" Her voice rises to a higher pitch as she arches backwards, her ass pressing against me and forcing my hand to rub against her again. My cock is suddenly trapped between her thighs, sliding against the soft damp flesh as she grinds her hips down into my palm. I can feel how close she is, her pussy swollen with it, her arousal soaking my hand as her clit pulses against my fingertips.

I allow myself to enjoy it for just a moment, her submission to my touch even without words, the feeling of my rigid, aching cock rubbing against her silky thighs, and the feeling of her hot, wet flesh yielding to my fingers. I'm so close, and I'm just waiting for her to be on the knife's-edge of climax, so close that she can't stop herself from tipping over.

"You want to come for me, Sofia," I whisper, leaning over her. "You know you do. You can tell me that you're not mine all you want, but you're lying. And you know what happens to girls who lie?"

"No," Sofia whimpers. Her hips are twisting against me now, and I can feel her inner thighs trembling, her desire trickling against my palm as I rub her clit hard. "No, Luca—"

She's on the verge of saying please. If she had, I think I might have let her come. The temptation is there to see my beautiful almost-bride tumble over the edge, to hear her moans and see her buck and writhe on my hand. But she clamps her lips shut instead, shaking her head even as her body strains against me.

"Girls who lie don't get to come."

I snatch my hand away right as she reaches the brink, her gorgeous ass arching upwards, her thighs splayed apart so that I can see the wet pink folds of the sweet, tight pussy that I so desperately want to sink my cock into. But instead I grasp the aching length in my hand, stroking once, twice, and a third time as hard and fast as I can, feet spread apart and braced as my hips thrust forward with a deep, shuddering need as I feel my long-overdue orgasm boiling up from my swollen balls.

"*Fuck.*" I groan aloud, my voice hoarse as my cock throbs in my hand, and I see the first splash of my cum over her perfect ass. Sofia stiffens immediately, the heat of it startling her. "Don't fucking move," I growl, my entire body shuddering as I stroke myself harder, the sight of my cum pearling over her skin almost dizzying. It's the hottest thing I've ever fucking seen, and I push the head of my cock against the soft cheek of her ass without thinking, groaning and still shaking with the sheer pleasure of it. As the last drop pearls against her creamy skin, I wipe the head of my cock on her ass, slapping it against her skin once enough to make her jump a little before I step back, looking down at her.

For a moment neither of us moves, and I'm treated to a longer look at Sofia Ferretti draped over my couch, her skirt up around her waist and my cum decorating her skin.

"You're mine," I murmur, my voice harsh and deep. "And now you won't forget it."

SOFIA

*H*is voice drifts over me like smoke, dark and thick and dizzying. I'm so embarrassed that I can't look at him, can't move, can't even bring myself to try to get up, despite the fact that he's no longer holding me down.

I wait for him to clean me up, to fix my dress, to reach for me, but a second later I hear the sound of his footsteps walking away, and although I wait a few minutes more, they don't come back.

That's when it hits me.

He touched me for the first time where no one besides myself ever has, brought me so close to an orgasm that I was *almost* on the verge of begging him for it, and then came all over my ass—and left me here.

Like a discarded blow up doll. A toy. Something to use and forget about.

I can feel myself flushing hot with shame and rage and humiliation. I'd come *so* close to pleading for him to keep going, to make me come—hell, for a minute I'd even fantasized about what his tongue might feel like, or even—

No. I'll never let him have that. I'll never let him inside of me. If I have my way, he'll never even touch me like that again.

But even as I stand up, pushing my dress down and walking gingerly towards my room, I can't stop thinking about the way his fingers felt against me. He played me as expertly as an instrument, drawing his fingers over my flesh the way I draw my bow across my violin, bringing me to the very crescendo of pleasure before taking it away.

And then spilling his own all over me.

I can feel my eyes welling up with hot, embarrassed tears. I can feel him on me still, sticky and cooling as I strip my dress off in my room without even turning on the lights, throwing it into the laundry hamper and hurrying to the bathroom. I feel dirty now, humiliated, but I hadn't felt that way in the moment. When he'd stood over me just after pulling his hand away, I'd just been overwhelmed with plea-sure, flushed hot with it, and the thought of him stroking himself above me had almost turned me on more, until I'd thought I might come anyway, even without his touch.

I'd been on the verge of finishing it myself, but something had told me that would only make him angrier.

That, and the fact that I refused to give him a show. Never in a million years can I imagine myself doing that for his pleasure, touching myself while he watches. Just the thought makes me blush from my forehead to my toes all over again.

But you wanted it, the tiny voice in my head whispers as I step under the water. *You wanted him to make you come. You liked how it felt.*

"No," I whisper, gritting my teeth. I don't want to admit it to myself, not out loud and not even in my head. I don't want to admit that his fingers felt a thousand times better than mine ever have, that the way he built it up, slow and teasing, murmuring filthy things above me as he held me down over his couch, was so intensely erotic that I'd been more turned on than I've ever been in my entire life. I don't want to admit that I'd liked being pinned down, unable to argue, made to give in to the craving that's been simmering inside of me since he had me up against his front door.

I don't want to admit that for just a moment, at the height of it, I'd wondered what it would feel like to let him take my virginity. To *really*

185

make me his, in a way that his fingers on me or his cum on my skin could never really accomplish.

Although right now, washing him off of me in the shower, I feel pretty fucking *owned*.

And a tiny part of me, one that I don't want to examine too closely, likes it.

What would it be like to be really desired and loved by, really belong to a man like Luca? I'd never have to be afraid again. I'd never worry that he'd get tired of my rebelliousness, my stubborn refusal to give in, that he'd decide I was more work than I was worth. I could stop running, which if I'm being honest, is what I've been doing all my life. Planning to leave Manhattan after graduation was just a different kind of running away. Running from my past, my memories, all the things I didn't fully understand about my childhood and who my father really was.

Those answers are here. Safety is here too, if I allow myself to accept it.

But I don't just want Luca's tolerance. I don't want to give myself to him only to have him tuck me away in another apartment like a discarded sweater, a game he's already played, a story that he already knows the ending to.

There was a moment, a brief one, at the reception. One where I'd caught a glimpse of what it would be like if we were a normal couple, if we were getting married out of love instead of obligation.

Luca introduced me to his best friend, and Caterina's fiancé, a handsome red-haired, green-eyed man named Franco Bianchi—the only name I'd remembered—with pale skin and a freckled face that looked nothing like the other members of the family I'd met.

"Is he Irish?" I'd whispered when we'd walked away to find our seat at the table, and for the first time since I'd met Luca, I saw him struggle not to burst out laughing.

For the first time, I saw him as almost human.

In that moment, I'd caught a glimpse of what it would be like if we actually liked each other—even cared for each other. What it would be like to be married to him in some other reality, where we'd chosen this, and he wasn't heir to the mafia throne and everything that I despised, everything that took my parents from me. I could imagine, in that fleeting second, what it would be like to be at a party with Luca, whispering something inappropriate in his ear and watching him try not to laugh.

I saw the same realization in his eyes, too, when he looked over at me. The realization that I'd almost made him laugh—that I was a person, someone who he might actually like, if he took the time to get to know me.

Just as quickly as it had come, though, the moment had passed.

"Don't ever say that in his hearing," Luca had replied sharply—more sharply, probably, than he would have if we hadn't ever so briefly shared a moment. "It's a point of contention within the family. But no, he's not."

And with that, the subject had been dropped.

But I'd realized something in that moment, the same thing that I know now, standing in the shower and trying to shake off the memory of what just happened in his living room.

If I let him have me, *all* of me, I'd want him to love me.

And that's the most humiliating thing of all.

Because I don't think Luca Romano can love anyone.

When I'm clean again, the last traces of him washed off my skin, my hair sticking wetly to my shoulders, I get out and wrap a towel around myself, stepping out of the bathroom with a heavy heart.

If tomorrow were a normal wedding, I'd be spending this night away from our shared apartment, in some fancy hotel room with my bridesmaids. Ana and I would be laughing about something—probably her insisting on joking and teasing me about the upcoming wedding night. I'd be happy, joyful, anticipating one of the best days of my life.

Instead, I'm back in a bedroom that doesn't feel like mine, with a fiancé who has barely spoken to me in a week, except for at the rehearsal today, and then tonight to whisper filthy things in my ear until he came all over my bare ass. I'll spend the night alone in my strange new bedroom, and I won't see Ana until tomorrow, when she comes to help me get dressed.

I don't even know if Luca is dragging me onto a faux honeymoon, to keep up appearances. I'm guessing he won't—but who knows? It would be just like him to force us into spending a week avoiding each other in the Caribbean, or something insane like that.

After tonight, who knows?

It doesn't matter, I tell myself firmly as I reach for the lights. After tomorrow this whole mess of a wedding will be over, and we can go back to ignoring each other. Hating each other. Trying to spend as much time away from each other as possible. I can forget about what happened tonight, and we can move on. Luca can go back to fucking as many nameless women as he wants, and I can pretend like I was never close to begging him to let me come.

But now, with that memory still filling my head, I can't help but think of how tomorrow night could be different.

It's just my luck that he's fucking gorgeous. If he were older, or ugly, or losing his hair, it would be easy to avoid sleeping with him. But instead, I'm engaged to the most gorgeous man I've ever seen. A man with a jawline that could cut glass and piercing green eyes, a man who wears suits that fit him like a second skin, a man who kisses like he wants to eat and drink and breathe me all at once, like my mouth is the only thing keeping him from dying. Like he wants to devour me.

Thank God we're getting married in a church, I think grimly. If he kissed me like that tomorrow, I'm not sure what I would do.

Climb him like a tree in front of everyone, probably, and damn the consequences.

I flick on the light, and my heart stops in my chest.

The room isn't strange and unfamiliar anymore. While we were gone, it's been transformed. The grey quilted duvet on the bed has been replaced with my thick blue-flowered one, the sleek white hotel-style pillows have been replaced with mine from my apartment, and the cable-knitted, light pink blanket that I used to love curling up under on rainy days is thrown across the foot of the bed. My book-shelf is against one wall, filled with my books, and as I walk further into the room, I see my jewelry box sitting on the nightstand. Next to it is a flat black box and a smaller velvet one, and a note.

I don't move to read it yet, though. I feel like I can't breathe, and I can't stop the tears from welling up in my eyes.

My things are here. Not everything I owned, but everything important to me—or at least almost everything—

And then I walk around to the other side of the bed, and I see it.

My violin case, propped against the wall.

I reach up to touch the necklace at my throat, my heart racing in my chest. I don't know who did this for me, or why—but what I do know is that it couldn't have happened without Luca's approval. He had to have allowed this—if he didn't outright ask for it himself.

Confusion floods me as I sit down on the edge of the bed, smoothing my hands over my duvet, looking at my violin case with watery, stinging eyes. *I don't understand him,* I think, frustration welling up in me. I can't reconcile the man who coldly told me to choose between marrying him and death, the man who's avoided me for the last week, the man who wouldn't even look at me on the drive home tonight, the man who pinned me down over a couch and used me as a fuck toy, with the man who left dinner outside my room, who defended Ana, who now has given me a better wedding gift than I would have ever thought to ask for—the feeling of being at home in my own room, on one of the most difficult nights of my life.

As if he knew how hard tonight would be for me, how scared I am of tomorrow, and wanted to make it better somehow.

Slowly, I sink down to the floor, reaching for my violin case. For eight years, I've left the last letter that my father wrote me inside of it, because I couldn't bear to read it. But now on the eve of the wedding to the man that he promised me to, the man he *entrusted* me to, I know it's time.

Maybe it will help me understand, somehow. Because I've never felt more confused than I do at this moment.

The envelope is still tucked in the lining of my violin case, stiff and slightly yellow with age. I open it carefully, sliding out the sheet of paper with my father's spidery cursive trailing across it—the last words that he will ever say to me.

I can feel tears welling in my eyes before I even begin.

My dearest Sofia,

If you're reading this, it's because I'm no longer here. That's a cliché way to begin a letter like this, I know, but I don't know of any other way to start this off. It's breaking my heart to write this, because I can't bear the thought of leaving you so soon, of missing out on so much of your life.

You have so much ahead of you, my darling girl, and I want you to have all of it. I want you to have the life you dreamed of, to go boldly forward and pursue every talent and gift that you've been given. You are the smartest, most beautiful, most talented daughter that your mother and I could have asked for, and I have never regretted that you are my only child, Sofia, because it meant that all of the love I have to give is yours. You are the light of our lives, and if I have one regret, it's that my own choices might ever put you in danger.

And that, Sofia, is why I'm writing this letter. In the future, you may find out things about your dear father, things that might cause you to question who I am, and if I'm really the man you think you know. It's fair for you to question those things. But if there's one thing you never question, I hope that it's my love for you.

If events come to pass as I think they might, and this letter finds its way into your hands, know that I will have taken steps to protect you and your mother from what might come after. Know that I've done my best to make sure that you're provided for. And know that I have made a choice—one that you might not understand, one that might even make you resent me, but that I feel was the only one I could make, under the circumstances.

Marco Romano was my best and dearest friend, and it is my hope that he will raise his son to be like him, a man who does what he must, but who takes no joy in cruelty, a man with honor, who will keep the vow that I will ask his father to make. I can't tell you here what that promise is, but please know, my dearest daughter, that I would not have done it if I felt there were any other choice.

The tears are falling too hard and fast for me to continue reading, and I set the letter down, afraid of getting it wet and causing the ink to run. All I can think of is my father in his office at home, writing this letter with me in my room a few doors down, knowing that death was coming for him.

His heart was breaking, and I never knew it. There was so much about him that I didn't know, and I cover my mouth with my hand as the grief hits me all over again, my entire body shaking. I will never, ever know the other half of the man my father was, the part of him that he hid from us. All I have is this letter, and the knowledge that he trusted his friend to raise a son worthy of me, if the day came that I had to marry him.

So is Luca that man? Or did my father misjudge his friend? Did his friend fail? A half an hour ago, I would have said yes. But now, sitting here surrounded by the trappings of my bedroom, I can't help but wonder if *I'm* the one who has misjudged Luca. If there's something more under his cold, heartless exterior, the way Father Donahue hinted that there could be.

Gingerly I wipe my hand on my skirt, reaching for the letter again.

I say all of that to say this, however—Sofia, if you have the chance to be free, to escape this life, I hope with all of my heart that you will seize it with both hands. It is the one great regret of my life that I didn't take you and your mother, and run as far away from it as I could. There are some who will say that there is no leaving this life, and they very well might be right. But I wish more than anything that I had not been too much of a coward to try. If I had, perhaps I wouldn't be writing this letter to you now.

Be free, my darling daughter. Be all that you were meant to be. Sing, and play, and make music that the world will weep to hear, and remember, above all, the last gift that I gave you. Remember what I told you about fairy tales.

But more than that, Sofia, remember that I love you.

Your father,

Giovanni

For a long time, all I can do is sit there with tears leaking from my eyes, wrapped in a towel on my bedroom floor. And then I fold the letter back into its envelope and slip it back into my violin case, closing it gingerly and pushing myself to my feet.

I walk back to my nightstand, and the two velvet cases sitting there.

Picking up the flat one first, I open it to see a delicate gold bracelet, essentially a looped chain with sapphires set into the ovals. And when I open the smaller velvet box, there's a matching pair of earrings—oval-cut sapphires so richly blue that they're almost black surrounded by diamonds and dangling from gold posts. They're beautiful and look expensive, and well-loved. The gold is slightly burnished in places on the bracelet, as if someone wore it often and touched it.

With my heart pounding in my chest, I reach for the note next.

Sofia,

Anastasia tells me that it's customary for a bride to have something old, new, borrowed and blue. She also tells me that the necklace you wear, that you never take off, is very old—so I suppose that will be taken care of. Your ring and dress are new, so here is your something blue—a bracelet and earrings that belonged to my mother. You may also consider them borrowed, if you like, although I would like it very much if you would keep them. As my wife, she would want you to have them.

--Luca

I stare at the note and the jewels, my thoughts whirling with confusion. How can the man who brought me home tonight and the man who wrote this letter be the same person? How can he sometimes seem to hate me, to resent me or want nothing other than to break me to his will, and then give me a wedding present of his mother's jewelry?

Part of me wants to refuse to wear it tomorrow. I could—he won't see me until I walk down the aisle, and what is he going to do about it then?

But as I look down at the bracelet and earrings, his note still clutched in my hand, I know I won't. I feel worse than ever, anxiety and confusion churning in my stomach as I gingerly close the boxes and lay back on my bed, knowing that a sleepless night is ahead of me.

It was easier just to hate him. Just to see him as someone keeping me prisoner, a cruel man who I'd been given to against my will. The villain of the fairytale, the dragon at the tower. It was easier when it was black and white.

Now my emotions are a tangled mix of hate and fear and desire and curiosity, wondering what tomorrow will bring and how we'll go forward after that. The thought of our wedding night makes my stomach clench all over again—now that he's touched me, what happens next? He said he wouldn't force me—but what if he doesn't have to?

What if, in the end, he convinces me to let him?

He awakened something in me tonight, an awareness of pleasure that I never had before. The idea of spending years, if not the rest of my life never being touched like that again makes me ache in a way I don't fully understand—but the thought of giving myself over to him completely feels just as impossible.

I wish, more than anything, that none of this had happened. Then I wouldn't feel so lost, so confused.

But it did. And tomorrow, I'll be Luca's wife.

SOFIA

$\mathcal{I}$'m woken up by Ana's hand on my shoulder, shaking me awake as the sunlight streams in from the curtains she must have opened, sprawled on the side of my bed. "Wake up, sleepy," she says with a grin. "It's your wedding day."

"Those aren't really the words I wanted to wake up to," I groan, rubbing a hand over my face.

"I know." Ana pushes my hair out of my face, looking down at me sympathetically. "But at least I'll be here for part of it. I picked up your dress on the way over."

I can see it hanging on the closet door, wrapped in the cheerful pink and white garment bag from the bridal shop. I push myself up to a sitting position, feeling tired and sore from being tense all night. Glancing over at Ana, I wonder what she would say if I told her what had happened last night between Luca and I. There's no way I ever could—I can feel myself flushing red just thinking about it. But after so long of hearing about her sexual exploits and her teasing me about my lack thereof, I can't help but wonder what her reaction would be.

Before she can see that I'm blushing, I get out of bed and quickly walk over to the dresser. But when I open the top drawer, I see that instead of the mostly plain cotton and few pairs of silky underwear that I'd picked out during my shopping spree, the drawer is also full of all the lingerie I'd skipped over, satin and silk in lace in white and pink and blue and red and black, frothing over the edge of the drawer as I open it. There's got to be thousands of dollars of it just in this one small spot.

"Sofia? What's wrong?" Ana asks, seeing me tense, but I don't respond, striding across the room to the closet. When I yank open the door, sure enough, there's new velvet hangers there with silk and lace robes and matching silk babydoll nightgowns. I stare at them, unsure whether to scream or cry or rip them off the hangers and throw them down the stairs so Luca can trip over them.

I hear her footsteps as she walks over to me. "Oh," she says softly, seeing the lingerie in the closet and the rest of it spilling out of the drawer. "You didn't pick this stuff out, did you." It's not a question, Ana knows my underwear choices very well. She's seen me get dressed often enough.

"No," I say flatly. "And it wasn't here before I came back last night."

"Luca told me he wanted your things brought over," Ana says quietly. "I thought it was strangely—nice of him. But he must have added all of this too." She pauses. "Are you—going to sleep with him tonight?"

"I made him promise we wouldn't," I whisper. "That it would just be a marriage of convenience, not real in that sense—" I look at the silky white nightgown in front of me, short enough to graze the tops of my thighs, edged in eyelash lace with lace cutouts at the waist. It's beautiful and fragile and expensive, the kind of thing any bride would dream of wearing on her wedding night.

When I turn around, Ana is looking at me disbelievingly. "And he agreed to that?"

"Originally, yes, but—"

"Sofia." Her face is very serious. "If you don't sleep with him, your marriage can be annulled. You know that, right? If he changes his mind about keeping you safe, if Rossi pressures him after the fact, he could make your marriage disappear just by admitting to that. Hell, if the Bratva got their hands on you again, you're more valuable if you're still untouched—" She looks slightly pale. "Sof, just sleep with him once. You'll be so much safer."

"I can't," I whisper, shutting the closet door so that I won't have to see the dress. "I just can't."

"Do you not find him attractive?" Ana cocks her head sideways. "Do you not want him like that?"

"I—" The memory of last night sears its way into my brain again, the memory of his fingers intruding where no one else's ever have, the way he stroked me until I was trembling, shaking, desperate for more. The feeling of him trapped between my thighs, making it so easy to imagine the way he might feel sliding inside of me. He was so hard, so thick—almost frighteningly so, but it had turned me on, too.

"You're blushing." Ana narrows her eyes. "Because you do want him, or because something happened?"

She knows me too well. "Something happened," I mumble. "Last night."

"Oh my god." She grabs my elbow, steering me towards the bed. "What?"

"I wandered off from the rehearsal dinner, and he was angry when he found me. He thought I was leaving. He said I embarrassed him— so I guess maybe he wanted to humiliate me, too? He brought me back here and kissed me—"

"And?" Ana prods. "You can tell me, Sof, I've told you so many things I've done. I'm not going to be shocked."

She's right, of course—she's shared the dirty details of so many of her hookups gleefully, right down to their dick size—or lack thereof— and the weird things they did or wanted to do in bed. But *I* never have before.

"He bent me over the couch and touched me—" I wave a hand vaguely below my waist.

"Did he make you come?" Ana stares at me. "You've really never done more than kiss before, have you?"

I'm blushing furiously now. "No," I whisper. "And no. He got me close—and then he stopped. He wouldn't let me."

"What a dick," Ana mutters. "But that's a hell of a way to get his point across, I guess. What else?"

"He—" I can't even form the words. "He finished, on my—on me."

"Oh shit." Ana covers her mouth with her hand. "I mean—normally I would think that's kind of hot, but without asking, I guess—no, I'd still think it's kind of hot. But for you—"

"I was just embarrassed," I whisper. "Maybe it would have been different if he'd stayed afterwards, if he'd made me...come...too, or acted like he cared at all. But he just walked off. Left me there bent over the couch with my dress up and left as soon as he'd finished. Like a used sex toy or something."

Both of us are very quiet for a long moment. Ana looks at me sympathetically. "I don't think he knows how to do anything else with a woman, honestly. From what I've heard about him, he's been fucking and discarding women all over Manhattan since he was old enough to get boners."

"So you see why I don't want to sleep with him," I say dryly.

"Don't want to? Or won't?"

That really is the question, isn't it? "Won't," I finally admit. "Of course I think he's gorgeous, Ana. He's the hottest man I've ever seen up close. And he knows what he's doing when it comes to—" I bite my lip, trying to push the memory of last night out of my head.

"So why?"

"It's the only thing I can keep," I whisper. "I can't finish my education. My plans for my life are gone. I live here now—soon I'll live in an apartment he chooses for me. I have to marry him, obey him, act like I'm happy to be his wife in public—all so that I can live. So I don't have to spend the rest of my life looking over my shoulder. The only thing I can control is whether or not I sleep with him tonight."

Ana chews on her lip for a moment, looking over at me. "That makes sense," she says finally. "I'm sorry, Sofia. If I could think of any way for you to get out of this—"

"I know."

"Just be careful." She leans over, wrapping her arms around me in a tight hug. "Be smart. Don't let your emotions get the better of you."

I hug her back, clinging to her for as long as I can. She smells like her sweet vanilla perfume, and I'm taken back briefly to afternoons spent in her room while she got dressed for a date, or snuggling together on the couch watching a movie, or hanging out in the kitchen together trying to bake something new. An entire life, a friendship, pulled away from me in an instant. Luca might let her visit me still, or go out under heavy security, but it'll never be the same.

"Come on," Ana says, and I can see that her eyes are as misty as mine are. "Let's get you dressed."

* * *

AN HOUR LATER, my hair is curled and pinned back and my makeup is applied, soft and rosy so that I look like I'm glowing. Ana zips up my dress and does every single one of the buttons down the back, and then slides a small gold and diamond comb into my hair, attaching the veil to it. "This was my grandmother's," she says. "You can give it back to me later, but for now it can be your something borrowed."

The jewelry. That reminds me of Luca's gift. "Thank you," I tell her, turning gingerly in my high heels to hug her again. "My something blue is in those boxes."

Ana's mouth drops open when she flips up the lid on the smaller one. "Oh my god—these are *gorgeous.*"

"They were Luca's mother's," I say softly. "He left them and the bracelet that matches last night."

Ana looks as confused as I felt. "I don't understand him," she says, shaking her head.

"I don't either." I turn to face the mirror, pushing a stray curl out of my face. "But I'm marrying him today."

By the time we're done, I'm the vision of a perfect bride. The dress fits flawlessly, my hair and makeup are perfect, the diamonds and jewels at my ears and wrist and finger sparkle in the light, and the veil floats out behind me like a soft cloud of tulle.

I reach up, touching the cross at my throat, the only piece of jewelry I'm wearing that looks slightly out of place—although I couldn't care less. "I wish my mother were here," I say quietly. "And at the same time, I'm glad she's not, so that she doesn't have to know this is happening."

"I'm so sorry, Sofia." Ana looks as if she's struggling to hold back tears. "I wish this could be a happy day for you."

"I'm just glad you'll be there at the ceremony." I take a deep breath, looking in the mirror one final time. "Alright. Let's go."

I'm glad that I don't have to worry about seeing Luca as we leave. The limo driver is waiting for us at the elevator, and the limo is in the parking garage, gleaming and black under the lights. Ana doesn't bother getting out the champagne once we slide inside—neither of us feel like celebrating. Instead I watch the traffic slide past as we drive to St. Patrick's, thinking about how I'm going to get through the next hour, the reception after that—and tonight. We're staying at the Plaza Hotel tonight, along with the rest of the major wedding guests, and Luca informed me the day I signed the contract that we would have to spend the night in the same room, regardless of my conditions.

Even if he sticks to his promise not to touch me, I still have to spend an entire night with him. There's no way out of that. It would bring up too many questions for me to have my own room, even if we spent enough time together in his to fake a consummation. I know there's no chance of escaping that part of the night.

The sky is grey and cloudy as we step out of the limo, the cathedral looming over Ana and I as we walk up the steps. Caterina is waiting for us in the vestibule, wearing a deep blue lace gown and holding a bouquet of white roses and baby's breath. She hands me a larger bouquet, looking at Ana nervously. "I'm sorry," she says softly. "I'm supposed to stand up with her as her bridesmaid. It should be you, but—"

"Can't have the Russian girl standing up in front of a cathedral full of Italian mafia," Ana says dryly. "I get it." She leans over, pecking me on the cheek before drawing the veil over my face. "You can do this, Sof," she says gently. "You're stronger than even you know."

"Only because of you." I squeeze her hand. "I'll try to catch you before we leave the church. And I'll see you soon, I promise. I won't let Luca keep us apart."

"I hope not." Ana gives me a sad smile before slipping into the church to find her seat, avoiding Caterina's eyes the entire time.

Caterina bites her lip. "I'm so sorry," she whispers.

"It's okay." I take a deep breath, forcing a smile as I clutch the bouquet. "It's not your fault."

"I—"

Whatever Caterina was about to say is interrupted by Franco stepping through the doors. He whistles as he sees me. "I'll never understand why Luca has such a long face right now," he says with a laugh, reaching for Caterina's arm. "Come on, love. I'll escort you up."

Caterina gives me a last tight smile as the wedding march begins, drowning out anything that either of us might say.

My heart is pounding in my chest as I wait for it to be my turn, my stomach twisting in knots. *Don't trip*, I think wildly as I wait at the doors. *Don't cry.*

Don't be afraid.

I can see Luca when I start to walk down the aisle, carefully timing my steps to the music. I'm glad for that, it gives me something to concentrate on, but I can't tear my eyes away from him. He looks more handsome than ever, tall and lean in a perfectly tailored charcoal suit, but his face is hard as stone. I can't see any emotion there when I finally come to stand at the end of the aisle, hoping that my bouquet hides the trembling in my hands.

Father Donahue clears his throat as the music dies away. "Who gives this bride to be married?"

The words stick in my throat. For a moment I think that I won't be able to speak, and my gaze flicks to Luca under my veil, wondering what he's thinking. I remember his words from the night before. *One phone call, and you would be dead.*

"I do." I manage to say the words aloud, firmly, not in the whisper that I was afraid they would come out as. I think I see a flicker of admiration in Luca's eyes as I step up to stand in front of him, but I can't be sure.

The Mass goes on for what feels like forever, the communion, the prayers, the Scripture, the words. I focus on the motions of it, remembering the kneeling and standing, when to face Luca and when to face Father Donahue, just to get me through. The less I think about what's really happening, the better.

As Father Donahue begins to say the vows, I can barely focus on the words. Luca's broad smooth hands grasp mine, holding me there, although not as tightly as I'd expected. I hear him repeat *love, cherish, honor*, and it's all I can do not to laugh. He plans to do none of those things, and I can't help but wonder why it's *my* virginity that could make our marriage null, when every word that Luca is saying in this supposedly holy moment is a lie.

When it's my turn, I can feel my pulse rising into my throat, threatening to choke me. "I, Sofia Natalia Ferretti, take you, Luca Antonio Romano, to be my husband." The words come out calmly, evenly, and I don't know how I'm even managing to say them aloud, let alone as if everything is fine. As if I want to be here, saying these vows. "I promise to be faithful to you in good times and bad, in sickness and in health, to love and honor—"

I pause. *Obey.* I can't bring myself to say it. I don't want to obey him. I don't want to belong to him—but last night I did. Last night my body arched towards him like a flower seeking the sun. *That was lust, not love,* I think. *Not obedience.*

Luca's hands tighten around mine warningly. I can see the look in his eyes through the haze of the veil, telling me that I'm on thin ice right now. That I should choose my next words carefully.

Behind me, someone clears their throat. Don Rossi? A wave of cold fear washes over me, and I choke out the words, tripping over them in my haste. "—to love and honor and obey you, all the days of my life."

Luca's grip loosens, and as I look up at him, I see something like relief on his face. *Is he really that glad that I'm going through with it? I* wonder numbly. *Does he really want me to live that badly? Why?*

The rest of the ceremony goes by in a blur. I barely register Luca sliding my wedding band onto my finger, barely make it through my own remaining vows as I clumsily slide his gold band onto his. Before I know it, I hear Father Donahue telling Luca that he can kiss the bride, and as Luca reaches for the edge of my veil, I feel faint.

His hand brushes against the side of my face as he pushes the tulle over my head, sending it cascading over my hair, and then his palm is pressed against my cheek as he tilts my face upwards, his lips brushing over mine in a sweet, almost chaste kiss.

I can feel tears burning the backs of my eyelids. *This is what it would be like if this were real. If he loved me. If I loved him.* The kiss is gentle, the way you kiss someone you love, and my heart aches painfully as I savor it for just a second, knowing that it might be the only time for the rest of my life that anyone kisses me that way.

It's a lie, but I let myself take a second's pleasure in it, just the same.

And then we're turning, facing the clapping audience in their pews, and I hear Father Donahue's voice behind us.

"I present to you, Mr. and Mrs. Luca Romano!"

It's done. The vows are said, the marriage is witnessed.

I'm Luca's wife.

For as long as we both shall live.

LUCA

I'm a married man.
Finally.

Not to the marriage itself, of course. I would have been very happy to spend all my days as a confirmed bachelor. But now that the deed is done, witnessed and signed and sealed, I can turn my attention to eliminating the immediate Bratva threat, sending them crawling back to their own territory, and then putting Sofia in a nice, luxurious apartment as far from me as possible.

I can forget about her. About what happened last night. About how fucking *good* it was, how it turned me on more than any sex I've ever had, despite how little we actually did. Last night did nothing to satisfy my desire for her. If anything, it stoked the flames even higher.

Which is why I need her out of my sight as soon as possible, before I repeat what happened last night. Worse, before I lose all control together.

The reception is a grand affair, entirely put together by Caterina and Giulia Rossi. Sofia looks slightly forlorn as we walk in, and I turn towards her, forcing myself to look as pleasant as possible. "Neither of us is going to enjoy this," I tell her flatly. "But at least try to not look as if you're going to burst into tears."

Sofia says nothing. Her face looks paler than normal. "Let's just get this over with," she murmurs, not meeting my eyes. "I won't wander off this time."

There's a cutting edge to her voice that startles me, but I choose to ignore it. Instead I take her hand, which sits limply in mine, our fingers barely linked as we walk through the wide double doors into the reception hall.

It's all gold and white, with expensive looking linens and chairs and china throughout the room, sprays of white and pink flowers on every possible surface, and our table at the front of it all. "The sweetheart table," Sofia murmurs with a hint of sarcasm, following my eyes. For once, I agree with her attitude towards it.

Everything has been planned out to the most minute detail, and none of it feels personal to either of us, which seems fitting. I keep a pleasant smile on my face as we pass through the guests, and to my surprise Sofia does as well, but inwardly all I want is for this to be over. I'm already calculating the minutes until I can escape to the hotel.

Not that that's going to be more relaxing, really. Sofia and I have to spend the night together, which means it'll either be awkward as hell, or some variation of last night, where neither of us leaves entirely satisfied.

All of that, combined with my new undesired status as a husband, has me in a dark mood. But I didn't get to where I am by not controlling my emotions, and so there's not a person in the room who would realize it.

Except maybe Sofia. Surprisingly, I catch her looking over at me from time to time as we take our place at the table and dinner begins to be served, a slight concern in her eyes. *Is she worried for herself, or for me?* I wonder grimly, stabbing at the filet on my plate.

The food is delicious, five-star and undoubtedly expensive, but it does very little to improve my mood. I've spent my whole adult life dining in fine restaurants, so a pricey meal on my own dime isn't exactly a treat. Sofia and I barely speak to each other, using the food as an excuse, but that can't last forever either. Eventually the time comes around for ridiculous wedding traditions like our first dance, and I have to face the necessity of touching my bride, again.

Not that I don't want to touch her. Precisely the opposite, actually. The memory of what we did last night is still burned into my thoughts, and I've had to struggle all day not to think about it purely to avoid the inevitable physical reaction. And the kiss in the church—

I'd barely managed not to get hard. I'd kept the kiss short and brief for exactly that reason, but even that brush of my lips against hers had made me ache for more. I'd never kissed her like that before, sweetly and gently, my hand against her face, cupping it as I kissed her tenderly. I'd done it for the sake of the people watching, to keep up the act, but in the end it had made me want something that I'd never known I could desire.

It made me think of what it could be like to have a wife I love, a real connection with someone, and for a brief moment I'd longed for it.

It's not possible, I remind myself. Truly loving something means the possibility of losing it. And I'm not certain I even have the capacity to feel that, for anything or anyone. It would make me too vulnerable, too raw, when I've spent my life training myself to be anything but.

The first dance song is something slow and sweet that I don't recognize, something about finding true love in strange places, probably something on the top 100 chart that Caterina picked. When I take Sofia in my arms I can feel that she's stiff and tense, and I lean close to whisper in her ear.

"Look like you're enjoying it," I murmur, swaying with her. "We're supposed to be happy."

Sofia tilts her head back a little, looking up into my eyes. For the first time I notice that hers aren't just brown, they're almost hazel, with small flecks of green and gold. I've never been this close to her and had the presence of mind to notice her eyes before.

"Don't you ever get tired of lying?" she asks softly. "Doesn't it just get exhausting?"

"Most of my lying has been done since I met you." I raise an eyebrow, looking down at her, and she frowns, obviously confused.

But before either of us can say anything else, the music ends and a more upbeat song begins, signaling time for everyone else to start flooding onto the dance floor.

Don Rossi appears at my elbow, smiling broadly. "Can I have a dance with the bride?" he asks, his tone almost jovial, and I have no choice but to hand her over. Sofia goes slightly pale again, but I just keep my pasted-on smile, my hand gliding over her waist as I pass her off. "Enjoy," I whisper wryly, and stride back to the table where my drink is waiting.

It's gone far too soon. I take a last swig of the expensive scotch and head towards the bar, which is four-deep with guests waiting for their drinks. I can't begin to count how many are here—the Rossi women certainly did their due diligence in making sure that *no one* could possibly feel slighted by not receiving an invitation.

I, on the other hand, might feel more than a little slighted once I'm handed the bill.

With Sofia occupied, I take the time to wander off on my own, making a trip to the men's room with glass in hand, and walking slowly back in no hurry to rejoin the party. But it's on the way back that I turn a corner and find myself face to face with Don Rossi, who has a darker expression on his face than I've ever seen when looking at me.

"Luca." His voice is cold and hard, making me flinch a little despite myself. I've heard him speak in that tone before, and what usually follows after isn't something that I'd ever want directed my way. "We need to talk."

"Well, that's a sentence no man ever wants to hear, especially at his wedding." I grin, hoping to lighten the mood, but Rossi doesn't so much as blink.

"Somewhere private."

"Well, I just came from the men's room." I try again, but if anything, his expression only darkens more.

"This isn't a joke, Luca. Let's go, now."

We end up standing in a far corner of the hotel lobby, far from where passing guests or curious ears could overhear anything, and especially far from the reception. I frown, looking at him curiously. "What's going on? Is it the Bratva?" Far from keeping the wedding and party under wraps, we'd done all we could to broadcast it. We wanted every Bratva man from Manhattan to Jersey to Baltimore to know that Sofia Ferretti had been wed, and was no longer a piece in the game.

"No," Rossi says curtly. "Something much closer."

"I've had too many scotches for you to talk in riddles," I say flatly, a tiny bit of irritation creeping in. "What is it?"

"You'd do well to watch your tone with me, son." Rossi's voice is colder than I've ever heard it when we've talked, even on the rare occasion that he's been displeased with me. "Do you know what I do to men who lie to me?"

With those words, my body goes cold as the grave. *Fuck*. I don't know how he could have discovered the truth, or why he'd gone digging, but I know exactly what's coming next. And worse yet, I have no excuse.

No excuse, other than the fact that you're besotted with the girl, which is something he'll view as weakness. And if Rossi thinks Sofia makes me weak, he'll see her as even more of a liability. Just because we're married doesn't mean that she can't ever meet with an accident—and if Rossi thinks my loyalty is compromised, he won't hesitate.

This is why I can't love. Why I can't get so close to someone that they distract me. Why every woman I've ever taken to bed has been promptly kicked right back out.

Love is weakness. And weakness is not tolerated here.

"You told me Sofia wasn't a virgin. That there was no need for witnesses the morning after because she would leave no stain. And now, Luca, I find out that you've lied to me."

I don't bother asking him how he knows. If I had to guess, he cornered Sofia somehow and tricked her into admitting she was a virgin. I should have told her that I'd lied for her, but it's always been my experience that the more people who know about a lie, the worse off you are. And yet here I am—worse off.

All I can do now is try to salvage the situation.

"I don't know why you're trying to get out of going to bed with your wife," Rossi says disgustedly. "God knows she's beautiful enough, young and innocent—that ought to be enough for any man. Maybe she's conned you into agreeing not to touch her somehow—don't tell me if she did," he adds. "I respect you, Luca, and I don't want to be given any more reason to feel differently. But whatever the reason, it doesn't matter."

"I don't like the idea of forcing a woman," I say quietly.

"A man with morals." Rossi shakes his head. "I've never denied that every man should have his code, but this isn't the time, Luca. There can be no question about the legality of this marriage. I've told you that already. So I don't care what you have to do in order to get your cock up her, but that girl best be made a wife by tomorrow morning. We'll view the bridal bed as is custom." He pauses, and the look in his eyes sends another chill down my spine.

"I'm going easy on you this once, son," Rossi says, his voice emotionless and hard. "You've always been loyal and honest, and you've worked hard for me through the years. I couldn't have asked for more from Marco Romano's son. But if you lie to me again—" he shakes his head, and I know that whatever he says next, it will be the absolute truth.

"You'll die. And you'll die slow. I don't tolerate liars—especially not from those who stand to inherit everything I've built."

"I understand," I say quietly. "I'm sorry, sir." There's nothing else to say. Anything more is excuses—the damage is done. All that's left now is to repair it as well as I can manage.

"You'll take care of it?"

"Yes." I pause. "Can I ask you a question?"

Rossi shrugs. "Go ahead."

"Why do you care so much about keeping this promise? Why is it so necessary that Sofia dies, or marries me and becomes my wife in every way? You cared for my father and hers, I know, but you've done far worse than break promises to a friend. We both have. Why not send her away somewhere? Why not give her fake papers and a new life? Surely all this cost so much more."

I hadn't asked all of this before because this solution seemed simpler—I hadn't wanted to give Rossi a reason to think that I didn't want to marry her and choose his preference instead...eliminating her entirely. But the marriage is done now. And I can't help but wonder why there were only two options.

"If she's not dead, she needs to be able to be watched. We need to know where she is, always. Allowing her to disappear would mean that there was always a chance the Bratva could track her down and take her without our knowing."

"But again—is she really so valuable?" I haven't pressed him before, but now I push, despite his anger with me. He's been cagey about this all along, and if I'm going to tell Sofia that she has no choice but to go to bed with me tonight, I need to know the truth. I need to know as much as he'll tell me.

He only gives an inch. But it's something.

"She could be the downfall of the whole family," Rossi says grimly. "All I've worked for, all I've built, gone to the Bratva if they get their hands on her."

"How?"

I see his jaw clench. "Some things you don't need to know yet, Luca." He pauses, draining the last of his drink. "Just do your job. Fuck her, or else."

Rossi raises his glass in a mock toast then, turns on his heel, and leaves me standing there dumbstruck.

I thought I'd done all that I'd have to do. I'd sheltered her, lied for her, and married her.

But now I have to do something else altogether.

And she's not going to be happy.

SOFIA

S urprisingly, the reception turns out to be more enjoyable than I had expected, aside from my dance with Don Rossi. Everything he said to me made me feel uncomfortable, eager to be away from him, but once the song ended and he passed me off to another guest, I felt myself begin to relax just a little. It takes me a long time to even notice that Luca hasn't returned, I'm so busy dancing with everyone who wants a turn with the bride. I know I don't have a choice but to be gracious and participate in all of the pageantry, and even though I've never been one for big parties or dancing, I have to admit that the experience is better than I'd thought it would be.

If I forget that they're all either members of or affiliated to this family that has trapped me in an unwanted marriage, it's not so bad. Everyone is kind and congratulatory, laboring under the assumption that Luca and I want this marriage, and it's a pleasant change from feeling unwanted. Even Franco, who I would have thought would be aware of the entire situation, twirls me around the dance floor as happily as any best man might, congratulating me on marrying into the family.

It's not until Luca comes back that I know something's off.

He's always alternately cold and hot with me, wanting me one moment and closed off the next, but there's something different about him when he returns. He won't meet my eyes even when we cut the wedding cake, kissing me quickly on the cheek for a photo and not quite looking at me when we feed each other the obligatory piece of cake. He looks almost—guilty, as if he's keeping a secret that he doesn't want me to figure out.

We're staying at the same hotel where the reception is being held, and it goes on for what feels like hours and hours. For a family largely made up of middle-aged and older adults, they can certainly party, and by midnight everyone is well and truly drunk, feasting on the late night food that's passed around the reception.

"Caterina and Mrs. Rossi really outdid themselves," I whisper to Luca, trying to get him to say something, but he just grunts, ignoring me in favor of taking another swig of the scotch that's seemed to be in his glass continuously throughout the night. I can't tell if he's drunk or not, but he's at least got a decent buzz going on.

I, on the other hand, have remained stone cold sober. I don't trust myself not to say something out of turn, or maybe just burst into tears if I have more than one or two glasses of champagne. For all that the night hasn't been as terrible as I expected, it's still a reception for a marriage I didn't want, and there's not a single person I know here except for Caterina and Luca—which isn't saying much. I like Caterina a surprising amount for her being Don Rossi's daughter, but she's far from being what I would call a *close friend.*

It's not until we're sent off with cheers and applause and rowdy shouted jokes and in our room, the door firmly shut behind us, that Luca turns to me with an expression like someone just walked over his grave.

"We have to talk," he says quietly. He sinks into a nearby chair heavily, pulling at his tie, and I can see that he's a little drunk.

My heart skips in my chest, my throat tightening. Nothing about his tone suggests that it's something good, and I bite back my frustration. *I thought marrying you today meant everything would be okay,* I want to snap, but I don't. For once, Luca doesn't look cold, or irritable, or combative. He just looks exhausted.

As I stand there, waiting for him to say something else, I see his gaze trail over me, from my face all the way down my dress to the floor and back up again. There's nothing cold or assessing in it though, nor is there the hot desire that I've seen there before, the desire to possess me, to force me to bend to him.

"You look beautiful," he says softly, and all I can do is stand there speechless.

This isn't the Luca I know.

"What's going on?" I ask, my voice trembling a little. "Is there some problem? Has something gone wrong?"

"It's Rossi," Luca says, leaning forward.

"What about him?" I keep my voice carefully neutral, even as my heart starts to race. I can feel that old familiar pinging sensation, that warning of danger, and it's all I can do not to run out of the hotel room. But whatever Luca is about to tell me, whatever is about to happen, there's one thing that I'm certain of.

I'm not going to be able to escape it or outrun it. I can see it in his face.

"He knows that you're a virgin," Luca says carefully. "I don't know how he found out, but—"

I feel my blood turn to ice. For a second I can't breathe, the room swirling around me. I remember the conversation I'd had with him on the dance floor, and suddenly it all makes sense.

"It's my fault," I whisper. "I didn't know that he wasn't aware—"

Luca is on his feet in an instant, striding towards me. "What happened?" he asks sharply. His gaze meets mine, bright and intense, and I suddenly feel very small beneath it.

"He asked me if I was nervous." I pause, chewing on my lower lip. "I wasn't sure what he meant, and he said the wedding night—he wondered if I was worried about the first time."

"Did you tell him that I'd agreed not to touch you?" Luca's voice rises, deep and thunderous. "What the fuck did you say, Sofia?"

I shrink backwards. "Not much! I thought it was weird that he was asking me about having sex with you. I just said that I wasn't really nervous, that I was sure you knew what to do and that you'd help me through it. And then he just nodded like I'd answered some question for him, and passed me off to another guest who wanted to dance. I thought it was strange, but—"

The memory of my dance with Don Rossi comes back to me, the way he'd looked down at me with that charming smile on his face, his eyes flicking over me as if sizing me up. The way he'd casually asked "Are you nervous, little one? For your first night with a man like Luca?"

I'd said no, of course, that I wasn't nervous at all. "It's supposed to be something to look forward to, right?" I'd said cheerfully. "The first time with your new husband?" And he'd smiled knowingly, as if I'd just told him something he'd been curious about.

Which, of course, now I know that I had.

I look up at Luca, twisting my hands together to keep them from trembling. "What's going on?"

His jaw clenches tightly, the muscles there working, and I can see him holding on to his self-control. It makes me almost dizzy with fear, because I can tell that this is more than just him being irritated or pissed at me. Something is very, very wrong.

"I lied for you," he bites out, looming over me. "Do you know *anything* about the marital customs of mafia families, Sofia?"

"No," I whisper. "I never needed to, I—"

"The custom," he says sharply, each word coming out punctuated, "is that the parents of the bride and groom, the maid of honor and the best man all come up to the bedroom the next morning, to see that the marriage has been consummated. It's tradition, to prove that the marriage is real and legal, and that the bride's virginity has been taken by the groom. It's old and outdated," he adds, seeing the look on my face, "but it is custom. And since you insisted that I not touch you as a condition of our marriage, well—you can see how that put me in a difficult situation."

"You should have told me," I whisper. I feel as if I can't breathe.

"You're right," he admits, and I can feel my eyes widening just from

213

the shock of that admission. "But it's my experience that the more people who know you've told a lie, the more quickly that lie is found out."

"So what now?" I wrap my arms around myself, the soft lace of the dress rubbing against my skin. "What happens?"

Luca looks down at me for a moment, and the silence stretches out between us. "We have to sleep together tonight," he says finally.

I stare up at him, speechless. My first, immediate thought is that he's lying to *me*, so that he can get me into bed. But looking into his eyes, I can see that isn't the case. I've seen hunger in his eyes, and desire, and lust. I've seen the way he looks at me when he wants to make me beg for him, when he wants me to bend to his will. This isn't that. He looks almost defeated, like a man who is backed into a corner with no recourse.

I'm actually not sure which is worse. I didn't want Luca to force me, but I also don't want my first and possibly only experience in bed to be with him behaving like a man being led to his execution. "What happens if I say no?" I blurt out. It's the only thing I can think of to say.

"Then we're both dead," Luca says tiredly. "Rossi won't tolerate any chance that the marriage might be able to be annulled, however slight. And if he thinks my loyalty to you outweighs my loyalty to him, he won't tolerate that either. If somehow I survive it, it won't be with all my body parts or my position intact."

He says it so tonelessly, as if he's telling me that the sky is blue, or that it's spring. I, on the other hand, shrink back in horror. "But you're his heir," I whisper. "He'd dispose of you, one way or another, just like that? Over one lie?"

"Loyalty must be absolute." Luca gives me a small, tight smile. "We like to think that we're better than the Bratva, more cultured, but in our own ways we're equally as cruel. And Rossi can be a brutal man in his way." He looks down at me, and I can see in his expression that there's no way out. "Sofia, rape is very far down the list of things that Rossi would hesitate at. And while it's against *my* personal moral code, it's exactly what he expects of me tonight, if I refuse."

"So what do you want from me?" I whisper.

"I want you willing." He says it simply. "And if you're not—then I don't know what we do. I can't live with myself if I force you, Sofia. I can do a great many things, but not that. But I don't want to die slowly, either. So you see, I'm at an impasse."

It's the longest conversation we've ever had, and the most serious. It's the first time I've ever felt that he's spoken to me as an equal. It doesn't make me love him, not even like him, but it does make me hate him a tiny bit less. It makes me feel, for the first time, that he doesn't think of me as something to be used and managed. He at least, for once, is asking for my cooperation instead of demanding it.

I don't want to be married to him. I don't even want to know him. I want to be as far away from this as I can possibly be.

But that doesn't mean I want him to die, let alone in the ways I can imagine Rossi could come up with—and probably ways that I can't imagine. And I don't want to die, either.

"I'm sorry," I say simply.

His face pales a little, and I realize that he thinks that I'm telling him no, apologizing for not being able to give in. The momentary upper hand feels like a small victory, and I grab onto it as something to cling to.

"I'll do it." I bite my lower lip, feeling my skin tingle with fear and —although I don't want to admit it—a little anticipation. "I don't want this—but I don't want either of us to die. I just wish you'd told me that you'd lied," I finish softly. "After all, I am your wife."

The corner of Luca's mouth twitches just a tiny bit. He reaches out then, pushing a curl of hair off of my shoulder, the tips of his fingers tracing over my collarbone. It makes me breathe in sharply, and his eyes close for a moment.

"I'd prepared myself to sleep in a chair tonight," he says wryly. "I'm not sure that I wouldn't have touched you at all, Sofia, especially after last night. But I need you to know—" He takes a deep breath, and there's something unreadable in his eyes, something that I can't quite decipher. "I would never have taken your virginity against your will,

Sofia. I am not a good man, but there are some things even I wouldn't do."

"I know," I whisper. I can feel my pulse racing, and my mouth is dry, my hands shaking. "I—" *I'm scared,* is what I want to say, but I can't admit that to this man, this gorgeous, mercurial man who is looking down at me, preparing to take me to bed for the first time. I don't know him well enough—I don't *trust* him enough.

"I'll be as careful as I can," Luca says, his voice dropping an octave. I can hear it deepening, growing rougher, and it sends a quiver through me that might be from fear or desire, I'm not sure which. "But I can't deny that I want you, Sofia. And when the moment comes—"

I shouldn't want him. Nothing about this man should turn me on. But something about the roughness of his voice, hearing him say that he wants me so badly that he can barely control himself—this man who can have any woman he wants, arouses me despite myself. I can feel the dampness on my thighs, my skin tingling as his fingers trail down to the space between my breasts, down to the edge of my neckline.

"You are beautiful," he murmurs. "I mean that. You're a beautiful bride, Sofia."

I look up at him, watching him as his gaze trails over my breasts, and his face is utterly unreadable. I can't tell what he's thinking, what he's not saying, and my chest squeezes with anxiety. The few times that I'd tried to imagine my first time, it was nothing like this. Sometimes I pictured it happening out of nowhere, tumbling into bed with someone overcome with passion, other times I pictured it planned, sweet and slow and intentional.

Instead I'm in the most expensive, luxurious hotel room that I've ever been in, with the most gorgeous man that I've ever seen touching me like I'm a fragile treasure, instead of handling me roughly like he has before. He's trying to make this easier on me, I can tell, and somehow that makes it worse—because I know that he doesn't really care about me. In the end, he's just saving his own skin.

Luca looks up, meeting my eyes. "What do you want?" he asks, his voice low. "Do you want me to take my time? Do you want—" he breaks off, but I know what he's offering. A night of pleasure, of him treating me the way he would any woman that he brought home to bed, a night of discovering all the delights that can be had with him. All of the mysteries of sex, unveiled to me in a single night.

And a part of me wants it. I can't deny that. My skin is electric with his touch, my lips already tingling with the memory of his kiss. I've had a taste of what he can give me, and if my mind and heart are still resisting, my traitorous body is quicker to give in.

But as always, I have a choice. Maybe not as much of one as I'd thought, but I can choose how this night unfolds. How much I give him.

I want pleasure, but not if it means giving him something that I can't get back, something that I'll never get in return. And I know that if I open myself up, if I let myself indulge and lose myself in him for a night, I might lose everything.

I might lose more than just my innocence.

Luca is not a man who can ever love me. Not a man who can ever be my husband in any way except the strictest definition.

And I can't give him what I would, if he did.

"Just get it over with," I hear myself saying, my voice more emotionless than I've ever heard it. Even as I say it, I can feel my body rebelling, wanting more than just a quick deflowering, but I refuse to give in. "Do what you have to."

Luca tenses, his hand going very still above my breasts. I can almost see him reshaping, turning back into the cold, hard Luca that I know so well, and not the almost-vulnerable man of the past half hour. "Very well," he says, his voice flat, and I feel a chill in my stomach as I realize what I've done. I've turned tonight from something we could both take at least some pleasure in, back into a chore. A duty that neither of us wants. And now that Luca isn't trying to be gentle, he could be something far worse.

He turns me away from him then, his fingers pulling the buttons of my dress loose one by one, until the zipper is laid bare. The room suddenly feels very cold, and I shiver under his touch as he pulls the zipper down, inch by inch, revealing the smooth skin of my back to him. When the dress is open, the straps sliding slightly off of my shoulders, Luca lays his palm against my back. His hand trails downwards, the heat of it burning into my skin, and then he reaches up, pushing the straps off of my shoulders.

With a slight movement, the dress slides over my hips, pooling around my feet on the floor. For the first time, I'm standing in front of a man in nothing but my underwear. I suddenly regret wearing the lacy white panties that I'd chosen. They were for me, to make me feel beautiful, not for him.

As if he read my mind, Luca runs his finger over the edge of them. "You must have had some idea of what might happen tonight," he says dryly, hooking his fingertip in the lace. "Such delicate lingerie for a bride who planned to stay virginal."

"I wore them so I would feel good," I snap, crossing my arms over my bare breasts. "Not for you." I can feel my defenses going up again, now that I've chosen this path. My means of keeping myself safe from him.

Luca doesn't reply, but in the next instant he yanks them down with that one finger, letting them fall to the floor. I suck in a breath, realizing with a sudden wave of shock that I'm completely, entirely naked.

He reaches up, plucking the comb out of my hair so that it falls down loosely around my face, tumbling out of the twist that Ana put half of it up in. "Be careful!" I gasp. "That's Ana's—"

I hear it clatter as he drops it atop the nearby dresser. "Turn around," Luca says, his voice toneless. "I want to see my bride."

I bought you. I remember him saying those words to me last night, and they've never felt so real as they do now. The fact that my life is at stake has never been so harshly obvious as it is now. I'd wondered once what I would do if it came down to my virginity or my life—and I guess I've found out.

Slowly I turn to face him, my arms still crossed over my breasts. I'm acutely aware that everything else is visible to him, but Luca doesn't look further than where my arms are tightly wrapped around myself yet. He doesn't say a word, only reaches out and grabs my arms, pulling them down in a quick movement that leaves me entirely, completely bare to him.

I expect something. He's never failed to show me that he wants me before, never hidden his obvious desire. But now he simply looks at me appraisingly, and nods, as if I've met some standard I wasn't even aware of. And then he jerks his head in the direction behind me, his face still entirely unreadable.

"Go to the bed," he says harshly. "Pull the blanket back, lay down on the sheet and turn on the bedside light."

My breath catches in my throat. *I don't know what I wanted, but it wasn't this.* This isn't gentle or tender, but it's not the forceful desire of last night either. There's something cold and clinical about him, and I want to tell him that I've changed my mind, that I want him to make it good for me—for both of us, but the words stick in my throat. I can't quite manage it.

Slowly, I crawl onto the bed, laying back against the soft down pillows. The sheet feels silky against my bare skin, and I feel completely exposed, more vulnerable than I've ever been. I flick on the lamp by the bed, and Luca switches off the brighter overhead lights, leaving us in dim, more romantic lighting.

There's nothing particularly romantic about this, though.

Luca watches me as he pulls his tie loose, tossing it to the floor as he shrugs off his jacket. His eyes never leave me, drifting casually over my naked body as he starts to undo his shirt one button at a time, revealing the bare skin of his chest. At first it's just the lean, tanned, muscled flesh that appears, but as he pulls the shirt free and slides it off of his shoulders, I see to my shock that he's tattooed. There's a saint etched on one upper arm, and an intricate design on the left side of his chest, stretching up over his shoulder and partway down, all of it in blacks and greys, swirling over his smooth olive skin.

But that's not all that I can't stop staring at. Clothed, he's gorgeous, but shirtless he's something else altogether, something that I don't even have words for. His chest and abs are perfectly muscled, lean and rippling, the lines on either side of his abs disappearing into his suit trousers in a way that makes my mouth water despite myself. As his hands reach for his belt I can see that he's hard despite the fact that we've barely touched, and despite the fact that he's clearly trying to make this as impersonal as possible. He's still aroused by me—the thick, hard bulge that ruins the perfect line of his pants gives that away.

Luca sees my gaze flick downwards, and smiles, though it doesn't reach his eyes. "Like what you see?" he asks, sliding the fly of his pants down as he reaches for them and his underwear. Before I can say anything, he pushes it all down his hips, revealing the muscled curve there before he shoves them down and lets them fall, letting me see him entirely naked as well—my first time seeing a naked man in the flesh.

His cock springs up from between his muscular thighs, long and thick and hard, the tip gleaming with his arousal, and when he sees my gaze fix on it he reaches for himself, wrapping his hand around the length of it and stroking slowly as he walks towards me. "You wanted this last night," he murmurs hoarsely, his green eyes dark with lust as he approaches the bed. "You can't tell me that you didn't. I felt it. I felt how wet you were when I slipped between your legs—"

I feel breathless as he stops at the edge of the bed, afraid and turned on all at once, and I can't take my eyes off of him. I'm wet now, despite myself, my skin tingling, my nipples hard and stiff without his ever having touched them, and I wish that I didn't want him. But watching Luca walk towards me, sculpted like a Greek god with his rigid cock in his hand, I can't deny that my body is aching for him. I want to finish what we started last night—and it helps that I have no choice. I have to do this—and an ever-growing part of me wants to enjoy it.

He climbs onto the bed, and I breathe in sharply as he leans over me. I feel small in the shadow of his body, fragile and vulnerable, and as he kneels between my legs, I lay very still, like a rabbit hiding in the grass.

Luca looks down at me, his face smooth and unreadable, and I wish more than anything that I knew what he was thinking. His hand grazes my waist and I shudder, my body twitching under his touch as he drags his palm down to the curve of my hip. "This will hurt for a minute," he murmurs, his other hand sliding between my legs. "But I'll try to be gentle."

My heart is pounding. *He's not going to kiss me,* I realize. I'd asked for him to get it over with and that's exactly what he's going to do. He's following my wishes, which in a way is its own kindness, but my stomach knots with anxiety as I feel his fingers slide up my inner thigh, brushing over the soft, warm flesh between my legs.

I see his eyes darken with lust as he touches me. "Good," he says with satisfaction. "You're ready for me."

He's trying to make it sound cold, clinical, but even he can't quite manage it. I can hear the drop in his voice, the husky, rasping sound of desire as his fingers trail over my skin and my body responds despite everything, my hips arching up to meet his touch as I gasp softly. His hand moves, and I look down to see him tearing open a condom, rolling it down the length of his shaft as he doesn't meet my eyes.

No children. I remember the contract then, and I'm suddenly very glad he was prepared—until I remember that he never meant to have sex with me tonight. That condom was meant to be there for some other random encounter, some other woman, and I feel a sudden tightness in my throat, my eyes stinging with tears.

I shouldn't care, but I do.

Luca says nothing. He spreads my thighs wider, angling his cock towards me, and I feel my entire body stiffen as I realize that it's about to happen, he's about to—

"Relax," he says, glancing up at me. "It'll hurt more if you don't."

I feel the tip of his cock pressing against me then, and I squeeze my eyes tightly shut, my breath coming in small, short pants. I try to relax, but all I can think of is how *big* he is, how hard, and that there's no way he'll possibly fit—

"Oh!" I cry out as there's a sharp pain, a sudden pressure, and I realize that the first inch of him is inside of me. My eyes fly open and I see him kneeling there in the dim light of the room, his face shadowed, his body shuddering slightly as his hands cling to my hips. His eyes slide shut as he moves forward another inch, and a groan spills from his lips.

"You're so fucking tight," he moans, and I can see his hips jerking slightly, the effort of going slowly almost too much for him. I feel a sudden, sharp flood of desire through my body, a response to seeing him hovering on the edge of control.

I'm doing this, I think dimly. *Me. My body. It feels so good that he can barely control himself—*

"Oh fuck," he moans again, and I can feel that my body's reaction has made it easier than before for him to keep going, to slide another inch and then another, until suddenly he's leaning forward over me, his eyes still closed, and I realize that every inch of him is buried inside of me.

It did hurt. It still does, a little, but I can already feel the pain receding, replaced by something else—an ache, all the way down to my core, a need for something that I can't quite describe.

"Luca," I whisper, his name spilling from my lips despite myself, and his eyes fly open, meeting mine, his body trembling above me.

I see the moment that his control breaks. I see him trying to rein it in, trying to remain detached, trying to make this the cold duty that he framed it as earlier. But when he hears my voice whispering my name, I can almost *feel* what snaps inside of him, his entire body jerking as his hips arch against mine, and he lets out a deep, shuddering moan.

"Sofia," he groans, and then his lips come crashing down onto mine.

What am I doing? The thought screams through my mind, but my body is already reacting, my arms winding around his neck as his mouth slants over mine, his tongue thrusting between my lips as his cock thrusts into me again, and I feel my legs spreading open for him, my hips rising up to meet him as he slides into me. It feels good—not what I felt last night, not that tight, building, aching need to come, but something tells me that it could be that, eventually.

And everything else—*oh, god.* His skin against mine, warm and hot and smooth, the taste of his mouth, the vibrating sensation of his moans against my lips, his hands roving over my body as he loses himself in me. Even last night, he was in control, but all of that is gone now. There's only the surging wave of his body inside of mine, his cock thrusting over and over again in long, slow strokes that get faster as his breathing speeds up, matching mine as I arch against him, wanting to be closer. I've never felt anything like this before, and I'm beyond thinking about what this means—for me, for us, for our future. All I care about is the heat of his body against mine, the press of my breasts into his chest, the way I can feel him surrounding me in every way, and I have the sudden, desperate thought that I never want it to stop.

"Luca, Luca—" I cry out his name suddenly, arching against him tightly as I feel something shudder through me—not an orgasm, but some deep, primal urge to be close to him. It's as if I know he's close, and I'm right, because in the next moment he suddenly buries his face in my neck, another deep groan spilling from him as he thrusts hard into me. I feel his hips rock against me, as if he wants to sink even deeper, his cock impossibly hard, and his hands dig into the pillows on either side of my head, his entire body convulsing with deep, wracking shudders.

The moment it's over, he goes very still. His body hovers over mine, not quite lying on me, and then just as quickly, he rolls off of me, standing up.

I feel cold at the loss of his touch. Just as quickly as he lost control he regains it, the connection between us severed. Luca doesn't look at me as he peels the condom off, striding towards the bathroom to dispose of it and leaving me there, naked on the bed. My body feels strange, still turned on and unsatisfied, suddenly hollow where he was a few minutes ago. I want to grab the blanket and cover myself, but I can't seem to move, frozen to the spot as I wait for Luca to come back.

He turns the lights on when he steps out of the bathroom, flooding the room with light, and I blink rapidly, my stomach tightening as he strides towards me. Every sign of the man who just lost control while he was inside of me, who kissed me and touched me like he was starving, like he wanted nothing more than me, is gone. His expression is

steely again, his green eyes emotionless, and he stops at the edge of
the bed, his gaze flicking down to the space between my legs.

I see his expression change in an instant, from flat to angry, his jaw
clenching, and I instinctively tense.

"What's wrong?" I whisper, looking at him nervously. "Luca—"

"You didn't bleed." His voice is cold, laced with the kind of cold,
passionless anger that's more frightening than raw fury.

"What?" I scoot away from my spot on the bed, sitting up and
pulling my knees to my chest. The sheet is still smooth and white. "I
guess I didn't—"

"You lied to me." He bites off every word, his stony green eyes
latching on to mine. "You fucking lied to me, Sofia. And you made *me*
lie, except it wasn't really a lie—" he starts to laugh then, bitterly,
shaking his head. "What a fucking mess—"

"I didn't lie!" I exclaim, staring at him. "I'd never been with anyone
before, surely you could tell that—"

"You were tight, but that doesn't mean anything. Maybe you just
weren't a slut, like your little Russian friend." His words are a hiss, his
anger rising with every sentence. "You fucking lied to me, you little
bitch, you almost got me killed—"

"I didn't lie!" I shriek the words, suddenly terrified at this new level
of anger. "I didn't lie, Luca, I swear."

"Then why didn't you bleed?" he roars. "I have to have *proof*, Sofia,
proof for Rossi in the morning that I fucked you, that you're my wife,
or we're both dead!"

I stare at him, unbelieving. My fear recedes suddenly in the face of
the absolute ridiculousness of this whole situation, this whole stupid,
convoluted worry about my fucking *virginity,* which only ever meant
anything to me because it was a way to keep some part of myself separate from him. Now he's gotten what he wanted, he's fucked me, and it's
still not enough. I start to laugh, almost hysterically, shaking my head.

"What's so fucking funny?" Luca snaps.

"You men," I say, shaking my head. "You stupid, self-involved, *arrogant* men. You're fucking idiots, you know that?"

Luca looks at me coldly. "What?"

"Not all women bleed," I tell him flatly. "I thought I might, and you were so insistent that we had to have sex, and I didn't even really think about it because I was so shocked and scared by the whole situation—but Luca, not every woman bleeds the first time. There's a million ways that can happen without ever having sex—hell, the ballet lessons I took as a kid might have done it. Yoga. Whatever." I glare at him.

"You're fucking kidding me."

"No." I stifle another round of laughter. "You men and your all-important dicks, you think you're so special, that we all just gush blood the first time you stick it in us?" I can't keep the anger out of my tone. "You were so desperate to take my virginity, but even that wasn't enough. You have to make sure I fucking bled for you."

"This isn't a joke, Sofia," Luca warns. "Rossi isn't going to care." He rubs his hand over his mouth, his features drawn with tension and worry. "It's an outdated custom by any way of looking at it, I already told you that. But he's an old-fashioned man, and he wants proof that you're my wife in every possible way. He said—" Luca stops suddenly, pressing his lips together.

"What?" I ask, my heart suddenly fluttering in my chest. "What did he say?"

"It doesn't matter," Luca says crisply. "What does matter is what we're going to do now."

My stomach tightens nervously. *He's serious*, I realize. Not that I ever doubted it, exactly—but this is a real problem, as massively stupid as it is. "We could do it again," I suggest hesitantly. "Without a condom? A doctor could prove it then—"

"No," Luca says sharply. "I want no chance of children. And besides, Rossi will want blood. Blood is our way of life, our—" Luca turns away, striding towards the leather duffel bag sitting by the dresser, which I can only guess is his. He bends over, unzipping it, and when he strides back towards the bed I see what's in his hand.

A sharp, gleaming hunter's knife.

"What the fuck!" I squeal aloud, scrambling back. "What the fuck are you going to do with that?"

"Relax." Luca rolls his eyes. "I'll cut your inner thigh, just a tiny bit. It'll leave a small blood spot, and Rossi will be satisfied."

"You've got to be fucking kidding me!"

"I'm not," Luca says coolly. "Would you like what is essentially a scratch, Sofia, or would you like something worse? Because I guarantee the latter is what Rossi has in store for both of us, if we don't obey."

I stare at him. *I'm so tired of the stupid death threats,* I think bitterly. Everything, everything out of his mouth is *do this or die.* I'm fucking sick of it. But once again, I can see that there's no way out.

"Lay down," Luca instructs. "As if—"

"I've got it," I say between clenched teeth. Any hint of desire is gone now. I close my eyes as I move back into place where I was before, my pulse racing in my throat.

Luca climbs back into the bed, kneeling between my legs as his hand slides up the inside of my upper thigh. Before it felt good, arousing even, but now I'm just angry and scared. I want his hands off of me—I want him to never touch me again.

"Don't look," Luca says, and I feel the cold press of a sharp-edged blade against my inner thigh.

It doesn't hurt that much. He was right about that. It's a quick sharp pain, like a pinch, not more than what I felt earlier when he slid into me for the first time. But the physical cut isn't what hurts. It's everything about the situation, the fact that I gave Luca everything, and it was all for nothing.

"You could have done this in the first place," I whisper brokenly, resentment filling my voice. "We didn't have to have sex, we could have faked it—"

I wish I'd thought of that. I wish I'd *insisted* on it. It hadn't even occurred to me in the rush of fear and emotion and shock that had accompanied what Luca had told me earlier, just like I hadn't pieced together that Rossi would specifically be looking for blood on the sheets. I hadn't really thought about *why* they were coming up to see us in the morning, only that they were and there was no way out of it.

"I thought—"

"What? That I would prefer sex with you to a little cut on my thigh?"

"You wanted me," Luca says defensively.

"My *body* wanted you! You're fucking gorgeous, and I've never been with a man, and you teased the fuck out of me last night!" I'm shouting again, my voice rising as I shrink away from his touch. "That doesn't mean I wanted to give you *the only thing I had left to keep!*"

"Sofia—"

"Leave me alone." I jump out of the bed, refusing to look at the spot on the bed. "Just fucking leave me alone!"

Luca says nothing, but I can feel his eyes on me as I flee into the bathroom, straight into the shower and the privacy of the hot water and doors between me and him.

When I finally emerge, every hint of his touch scrubbed off of me, the lights are off. Luca is on the far side of the king-sized bed, and while I can't see if he's still naked, he's far enough away from the other side of the bed that I can manage to sleep without touching him.

But as I lay down, curled up in the pajama pants and tank top I'd brought with me to wear, I can tell that it's going to be a long, sleepless night. My body aches, but not with the need for pleasure any longer. It just feels sore and restless, my chest tight with anxiety and a faint sense of betrayal, and I want more than anything to be far, far away from him.

I can't wait for this to be over.

LUCA

*M*y new wife hates me.

I can see it in her eyes when we wake up the next morning, in the way she refuses to meet mine, the way she shrinks away from me when I make even the slightest move towards her. The tension in the room is so thick that I could cut it with a knife—which is ironically a large part of the reason she's so angry with me.

I suppose I should have thought of that as a solution last night—but I didn't. And in the heat of the moment, with the opportunity to finally fuck my beautiful, innocent new bride—who can blame me, really? I wanted her, and I had her.

It was better than I could have imagined. Her naked body was more perfect than I'd dreamed, her pussy the tightest I've ever felt, so much so that I'd lost all the control that I'd planned to have. She'd asked me to make it quick, and that had been embarrassingly easy, but I'd touched and kissed her in ways that I hadn't planned on doing. I'd meant to make it reserved and cold, and instead I'd fucked her with the abandon that I'd so carefully tried to avoid.

She'd just felt so fucking good. Better than any sex I've ever had, better than any woman I've ever touched. All I want is to take her to bed again, to explore all the curves and valleys of her body that I didn't get to last night, to touch and taste her and learn every inch of her.

But that's not in the cards, and I know that. I got one night, which was more than I'd expected.

Now it's time to get the fuck over it.

With the way Sofia is behaving, it doesn't seem like I'll have much of a choice. She dresses in the bathroom, careful not to give me another glimpse of her naked, and emerges in a knee-length, bright green dress that sets off the color of the stones in her ring and makes her skin and hair glow even more than usual. She's the most beautiful woman I've ever seen—and I'm married to her.

Not that that seems to matter, really.

Tomorrow I'll begin making plans. I'll find her an apartment, set up a security team just for her, and as soon as a week or so has passed without movement on the Bratva's part, I'll have her moved into it. We can avoid each other until then. She'll be safe, which was all I was ever supposed to worry about.

I wasn't supposed to want her, or care about her, or feel anything for her other than what I always have. She's a box to check off, a line item to deal with. I can't think of her in any other way.

But it's impossible to go back to that now. Now that I've seen her, now that I know her. She's rebellious, infuriating, stubborn, and stronger than I think even she knows. She doesn't know how to use it yet, how to navigate her place in this world, but there's something about that innocence that draws me, too. Not just sexually, but because it reminds me that I've never been that innocent. I both crave it and resent it all at once, the idea that there was ever a life outside of the one I was born into.

When Sofia comes out of the bathroom she doesn't say a single word. She packs her things, hanging up the dress and carefully avoiding my eyes, and then she sits in the loveseat furthest away from me, studying her phone as we both wait for Rossi and the others to come up. I sit on the edge of the bed, feeling more awkward than I have since I was a teenager. Outwardly I don't show it, but the fact that I'm sitting on the bed of our honeymoon suite with my new wife studiously ignoring me, waiting for my boss to come up and see the proof that I fucked her last night has me feeling more than a little uncomfortable.

When the knock at the door comes, I see her flinch. She doesn't move to get up, however, and I cross the room to open it, careful to keep my expression smooth despite my own nerves. If Rossi suspects that anything is off, that'll be it for both of us—but I *did* sleep with her. It's not either of our faults that we had to make her bleed through other means.

Rossi walks into the room, followed by his wife Giulia and Caterina. two women look carefully blank-faced—I can only imagine what they think of this particular ritual—and Rossi has a thin-lipped expression, as if he's anticipating some problem. That I haven't obeyed . It makes my stomach knot, because no matter what, I've lost some measure of his trust. A flood of resentment rises up in me, towards both Sofia *and* Rossi. Sofia, because her naivete got us here in the first place, Rossi, because one stupid and unimportant lie has set back years of loyalty and work. All the blood on my hands, all the things I've done, all the unwavering devotion I've shown to him and to the family, called into question because I made the mistake of allowing this girl to get under my skin.

Rossi has known plenty of women in his day. I'd have thought he would have understood. But plainly he sees any failure, any faltering, as a possible sign that nothing I've done has ever mattered.

To be honest, it makes me angry.

There's one person I'd expected to see missing, and I glance over at Caterina. "Where's Franco?" I ask curiously.

"He said he was too hungover to get up," Caterina says with a slight twitch of her mouth, as if she's trying not to laugh. "I asked if he was coming down for breakfast with everyone, but he wasn't sure if he'd be able to make it. He was throwing up when I left."

Giulia wrinkles her nose, but Rossi just laughs. "Ah, to be young again, eh?" He claps me on the shoulder, moving past me towards the bed. "Let's witness this and be done with it. I'm starving."

He strides towards the bed, the two women behind him, and yanks the blankets back. It's there for all of them to see, the small dried bloodstain on the bed, and it takes everything in me to appear relaxed. There's no reason for him to doubt it, but I can't help but feel that he'll see through it somehow. He studies the stain for a long moment, and I can feel the hard thump of my heartbeat in my chest.

But then Rossi turns to me, a broad grin on his face. "Passed a good night with your new bride, eh, Luca?" He claps me hard on the shoulder again, and I catch a glimpse of Caterina's face—it looks so carefully blank that I can't help but think she must have had some idea of how Sofia felt about the whole situation.

I suppose I should feel irritated about that, but I don't. If anything, it's good if Sofia feels she can confide in Caterina. Caterina is a good daughter, a good mafia woman, and if I'm lucky she'll help instill in Sofia some of the values of a good mafia wife—teach her that resisting the way things are is hopeless.

Sofia got a lesson in that last night, already.

Rossi jerks his head sideways, indicating to me that he wants to speak to me out of earshot of the others. I follow him out into the hall, and as we step out I can hear the faint sound of Giulia speaking to Sofia. I can't make out Sofia's response, but her tone is reserved and cool.

Fine. As long as she's polite.

Rossi looks at me as he closes the door behind him. "You obeyed orders, Luca. I'm pleased with you."

"It was never my intent to make you distrust me," I say quietly. "I wanted her to feel safe, that's all."

"You must always remember that your first loyalty is to the family," Rossi says firmly. "Not *your* family, Luca, but the greater family, the one that has raised you up and given you wealth and power and your place in the world. You've fought for it and bled for it, don't lose it all over a woman. There's a great many women in the world, and none of them are worth losing your head over. Literally or figuratively," he adds with a smile, but there's a warning in it and in his tone that I don't miss.

"We'll forget it ever happened," he adds. "You've never given me any reason before to doubt you, Luca. It was an error, a misstep. We all make them."

"Thank you, sir," I say quietly, but inside I can feel my gut clenching. Rossi might say it's forgotten, but I know it's not. There's a strike against me now, and in this world, you don't always make it to three before you're out.

"Come on," he says, nodding towards the door. "I want to speak to your new bride. And after that, I'll see you down at breakfast. I'll understand if it takes a little longer for you both to come down, eh?" He grins at me as he pushes the door open, and I see Sofia's face plainly as she looks up when we step inside.

It's an expressionless mask, her body tense, her eyes flat and cold. *It's better this way*, I tell myself. The more she freezes me out, the more she avoids me, the easier it should be to put her out of my head. To wash my hands of this whole messy business.

But as she looks away, responding to something that Caterina quietly says, I know it's not going to be that easy. Just looking at her delicate profile, the soft curve of her lips and the shape of her sitting there, I can feel my chest tighten and my cock twitch, my body wanting her even as I try to put her out of my mind.

I know last night isn't going to be something I quickly forget.

SOFIA

I'm still seething over last night. The cut on the inside of my thigh stings, but it's nothing compared to the sting of knowing that going to bed with Luca last night wasn't even necessary, that I gave up the thing I'd tried to cling to over nothing.

It stings even more that he was right when he said that I'd wanted it. I *had*. It would be a lie to say otherwise—but never again. I'm so angry right now that I can't even imagine feeling that desire again, but even if it comes up, I won't give in. No matter what Luca does, no matter if he kisses me, teases me—*nothing* will make me let him have me like that again. If I had to do it once, then once is all it will ever be.

I'm polite when Rossi walks back into the room and straight over to me. I know better than to not be—I might be angry with Luca, but I know to be afraid of Rossi. I stand up, holding out my hand to shake his and greet him, but he pulls me into a hug instead. "Welcome to the family, Sofia," he says, loudly enough for everyone to hear, but then more quietly, as his arms wrap around me like a pseudo-father's, he murmurs in my ear.

"Don't ever try to turn Luca against me again," he warns, his voice low and so dark it sends a shiver down my spine. "Your marriage protects you for now, but at the end of the day, it's a ring around your finger and a piece of paper. Easily dissolved, easily shredded. And you can quite easily disappear."

He lets me go then, holding my hand between his two broad ones. "It's almost as if I have a younger daughter," he says, that same broad smile on his face. "I'm so glad to bring Giovanni's daughter back into the family. He'd be so proud, if he could be here today."

It's not true. None of it is. And my father didn't want this for me, not if he could help it—I know that now. But I just smile, my face hurting with the effort, and squeeze his hand in return.

"Thank you," I say softly. "For the wedding, for everything. For my marriage. I'm so glad to be home."

I catch a glimpse of Luca's face before he looks away. He sees right through my act, of course. But it doesn't matter. I know now that he's not the real danger. Whatever his reasoning for not letting Rossi do as he pleases, I feel confident that he won't have me killed.

That doesn't mean our life together is going to be pleasant, though.

I refuse to speak to him, pasting a smile onto my face as we walk together into the room reserved for the post-wedding breakfast. There's a delicious-looking buffet spread out along one wall, but I can't imagine wanting to eat. My stomach feels tied in knots, and all I want is to be as far from Luca as possible. My own apartment can't come soon enough. All of this—Rossi's warning wrapped in fake pleasantries, the unexpected drama of last night, the fear that won't leave me even though I'm supposed to be safe now—I can't help but feel that it would be less oppressive if I had my own space, at least. Somewhere to escape from it. Not Luca's penthouse, a luxurious bachelor pad in every sense of the word, where I feel so completely out of place.

This party is smaller, just the immediate members of the family and the highest-ranking men under Rossi and their wives, but I still feel a little overwhelmed by all the congratulations, the hand-shaking and the names I can't possibly remember. It does at least distract me from the memory of last night, of the warmth and weight of Luca's body on mine, of the sounds he made, the way he lost control while he was inside of me. I have to forget about it, to pretend as if it never happened, to separate myself from everything that occurred last night.

It's the only way I'll be able to move on. I'm certain that he already has.

And I wish, more than anything, that Ana were here so that I could talk to her. I've never felt more lonely than I do in this room, surrounded by people I don't know, who don't care anything about me. Caterina is the best I have here, and even she has been carefully quiet and polite this morning, due to her mother's hovering presence. Everything she said to me in the hotel room were bland comments about how nice the wedding was and how happy they are that I've married Luca, how happy *I* must be about all of it.

And of course, I nodded and smiled and said yes, I'm so happy. Because from now until the day I can escape, if that day ever comes, I have to pretend to be happy. A content, dutiful wife.

"You have to eat," Luca murmurs in my ear. "I'm sure you think you don't want to, but get something, even if you pick at it. The others will notice."

Resentment burns in me at that, the idea that I should give a single shit about what anyone in here thinks. That I have to do anything that I don't want to in order to mollify Luca and his family.

But that was what last night was all about. And it's going to be the rest of my life, for as long as I'm with him.

I suppose if I have to play this part, though, I might as well not do it hungry.

I get a plate from the buffet, putting bits of food on it without really paying attention, and retreat to our designated table. Luca chats with someone on his right, giving me the opportunity to withdraw into myself, staying as silent and unnoticed as I can. I don't want to talk to anyone, I don't want to pretend to be happy. I just want this to be over with.

I'm so deep in my own thoughts, so preoccupied with pushing the bits of smoked salmon and scrambled egg around my plate, that it takes me a second to register the sound of the explosion.

In fact, for a split second as I go flying backwards through the air, my ears ringing and throbbing with pain, the sound of glass windows shattering and screaming all around me, I don't completely grasp what's happening.

Not until I land flat on my back, my head striking something hard, and pain floods my body as I try to keep my eyes open, to see what's happening. My head feels fuzzy, muddled, and I try to get up, only to hear Luca shout my name.

"Sofia!" He launches himself towards me, flinging his body atop mine, his arms cradling my head. "Stay down! Don't fucking move!"

The next explosion feels as if it shatters my eardrums, my head, and I can feel the faint trickle of something warm down my cheek. My body is wracked with pain, aching in every limb, and I feel the heavy weight of Luca atop me. Faintly I can still hear crying and screaming, but it sounds very far off, like something heard through a tunnel.

Smoke fills the room. In my peripheral vision, I can see someone crawling past me, but that's quickly forgotten as my vision briefly comes back into focus, and I see that Luca is slumped atop me, blood running from his nose and mouth, his arms still flung upwards as if to protect me. My arm is trapped beneath him, and when I try to pull it free, I feel something warm and wet on his side, sticky on my fingers.

I should get up. I should call for help. I should do *something*—but I can't move.

I can hardly think. All I can feel is pain, and my vision swims again, narrowing as I gasp for breath underneath Luca's weight, knowing that he could be dead, he could be dying, and in his last moments for some reason, he chose to protect me.

The wife he didn't want.

I can't make sense of it. But I can't make sense of *anything*, my mind feels thick and foggy, and my vision is still narrowing, going dark at the edges.

I have one last flash of memory, of the first time I saw Luca's face when he opened that closet door, his shirt blood-spattered and his face hard, a gun clutched in his hand just before I passed out.

And then, everything goes black.

* * *

Don't miss the next installment of Luca and Sofia's story in the second book of the Promise *trilogy,* Broken Promise!

ABOUT THE AUTHOR

Join the Facebook group for M. James' readers at
https://www.facebook.com/groups/531527334227005

Printed in Great Britain
by Amazon